CURVEBALL

Life Never Comes At You Straight

Gustav Preller

What Thomas Bland, formerly senior manager now plain senior, expects upon his retirement in the seaside city of Durban isn't remotely what he gets. His wife, Caro, leaves him, and he loses friends through betrayal, illness, and murder – events that threaten to destroy what little relevance he has left in the world. All the while, socio-political storm clouds are gathering over South Africa with most of its citizens, including Tom, either inured to them or choosing not to see them. His dream shattered, Tom seeks love before it is too late. This time he gets more than he hopes for. After decades in a straightjacket at the office, his edges blunted by corporate convention, he goes on a hedonistic trip of Roman proportions. He also finds a dream island in the tropics, a surfing paradise, where he spends happy days. But matters reach a tipping point as Tom's personal journey and the fate of the country converge. Tom gets caught up in events bigger than he could ever have imagined, and he has to fight for his life, and love.

GUSTAV PRELLER worked for multinational corporations in South Africa, Germany, Switzerland, and the UK in the fields of fast moving consumer goods, advertising, sports goods, and banking. He is the author of three novels: *Icarus over Hong Kong* (2009), *The Twelfth Delegate* (2011), and *Last Train to Retreat* (2013). He lives in South Africa on Kwazulu-Natal's north coast. *Curveball: Life Never Comes At You Straight* won the Proverse Prize 2015.

CURVEBALL

Life Never Comes At You Straight

Gustav Preller

Winner of the Proverse Prize 2015

Proverse Hong Kong

Curveball:
Life Never Comes At You Straight
by Gustav Preller.
Copyright © Gustav Preller, 2016.
2nd pbk edition published in Hong Kong
by Proverse Hong Kong, 2016,
under sole and exclusive right and licence.
ISBN: 978-988-8228-50-8
Available from https://www. createspace.com/6499379

1st published in Hong Kong by Proverse Hong Kong,
22 November 2016, under sole and exclusive right and licence.
Copyright © Gustav Preller, 22 November 2016.
ISBN 978-988-8228-49-2

Enquiries: Proverse Hong Kong, P. O. Box 259,
Tung Chung Post Office, Tung Chung, Lantau, NT,
Hong Kong SAR, China.
E-mail: proverse@netvigator.com
Web site: www.proversepublishing.com

Cover design by Pami Preller.
Page design by Proverse Hong Kong.

British Library Cataloguing in Publication Data.
A catalogue record for the 1st edition of this book is available
from the British Library.

Permissions

The author would like to express his appreciation to the following publications and organisations for permission to use the quotations included in this novel and which are listed at the end of this book in order of appearance.

BizNews.com, Chapter 32; *Business Day*, Chapter 24; *Business Report*, Chapter 17; *Crime Stats South Africa*, Chapter 19; *Independent Online News (IOL)*, Chapter 6; *Institute for Security Studies (ISS)*, Chapter 20; Mind of a Fox website, Chapter 10; *SWEAT* website, Chapter 25; *South African Civil Society Information Service (SACSIS)*, Chapter 3; *Statistics South Africa. General Household Survey*, Chapter 5; *The New Yorker*, Page 2; *The Mercury*, Chapters 4, 12, 13, 16, 18, 26, 27, 28; *The Star*, Chapter 30; *Time Magazine*, Chapters 2, 8, 31.

Acknowledgements

The author would like to thank Proverse Publishers Dr Gillian Bickley and Dr Verner Bickley for their help with the novel's structure, for their perceptive and thorough editing, and for creating the Proverse Prize as an incentive to writers across the world to *write*.

Author's Note

Two narrative threads run through the novel: the fictional (Tom's story), and the actual as represented by quotes on the country's socio-political situation. For a large part of the novel Tom's life seemingly is unaffected by what happens in the country. However, as fiction and reality begin to merge, this changes, forcing Tom to confront his secret-ridden past as well as the unfolding situation in South Africa.

Towards the end of the story the need for quotes falls away for this reason. As the prophecy of the quotes is fulfilled and the country unravels, it also makes the man.

When I wrote the first one (*Casino Royale*), I wanted Bond to be an extremely dull, uninteresting man to whom things happened … when I was casting around for a name for my protagonist I thought by God, James Bond is the dullest name I ever heard.

— Ian Fleming, in a 1962 interview in *The New Yorker*

PART ONE

GRUPUK, SOUTH LOMBOK, INDONESIA

CHAPTER ONE

Why should a sea krait be revealing itself to me on this day and in this place – my paradise on earth? Head up like a periscope, its black-banded beauty ruffling the water's smooth surface. I remain still on my board. Maybe it's just curious, but these snakes are highly venomous.

I watch it. It neither glances my way nor veers from its path, as if it knows it is master of its world and I am not.

Pumped from riding eight-footers, my breathing deep from all the paddling, I'm taking a break away from the other surfers. Plugged into what it means to be alive, giving thanks without need of middleman, holy garb, or ritual. To my right, *perahus* at anchor leaning on their bamboo outriggers, out of reach of the white water's turbulence.

I flip onto my back on my longboard, the sky on top of me it seems yet utterly out of reach. Blue eye of the universe, deep and mysterious, indifferent I suspect about me, Thomas Bland, and all that happens down here – can beauty so absolute be preoccupied with anything but itself? The thought is fleeting, lulled as I am in my hammock of the moment, of tropical sea and sun and sweet air.

Then I hear it – the sound of a roaring engine from the sea. I see no jet or contrails, and sit up sharply as the water around me explodes in white foam, and tall trees sway violently at the shoreline. Like a squadron of top fighter pilots sea gulls swerve in unison. Surfers shout and start paddling for their *perahus.* More thunder, like a freight train this time, sensation of a giant force vibrating through the air.

The ocean suddenly a stranger, waves not breaking normally, and surging around me. My mind struggles to take it all in. I scan the horizon. Where is Doni, he should be back by now! Boatmen frantically pull up boards, surfers, anchors, and fire up motors. I shout at Separ, 'Go, man, but call the clinic in Kuta, you know the one! Tell them to run for Ashtari. And everyone in Grupuk, they must stay off the road, go to the hills!'

Separ nods vigorously. 'But your boat, where is it? You come with me?'

I stare at him, the urge to jump aboard powerful. I'd be in Grupuk in fifteen minutes then make a dash on my moped to Kuta, and find her. Everyone would understand that Udin had tasked his son to retrieve a lost anchor, that Doni took too long, and that I had no choice but to return with Separ. As for a *perahu* going out to look for Doni, how can anyone expect it in the face of a tsunami? Not for one man.

'No, Separ, I can't, gotta find Doni. Just phone the clinic, okay?' I think of Doni out on that sea, and know I can't go back to Kuta now, look her in the eye, and make excuses why I didn't try. As I think it I realise I might never see her again. Or she, me. *'You'll do that for me, bru?'*

Separ gives me the thumbs up. A surfer screams, 'Let's get the hell outta here!'

I check the horizon. They say tsunami waves take anything from minutes to hours to arrive, and the first isn't always the biggest. Nothing can be less helpful right now. And it's not as if you can ride these waves – no face for the board to grip, just a wall of white water with the entire ocean behind it and death on the rocks, if the debris doesn't kill you.

I start paddling out to sea. Flutters in my stomach, relief that I'm lying down – my legs might not hold me up. My arms like windmills, my longboard cutting through the water. What if Separ doesn't make it, or doesn't call the clinic? What if he calls and no one answers? What if she elects to stay until she has helped everyone else out? It would be just like her. Crazy that compassion can kill. Kuta and the clinic no higher than a man's head above the sea, and only a hundred metres from it. The town doesn't stand a chance. Neither does the village of Grupuk with its low stone wall as sole protection: Udin, his family, Badri, Kojak, the elderly and the infirm, the children, the surfers' beloved ones in the village – all are at risk.

The water now a deep blue, the sea pretending as if nothing has happened yet knowing that on the beaches the curious will be tempted to walk out as it pulls back to reveal its treasures.

They would stare in awe, and then drown. A force that is full of trickery and malevolence after all? Is today my appointment in Samarra, on this island, not in my country on the other side of the ocean as I expected? Retribution for the things I've done and the secrets I've kept, not allowing God in, and not believing unquestioningly like Spirou did? Confronted in the end not by others, but myself?

I'm approaching the mouth of the bay. On the left is the headland where Doni said he'd be. Part of me wants to carry on straight, to deep water where I'd be safer. But I see her eyes again; it's as if she's looking into my soul.

I veer left. It appears shallower, rocky. Then I glimpse it, smaller than I remember – Doni's *perahu*? In a spot where people spearfish I recall. I see it – the lone figure in the boat, the orange buoy, Doni pulling the cord of the motor, over and over.

'It won't start!' he yells. He's still at anchor.

'How long you been trying?'

He kicks the motor, 'Too long, Mister Tom. My father will kill me.'

'If he doesn't, the waves will, Doni! Leave that anchor, and the boat, and our stuff. There's no time, come on!' He's freaking me out.

'But ...'

'Don't make me come and fetch you, bru!'

In that moment I see the terror in his eyes, a mere boy with no recourse to the swagger of stick fighting, the intoxicating drums and adoring shouts of the crowd, and a referee who stops bouts the minute blood flows. Here his adversary is the ocean, waiting to take him down.

I cannot tell him I've never been so afraid, and that having him in my charge magnifies it. I throw him a lifeline of desperate words: 'Doni, you are brave. You've proven it on land. You're a warrior, remember. Show me that man in the sea. Show me that no matter where you are, you're brave. Now come.'

I hold out my hand. He fixes dark, doubtful eyes on me, looks longingly at the shore as if he were a gull about to stretch out its wings and fly there. Then he jumps.

He lies at the front of the board, where the spider logo is, and I behind him, feet trailing in the water. Our paddling is sluggish and without rhythm. My eyes don't leave the horizon for a second. When the waves come they'll sense the shallower water around the headland first, slow down then rise to a dizzy height before smashing into this finger of rock pointing heavenward with such hubris. Get away from it, I tell myself. For once I regret the absence of a reef to break the tsunami's power.

'You okay, Doni?' I can't see his eyes. I need to know what's in his head.

'Yeah, man, let's go!' His shout is bold. I pray it isn't just bravado.

We head further out to sea at a pace far too slow for my liking, the spear-like rocks and the hapless headland, no longer a sentinel to me, still unnervingly close.

PART TWO

CHAPTER TWO
Durban, South Africa

A port city of beaches and lush parks where the buildings are painted in bubble gum pastels ... (it) is the corruption and political-assassination capital of South Africa.
— Alex Perry, *Time Magazine*

At the bathing area flags are hanging still, on the pier the black silhouette of a cormorant. Further out the sun is scattering diamonds across glassy swells, above it white puffs of cloud.

I conjure up the scene at North Beach from the study of my Berea home. The SMS fifteen minutes ago said only 'Get here, bru'. It's good enough for me – Dunbar reads the sea like a book.

Quietly down the steps now, avoid the creaks in the old floor boards – Caro still asleep. Bag with gear in one hand, unlock the door with the other, happy that on this day others are oiling the wheels of industry and keeping pension funds afloat.

Hadeda screeching at the pool, from the bedroom Caro's drowsy voice, 'Tom, we need bread. Agrippa and Precious are here today, there's a lot to do.'

'Haven't we done enough, honey? Builders, rubble and dust for months with me pretending to know more than I do. This old house is now just fine for us, time to enjoy don't you think? A new year it is and a new life!'

'But there's no bread.'

'What about cereal? Maybe some banana with it – potassium for working muscles, you know. Much healthier than that ghastly refined stuff they call bread. What else is there?'

'Only carrot cake ... let them eat cake, is that it?' Caro at the top of the stairs in her cream and ecru silk nightie, auburn bob framing her face and dutifully curling forward over her ears along her jaw line – everything in place always, no matter the time of day. Caro's carrot cake is, like all her food, to die for.

'Rather not tempt fate,' I say, 'keeping our heads at our age is everything.'

'Then please go to the shop before the beach. The rest can wait. Here's the list.' The foolscap page in her hand flutters under the fan.

Back up the stairs, my T-shirt damp in the February heat. Quid pro quo: I shop for ingredients, perform the odd sous-chef task, and rinse and stack dishes in return for Caro's heavenly dinners. Endearing morning puffiness under her eyes, soon to be exercised away in the gym. Chose me all those years ago, stuck by me even as I hid things from her. Strange how unshared secrets keep love's edges keen.

'And dark blue doesn't go with black.' Her head tilts as she appraises me. 'White with black or black with black is so much nicer. You *are* going to the shops.'

'Musgrave, Caro, not Tiffany's. The fact that *you* dress up every time is your choice.' She's worried about her friends spotting me, in my old baggies, tank top, and sandals. A posh lot they are – coffee at cafés and all that.

I glance at my watch, the call of the sea strong. 'I'm afraid it's either a change of clothing or the bread, the traffic won't allow for both.'

'Oh, get the bread then, Thomas!'

My wool suits attracting fish moths in humid cupboards, leather shoes and belts going mouldy, silk ties losing lustre – things that once told the world I was somebody on Gauteng's Highveld. Not high enough for Caro's Old Durban Family though – expecting CEO and getting Senior Manager instead, now plain senior. Let her down I think, she never says it outright. But how happy am I to have traded Armani and Boss for a cupboard full of Billabong and Reef.

I kiss her lightly on the eyes to sooth the swelling, and wonder why there isn't a union for retired men.

*

I'm gunning down Berea Road to beat the morning traffic. In the distance, between the city's buildings, tantalising patches of ocean. Beggars at intersections, some with bandaged limbs, others on crutches, all with fingers pecking at mouths except the man sucking on a harmonica, amplifier strapped to his shoulder, yellow money bowl in hand. Ahead, traffic lights out of action. No cops. Overloaded minibus taxi ignoring the rules of the 4-way stop causing me to swerve violently, hand on hooter, heart in throat. Driver flashing his finger from an arm that's been hanging out all this time, primed for such occasions.

I pull over onto the kerb to catch my breath from the near death experience. It could have been me wrapped around the lamppost instead of the headline, 'Police swoop in massive tender fraud.'

An old woman trudges along with brooms bunched up over her bony shoulder. Blue-gum sticks stripped of bark, now smooth to the touch, strips of dried grass fanning out at one end.

'*Sawubona, unjani?*' she asks.

How am I? I'm a *mlungu,* a white, in a rush and I've just survived a cruise missile on my way to the beach, in a nice car, with air-conditioning. I cannot tell her that.

'*Malini* brooms?'

'Forty rand each, sir,' she says, face wrinkled like old granadilla husk.

'I'll take that one. No, wait ...' How many taxis, how long her walk? And this evening back again, perhaps with unsold brooms. 'Okay, I'll take three – that one and those two.' I pass her a blue hundred and a red fifty, 'Keep the change, for the taxi.'

Woman doing a little Tutu dance. Sweat in the furrows of her face. '*Inkosi ikubusise!* God bless you!'

I pull off with a '*Hamba kahle*, old one.' If the saying is true that all taxi drivers are born of the same mother then she's not the one.

*

I cross over Warwick junction easily, only to find traffic heaping up on the other side from converging lanes. Waterman landlocked, rugged Wrangler trapped between sedate sedans waiting to break loose – a travesty of justice!

Sealed off in my cabin now with Neil Diamond, anger towards the taxi driver gone, just sadness at what was emblazoned across his vehicle, *Me Against the World,* and memories of me, small and carrying a rage beyond my years.

From the Marine Parade the club and the sea at last visible. Jan Pretorius guarding cars, squatting on a concrete refuse bin beneath a tree, his *tonfa* his only weapon – a hard plastic club with an angled handle. Matted hair, mahogany skin, cigarette bobbing between his lips like a sick bird's tail as he tells me there are waves today and the boys are out. He points to black-capped figures sitting at the backline, easy on their longboards like cowboys on horses.

I grab my gear. 'How goes it, Jan?'

'You heard about Peet? He died yesterday.' Jan takes a drag on his fag.

'Jeez! What of? I'm shocked.'

'Emphysema, they say.'

'*Vasbyt*, Jan,' I try to lift his spirits.

Lost his little flat in Gillespie Street last year, and now lives in a Winder Street shelter at forty rand a day – bed, breakfast and dinner – sharing a hall with a hundred men and women and no privacy at all, by day carrying surfers' car keys on a steel ring, with never a vehicle tampered with or missing, sharing shifts on this piece of tarmac with its white-lined bays.

My past is inerasable like rings in a tree trunk, and my mind retraces my sapling days whenever I see the likes of Jan, knowing it could be me sitting there guarding cars. Maybe it's why I ask so little of the future: an untroubled, peaceful retirement, blood cells that won't turn rogue on me, a P-gland that doesn't become a Trojan horse, or forgetfulness a disease, surfing with my friends, sleeping with my wife in the afternoons. Feeling wanted in this changed and diminished world of mine.

The air feels thick and humid as I walk to the club. It has become too still for my liking.

CHAPTER THREE
Durban

Once a culture of political assassination sets in, it can become the repressive tool of choice for individuals wishing to gain control of state resources, and to dispense with those who stand in their way.
—Jane Duncan, the South African Civil Society Information Service

'Y ou're late, been in bed with your wife?' Spirou swings his board around, paddles furiously to catch the next wave, shouting as he takes off, 'Heard the news, Cal's back!'

I'm relieved the first question requires no answer. Not since my birthday a month ago have Caro and I made love, and then a sort of perfunctory present without any of the elaborate packaging and ribbons of times gone by, a here it is and get on with it kind of offering. Then keeping her distance which upset me but I decided to let go, as long as we remain together for the rest of our days. If it sounds like Mills and Boon for seniors, it is how I feel about Caro.

Callum Ryder back after an absence of twenty years – *that's* news.

Close by dolphins cavorting. Mind the shark nets, you beautiful creatures, keep the smiles on your faces and the ragged-tooth Johnnies away. Dunbar paddling out in the rip next to the pier, Bones riding a foamie near the beach, arms out like wings of a gull. Only Russ not there – probably caught up in his writing. All accounted for. Anything could happen in the sea: a knock on the head from a board, a heart attack, a leash caught in the pillars of the pier, even a shark (in spite of the nets).

Dunbar now at the back line, arms embracing the sky. 'This is the life, bru.'

'Yeah, sure beats the office. I hear Cal's back. Did he call you?'

'Nah, he called Spirou. Looked him up in the book. No other Spirou here spelt like that.' Dunbar's broad chest, combative stomach now at rest beneath his black rash vest, twin vertical furrows on his forehead extra deep today because of the glare, long nose running down to a mouth that seldom cracks into a smile.

'Yes, they were buddies but then so were we, Dunbar, from our high school days.' Not that Dunbar would remember, or care, being years older and famous at the time – Springbok lifesaver and water polo player many times over. Chris, a first name somehow too soft for this man, so Dunbar it became. 'Did Spirou say how long he's been back?'

Dunbar scans the sea for the next set. 'A few weeks, running around something hectic it seems. He's coming the day after tomorrow.' Dunbar speaks in bullet sentences, not paragraphs, and when he's silent you're still aware of him. Not like Bones, whose presence you can easily overlook. That's why Dunbar never has to repeat himself and Bones does.

Why did Cal not call me? How many people with the name Bland in the directory? He could have got my number from Spirou.

*

We surf for two more hours, Bones the goofy footer taking lefts, the others riding the right shoulder, until the tide is too far out and the waves too gnarly for our longboards.

'Last in buys the tea!' Spirou's eyes lustrous like washed black grapes, nose curved, lips full, skin olive-brown courtesy of his Cypriot ancestral town of Paphos where he was christened George in the days of Archbishop Makarios.

Bones winces, his bald head the best around for slipping on a surfing cap. The pot of tea a question not only of pride but also pocket – retired pro lifeguard fixing dings on paddle skis and surfboards to supplement his meagre pension, at seventy his once taut, rippling hide hanging loose on him like an old dog's, the name Greg Marais all but forgotten.

Quiet now as we ready ourselves to be first on a wave. A swell pops up from the flat sea without warning, rising steeply with a wicked lip in the centre, broad shoulder building to the right. All four of us take it, the no drop-in rule thrown to the wind. A family wave we call it, not for rookies. I pretend to lose my balance and fall backwards knowing my leash will stop my board from crashing into them.

What's a little loss of face among friends on a morning like this, so I can buy them a pot of tea? They ride to the shore, whooping and yelling like teenagers.

Old longboards yellowing like nicotine teeth. Now hosed down and stacked away in their racks. Locker keys retrieved from their hiding places because combination locks have become too difficult to read. In the change rooms, under the shower, Spirou's soap drops onto a patch of sand on the tiles.

'Can you still get down there, bru?' Bones asks. As he says it his own soap slips onto the same spot; guffaws all round.

We walk past the notice board and the weekly duty rosters, up the steps past framed competition posters and headlines celebrating the club's victories, photos of the beachfront in bygone days, and granite plaques in memory of those who died young, to the wafting smells of coffee, and the deck with its wooden benches under large umbrellas.

*

'How do you put a condom on a marshmallow?' Spirou asks.

Hands curved around warm cups of tea, sunglasses hiding mischief. Down on the beach a sand artist sculpting breasts on a mermaid, on the promenade a skateboarder grinning at his mate.

'Haven't the foggiest, ask Bones,' I say.

All heads turn to Bones. He pulls his cap down. 'Why look at me!'

'We thought you'd know, being the oldest,' Spirou says.

'Come off it, what the …' Bones usually rises to ribbing like a shark to a seal and then somehow becomes the seal.

'You could ask the lady for help and understanding,' Russ says, appearing from the direction of the coffee shop. 'Okay, tell me the waves were great … always when I'm not here, eh.'

'You'd better believe it,' Dunbar says. 'Have a consolation cuppa, Tom's buying.'

Everyone moving up, making space for Russell Clack, bouffant hair like Donald Trump's that on windy days goes wild. He once let slip that his good hair came from using horse shampoo. Bones promptly bought some, used it religiously, and even smeared it on his head at night on Russ's advice, finally binning it in disgust. A neat beard, bushy brows and a false eye complete Russ's looks – the eye lost at New Pier when an angry fisherman cast a sinker at Russ who was out on his board. He squeezes out laughs like hard, sharp lemons. There's raw stuff in him, and in Dunbar ever since his return from the border long ago. There is in all of us. For instance, I can't tell Caro the marshmallow joke, not when I let her down in bed twice recently (I ascribed it to too much sun and surfing).

Spirou removes his sunglasses. 'Hey, Russ, how's the book? Sounds like you're going all soft and romantic. What if we don't like it?'

'Yeah, give us a trailer, like the movies, and we'll tell you what we think.' Bones's brown eyes, usually resigned like an old dog's, full of anticipation. 'Have you finished it?'

'Put down the last words last night, not without sadness, I admit. Tough saying goodbye to people you've created. It brought tears to my eyes.'

'Serious?' Dunbar asks.

Russ nods.

'That's radical, bru.' Dunbar looks impressed. 'Hey, you know Cal's back?'

'I didn't, thought he'd gone to Mars.'

Spirou checks an angry sun spot on his forearm. 'No, to Jo'burg before moving overseas, made it big in London apparently.'

'Why come back, and after all this time?' I ask.

Spirou throws up his hands. 'How do I know? He's working on some business proposal. Anyway, he's coming here day after tomorrow.'

'What if the surf's up?' Bones sounds indignant. 'He'll have to talk to me from the pier, that's what.'

'And why would anyone want to talk to you?' Dunbar gives Bones a knuckle punch to show he harbours no hard feelings.

Silence around the table. Billy the beggar like a scarecrow today with his hair wild and his clothes torn standing outside the glass walls of the fast food joint staring at patrons inside, knowing they'll buy him a burger or two before the morning is out. Threatening clouds from the south-west, umbrellas flapping, Russ patting down his flaxen hair, Dunbar fixing the curved blade of the horizon in his sombre gaze, and my thoughts running back to a time when the beaches were like golden brown sugar and my fortunes turned around – at last. Summer holidays, South Beach, fourteen, my first job as a fetcher of surf-o-planes – rubber surfing 'mattresses' with moulded ribs, handles on the nose, and a valve at the tail for inflating. Colour coded and numbered enabling Mr Savage, who owned the municipal concession, to rent them out for thirty or sixty minutes. Bathers would ignore the clock on the tower telling them their time is up, and I'd have to swim out and fetch their surf-o-planes. It taught me about the changing moods and colours of this ocean – from tranquil blue to angry anthracite – and its collaborators, the south-west and north-east winds. In my homemade swimming trunks, Speedo underneath, and my body slippery from all the Brylcreem, I'd apply tricks I'd learnt to separate stubborn bathers from their surf-o-planes, often experiencing surf rage that scared even me. There were complaints from swimmers, and reprimands from Mr Savage, but true to his name I think he liked my methods. For the first time in my life I could exact a little revenge for the treatment I'd received at the hands of so-called adults.

Addicted to LM Radio, whistling *San Francisco Be Sure to Wear Flowers in Your Hair*, I rode Corporation buses to the beach, the Roxy bio cafe (15 cents for a movie and a free drink, wearing shorts and T-shirt), and once in a while to the smarter Embassy and Playhouse theatres (in stovepipes, body-fitting jacket and twister tie). Spirou, Cal and I worked every school holiday for the money, our love of the sea, and the girls at the Little Top and the rock sessions across town – until the day came when we could each claim we had done the deed. Cal the first, who seemed to have it all: hazel eyes, shock of blond hair on either side of his middle parting, silvery tongue, pectorals and laterals filling out earlier (he was shorter, stockier). Spirou was next, hair thickly-curled from the humidity and so black the sun couldn't get a yellow streak in anywhere, his dark liquid eyes, olive skin, and foreign accent working wonders for him. It seemed natural that I should be last, the tallest but also the gangliest, a face over angled, and only one nice thing girls could say about me: that I had lovely eyes, sapphire blue one called them, deep and cool like the ocean (I was neither at the time, not that anything has changed). Cal from highbrow Mentone Road with a lawyer father, Spirou whose dad owned a restaurant in an arcade off Smith Street, and I with my new, untried father – a high school teacher from lower Glenwood – the three of us vowing we'd be friends forever, equalised by sea, sand and sex.

'Who's for a game of bulla?' Bones says.

'You mean boules,' Russ says.

'Known as *petanque*,' says Spirou, man from the Mediterranean.

We look up, sniffing the air like buck on a plain for signs of rain. The south-westerly still gentle, a friend that cleanses and grooms the sea when in a benign mood, but an ill wind when it comes up hard and reaches a tipping point, blowing away all prospects for surfing.

'No time for a board meeting,' I declare. 'Let's play while we can.'

But no sooner are the boules unpacked, the line drawn, and the piggy thrown than the sand starts to lash at our legs. Flags extend sideways, palms bend over at the waist and thunder rolls over the grey sea.

That's the thing about busters. Even when you half-expect them they surprise you with their suddenness.

CHAPTER FOUR
Durban

In the weeks and months before the death of ... Nelson Mandela, many South Africans were in despair as the ... ruling party trampled on ideals and values the great man so admirably represented. By their words and deeds, Nelson Mandela's heirs in government have been dismantling the solid foundation he so assiduously laid.
— Editorial in *The Mercury* at the time of Mandela's death

I'm attending to my surfer's hunger on the balcony of my house. In the distance the ocean whipped up white by the wind, the harbour with its cranes and ships hunkered between the Bluff and the city's skyscrapers. In the garden below Agrippa singing – Caro calls it Zulu *basso profundo* – his voice hijacked by screeching Mynas dogfighting above the pool, and monkeys thundering across the corrugated iron roof like wildebeest. Agrippa shakes his peppercorn head gone salty-white with the passing years. His name in ancient Latin meaning 'born feet first', carried proudly by the Roman statesman, general, and friend of Augustus, and now by this Zulu man tending to a suburban garden, no less proud.

Light footsteps up the staircase. 'Halloo, anybody home!' Caro's eyes, brown bob, and skin glowing as she kisses me on the forehead, in her Reeboks with pink stitching, hydrangea-blue track pants, and white T-shirt – ah, what a picture at fifty-six, after all these years still sending a little shiver through me when I haven't seen her for a while.

'Wow, looks like you had quite a workout.'

'A slave driver our Dylan, seems to delight in making delicate bodies suffer.' Caro dips a finger into my peanut butter and licks it in the most plebeian manner, but there's no mistaking the posh, private school accent. 'I swear my body has been eating into its own protein.'

'I'll double Dylan's fee if he keeps you looking so good.'

'How was the sea, honey, any waves?'

'Awesome – not many cities have streets that end in great beaches and surf, and ten minutes away. How often did I dream of it in my office ... '

'Dreaming indeed, have you seen the paper? Robbers tried to cut off a husband's fingers with pruning shears, and stabbed his wife with a pair of scissors. At another house a woman and her helper were shot, *after* the criminals had taken what they wanted. Then they raided the fridge, ate at the table using silver cutlery, and took that too! The helper survived. We should get out, Tom, find something overseas.'

'Hey, we've been through this. Live in a pokey flat, as tenants, because our currency can't buy us anything decent, without friends or medical aid, struggling with some tongue-twisting language, no thanks! I happen to like it here: the weather, the sea, my friends, and the lifestyle. Sure, we have to be careful, but where will I get this at the price? Panama, Costa Rica maybe, but who wants to go there? Take Spirou's family – fleeing Cyprus because of Makarios' silly war in the sixties, then coining it here in the restaurant business. Imagine if they'd gone back to Cyprus only to be zapped by that banking disaster! In any case, Carolyn, there's still Dad. I can't just leave him, you know that.'

Her eyes go hot. 'High walls, fences and razor wire – what a way to live, not to mention your loaded gun under the bed. This country has become so desensitised people don't see these things anymore!'

'Caro, at the next election we'll have a new president, probably the current deputy. Even now he's promising he'll target crime and corruption. He has support ... '

'Come on, it'll be more of the same. No true democracy would tolerate a ruling party like this one. Besides, he has enemies. '

My day is going badly when it should be all good. I'm retired, am I not? I change the subject: 'Guess what? Cal Ryder's in town, after twenty-five years, can't wait to see him.'

'Oh, Cal, yes, of course … don't get side-tracked, Tom. Remember when Mandela died? The grief and the gratitude, but also the foreboding, the future suddenly more uncertain – *two* decades after the great election of 1994! Then things deteriorating after the ANC won again. Mandela couldn't have died at a better time for them; they exploited his death.' She was on a roll.

'Caro, please …'

'Why aren't you more bothered? You seem switched off, the beach and your friends your only world. Thank heavens Franny and the twins are in Hong Kong.' She folds her sunglasses, a sign of worse to come.

'It's a world-class beachfront, I'll have you know.'

'You know, Tom, sometimes I think you're just like those people Roy Campbell wrote about, whose vision extends from the Berea to the Bluff and no further!'

Her words are cutting me up but I can't show it. 'Ah, poetry when what you really mean is I'm parochial – a man in baggies and sandals who spends his time with other men in baggies and sandals, shaving maybe every third day, mangling the language. Remember that?'

'I didn't mean *your* English …'

Something in me snaps. 'Are you like this because I'm here at home all the time now, underfoot instead of at work? No more romantic looking forward to my homecoming after business trips?'

'What hurtful things you say! You know I think you deserve your retirement.' Caro's eyes suddenly fill up with tears, her hands seeking mine. 'Sorry, honey, didn't mean it, I really didn't. I'm afraid being here, that's all. Wish you could take me away, right now, to an island with wide empty beaches where we can fly kites and not worry about being murdered.'

I bring my face closer, 'Yes, I like that, a tropical island, just the two of us.' She always smells nice, even after working in the garden on a summer's day.

'I'm cooking something new tonight.'

'You make so many nice things.' I steal a kiss.

'This one's out of my head – spaghetti with a medley of mushrooms: shiitake, portabellini, shimeji, king oyster. Then some rocket on top, drizzled with olive oil and lemon juice. Oh, and some crushed chilli.'

I don't let go of her hands. The taste of her lips mingles with my guava and yogurt – a heady cocktail for love in the afternoon. 'Busy after lunch?'

'Oh, having my hair tinted … unless you don't mind the grey showing.' In her eyes memories of lost youth, like when she looks into the mirror applying night cream after she's washed off her makeup. She used to keep her makeup on until after lovemaking, but hasn't bothered for years.

*

I'm lying naked in bed, Caro in a nightie, her head on my shoulder, both of us staring at the ceiling and the whirring fan. The sheet lifts and falls gently over us, the moving air cool on our faces that are still flushed from our melding.

I'm lulled to sleep by thoughts of al dente spaghetti and flavourful mushrooms, washed down by full-bodied cabernet, the two of us in bed afterwards, in harmony like veterans in a band – a bit like old times. Then Caro crying and saying sorry again and I do love you so, the second time she's cried in a day, but the first saying she loves me in months. Sudden and desperate, and somewhat perplexing, but I don't mind or question it, I take it when and how it comes. On this bountiful day all's well in the world. Worship these flavours of life I say, because there are none in heaven.

CHAPTER FIVE
Durban

15.8 Million South Africans – one in every three – receive a social grant from the state, double the number ten years ago. Cost: R118 billion.
— Statistics South Africa General Household Survey

In a coffee bar in Musgrave Centre my left fingers drum the table, my thumb opens my mobile phone to check the time once again. I find Tonderai Manyika's number and press it hard, as though it's an unresponsive doorbell.

Then his voice right next to me, 'Mister Tom, so sorry I'm late. Traffic on the N2, and can't phone and drive you know. Stay on the left side of the road and on the right side of the law, my daddy always says, ha, ha. And me *kugula ukugula* this morning– ah, these Natal curries, they can make you sick when they're new to your stomach!'

'Tonderai! Have a chair. Yes, you're late, on the rental too, third time as a matter of fact. Then there's the electricity I had to pay so you wouldn't be cut off, right? To say I'm concerned is putting it mildly … coffee?'

'Macchiato thanks, Mister Tom.' Tonderai puts his cell phone on the table. 'Still getting used to this new *chimbeva*, not like my old *chidhina* … ah, sorry, that's brick in town Shona.'

This man half my age talking too much instead of paying his rent, with his thin black moustache that looks pencilled-in like Robert Mugabe's, matched by a black-stubble chin. Cool shades and clothes and Shona slang, expensive new cell phone, a Rolex that seems too heavy for his delicate wrist. Tonderai Manyika, born in the shabby suburb of Chikanga on Mutare's outskirts in eastern Zimbabwe in the early years of independence, then to Harare where his father became a man of means and sent him to a private school where he no longer had to eat *sadza* and *matemba*, cattle hooves and yam – told proudly to the agent and me to assure us the rent wouldn't be a problem, backed up by his educated English, prompt payment of the deposit and first month's rent sent from his father's bank, with a letter saying the account was in good standing. No quibbles about the high uMhlanga rental required by our investor syndicate, or with me managing the lease as the only Durban based member.

'And I'll have a glass of milk thank you, very cold,' I tell the waitress who has long, shiny black hair. 'Tonderai, why can't you make EFT payments, like at the beginning? Paying in cash, and irregularly at that, doesn't work. I manage the flat on behalf of a syndicate … '

'Hey, sista, anyone tell you how pretty you are?' Tonderai says to her. She looks away, shy and pleased at the same time. 'Mr Tom, money is money but I confess I've been late in paying. My father sends it via his business associates in the Republic, and it doesn't come in a lump sum, you see. From next month my allowance will go straight to my own bank account. Of course, I hope to get a decent job soon.' He hands me a large brown envelope, flaps glued and sticky taped. 'Here's the rent ... and I still love the apartment, in case you wonder.'

'This is really awkward, Tonderai.'

'No need to count it in the loo. It's all there, no worries. Sorry, can't stay … meetings in the *tonaz*.'

He means 'town'. God, what kind of slang is this? Like the view from the apartment he called *bigaz* when he saw it for the first time. Big indeed – the long stretch of beach with its iconic lighthouse, the ocean, the giant curve in the land taking the eye all the way to Durban thirty kilometres away. I'm waiting for him to say I'm so *tolaz* or tall. Words that are simple twists of reality, childlike, inviting play as if straight from a Lego box, yet strangely unsettling – like the man himself. He doesn't have to talk like that – his English is too good – yet he does, as if he wants to emphasise he's no longer from the world of totems and Manicaland but from the street, tweeting and texting his way through the urban jungle. We drink our drinks saying little else, and I suddenly regret that I was persuaded by my fellow investors to take Tonderai Manyika as our next tenant. I don't have a good feeling about this man grinning at me, a moustache white with macchiato foam and still looking so young.

*

Tonderai has gone and I'm at the table waiting for the bill, checking my phone for messages. An SMS from Caro: 'Also get 2 ciabattas please.' There was a time when her messages would include 'darling', but that was long ago. Soon she'll send one from her bridge club saying 'fetch please'. Fido-like. Fetcher of surf-o-planes at fourteen, fetcher at sixty, a lifetime on its last lap, and so few years with so many joys still to be had.

Caro went to the gym again this morning. A bit compulsive at her age, I think, worrying about things like the little roll on her stomach. When I said so she said, 'Do you want me to look like Jane Fonda or Ugly Betty?' Her answers often force me to agree. I can't remember when last she slept naked with me. She's turned in on herself like a flower at night, sticking to inconsequentialities in our conversation that float like morning mist over a stream – staying above it for fear of being pulled in, shrouded in a sadness she can't hide. When I took her in my arms and asked what was wrong, she simply said, 'Not now please.'

*

I'm moving up and down the supermarket aisles unerringly finding packets, boxes and bottles on my list – a human Garmin with coordinates for every item. Checking sell-by dates, rummaging at the back of shelves for fresher stock, causing havoc among the displays made that morning. On to the tills with a warm sense of mission accomplished. And pensioner discount today. I wait for the question that doesn't come: 'Are you a pensioner, sir?' Cashier smiles kindly as if it's blindingly obvious. 'Plastic, sir?' she asks instead, making me suddenly feel old and weary like the people in the queue leaning on their sticks and trolleys. 'Yes, two bags, please.'

Outside, a summer's day but a strong north-easterly making palm trees bend away from the sea, and creating a haze over the city. If I were a dog my neck hairs would stand up. Thoughts of Tonderai and Caro have made me fractious, and I'm put out by Cal not making an appearance (said he had to go to Johannesburg on business, sent his SMS to Spirou, not me).

Then my dream last night (I get these disconcerting work dreams).

I'm standing in the pit of an auditorium shaped like half an amphitheatre, in the dim light eyes are visible in the front rows, higher up heads like dark blobs. I search for my presentation material that was on the table. I see part of it pushed to the side and in disarray, someone else's papers now in the centre. And Jack behind the table facing the audience. 'Jack, where's my stuff, Jesus, I'm opening this show remember?' 'It's over there, Tom.' 'No, that's only part of it, where's the rest?' 'Dunno bro, your stuff is your responsibility,' Jack getting ready, looking up at the audience. Another voice behind me: 'Where did you get this, Tom?' It's Donovan, holding up my presentation, now torn in half. 'That's mine,' I say. 'But Tom, this information is confidential, where did you get it?' 'From the files, you know that.' 'Sorry, Tom, you're out of line, it's for Jack to present, not you.' 'You know what, Donovan, I'm going to get up on this fucking table and tell everyone I've been shafted. That's what you want isn't it, to bring me down?' I get up on the table, stand in front of Jack. Faces staring from the lower levels; further back only the dark blobs, but I know all eyes are on me now – row upon row reaching up to heaven. But words fail me. Donovan leads me away. I can neither fight nor flee, both have been denied me.

You explain that, and my other dreams. I felt no rage when I retired, only immense relief that I had not been consumed by my world of work, or spat out, and looking forward to a life without toil and conflict.

*

On my balcony reading the paper – a carjacking in the area yesterday, following four last month, one fatal, and today Caro away longer than usual. Shouldn't phone her, it could make her feel hemmed in. Let the sweet bird fly out but leave the door open so that it is love that brings it back. God, how many disasters in the world – flooding in the Philippines and Thailand, tornadoes in Tennessee, an unheard of 240kph storm over Perth, earthquakes in Japan followed by a huge tsunami, a category five cyclone battering Queensland, flooding in the UK eclipsing even that of 2013/14, and famine, disease and conflict in so many places. And Caro wants us to leave Durban, this grand old home on the hill that no tsunami can reach.

Ah, the sound of the garage door opening. Light footsteps up the stairs, Caro appearing in her green and yellow frock with matching wooden necklace and yellow sandals.

'Good heavens, Caro, are you okay … your eyes!'

'Oh, the swelling … it's permanent eyeliner. No more doing it every day or having to buy any. Do you like it?'

'I suppose once the swelling's gone, yes. But then you've never used much make-up so I don't really understand …'

'It isn't just for you. I hate showering at the gym and then walking around with a bare face like when I wake up.'

'I've never had trouble liking you in the morning. Of course over a candle-lit dinner you do look extra sexy with your face all made up …'

'So you don't really like it!' Caro slips her dark glasses over her eyes.

'I didn't say that. How do they make it permanent?'

'It's like a tattoo.'

'My wife with eye tattoos, at fifty-six! What next and where? I can think of other places.' I get up to hug her.

'Oh, Tom, wait … I'm a little dizzy from the treatment, and a bit sore. Seemed like hours of needles going into me.'

Pages of the newspaper blown off the table by the wind, flapping on the floor, all order gone, no longer this page belonging here and that one there.

*

A quiet evening watching TV with dinner on our laps – chilli chicken breast cooked in olive oil and lemon with a maple syrup dressing, a glass of Sauvignon Blanc. Sound suddenly going up during ad breaks to make sure you get the message – good for another helping or a glass of wine, my thoughts on my wife, her newly tattooed eyes appearing dark and mysterious in the soft light of the bedside lamps. Here with only our gowns on.

'I do like your eyes. Bit like Cleopatra's when Elizabeth Taylor played her. No wonder Burton was smitten.'

Then, 'Tom, I've not been sleeping well … it's your snoring.' Caro's blackened eyes on me. 'I've been meaning to tell you. Please don't feel hurt but I think it's best if we sleep in separate rooms.'

'You can't be serious?'

'I am.'

I can't very well say I don't snore because I don't know – it's one of her hard-to-argue-against statements that I get now and then. 'It's a dreadful and depressing idea, Caro. I'll talk to the chemist. See if they have something.' I'm hoping the stress in her voice means she's open to negotiation.

'I already have, to save you the embarrassment. There's nothing I'm afraid, not with your kind of snoring.'

For a moment I'm Horace Rumpole listening to She Who Must Be Obeyed. Suddenly I have to contemplate life without sleeping in the same bed as my wife. It would be like losing a limb. 'From tonight, is it?'

She nods. 'In England the upper classes have always had separate bedrooms, Tom. It's nothing new. Lady Mountbatten I think it was, said, "You don't want to be bothered with snoring, or someone flinging a leg about; then when you are feeling cosy you share your room sometimes …" '

'I don't care if we're Elizabeth and Phillip. Dig me in the ribs, turn me over – anything. Wait … you don't have some dread disease you don't want to talk about? Or something else?'

'Hey, many of our friends are in the same boat, it comes with age. Doesn't mean they no longer have sex. Really, it's no big deal. Only chauvinists think wives can't have their own beds, and you're one of the least chauvinistic men I know. We're not living in Saudi Arabia.'

'What exquisite timing this eyeliner business, Caro. To make you presentable not for your husband, but a pack of gym rats! Honey …?'

'Yes.'

'I do love you … very much. You know that, don't you?'

I want her to see my eyes but she's looking away.

'No, Tom, I don't. I can't remember when last I heard you say it.'

*

I lie in one of the spare rooms, lights off, staring at the grey-black expanse that is the ceiling, the north-easterly gusting and howling through the hole in the windowpane (the one Caro asked me to fix weeks ago), the old Leopard tree scraping on the corrugated iron roof like chalk on blackboard. For the second time in a day imaginary hairs stand up in my neck. Something is amiss with Caro. Is it really the snoring? And what's with the eyeliner? My mind embarks on unwelcome, dark paths. All I'm aware of is my shallow breathing and the clamp around my heart. Unless – the thought comes as a blinding light in the night – she has found out about me, what and who I am, after all these years? I dare not ask, even indirectly. She would never trust me again, and it could exacerbate whatever is troubling her.

Tonight the mosquitoes are having a field day, turning heavy and black with my blood. I think I have the smell of distress about me.

By morning my sheets and pillows will resemble a battle zone.

CHAPTER SIX
Durban

National and provincial government spent R33.7 billion on consultants and outsourcing in the last financial year.
— Independent Online News (IOL)

Bones pulls up another umbrella, leathery limbs straining. 'Sure is a miff day,' he says. An intense glare coming off the sea onto the deck, the gentle southerly from earlier pushing hard, making the waves weak and ragged.

All eyes on Spirou and his water gun – a 9mm auto lookalike with silver handle and black snout. A large-breasted pigeon moves towards some sparrows eating crumbs from breakfast. Steam rises from the pot as Russ pours tea into our eager cups. The pigeon is close now, rocking belligerently to and fro, the sparrows too busy feeding. The pigeon oversteps the mark. A stream of water erupts from the gun's nozzle, cascading off the bird as it takes off in a flurry of feathers.

'Good one, bru!' I say.

'I can't stand them, always crapping on our boards,' Dunbar mutters.

'Good old Spirou, defender of the small and weak,' Russ says, putting the teapot on a document to stop it from blowing away.

'That your book, Russ? Read to us, will you?' Bones peers at it as though he's cribbing at an exam. On his T-shirt is printed *Old Guys Rule*.

'Have you sorted the title?' I ask.

'Amazing how it came, only at the end though. Had to write the damned novel first! I've called it *The Scent of Fraud*.'

'Ah, your auditing days … write what you know.'

Russ gives a self-aware little cough and picks up a page, good eye straining in the glare:

Justin Marlowe – with an 'e' he would always point out – bloodhound in the battle against card cloning, advance fee fraud, money laundering, and raising finance against non-existing assets, was not nearly as successful in matters of love. Crack forensic investigator that he was, he could only dream of it.

Bones throws his arms into the air. 'That's Greek, bru'.

'The Greek is still coming, man!'

'Let him finish!' Dunbar pushes a knuckle into Bones's arm, somehow always finding the same spot.

Bones winces. 'Hope you got medical cover, bru, is all I can say.'

We break down laughing. No one is a match for Dunbar. He handled the old wooden rescue boats as if they were made of balsa, lifted burly sailors against the wall with one hand at Smuggies (it was there, at this notorious pub in Point Road, that I scored my first brownie points with Dunbar: two sailors had come up behind him with knives and a serious grudge when I – underage drinker – tripped one of them and shouted a warning to Dunbar who finished them off).

'Order, order,' Dunbar says. 'Carry on, Russ.'

Russ coughs some more and resumes reading:

Life would have been tolerable had Justin not been able to put a face to his yearnings. But he could, in an antique shop in Parkhurst months earlier. She couldn't afford the pair of Edwardian crystal decanters on sale, and her anguish was palpable. On impulse he offered to buy one of them so that she could take the other, and she thanked him with a look that haunted him from that day on. His decanter would constantly remind him of her. The cut glass on his drinks tray would catch the sun and keep alive the fire burning in him.

'Bit of a *wuss,* if you ask me,' Spirou says, 'not getting her name and number.'

Dark looks dart Spirou's way. Russ continues:

Then he saw her again, waiting at the lift about to take him to the boardroom for his presentation. Suddenly he was Paris, Prince of Troy, gazing at the face of Helen, Homer's words pulsing through his head: 'Fair-skinned, with a wide, firm mouth, strong, rounded chin and deep, dark eyes under a smooth brow, a flower to melt man's heart with wonder and desire.' Then he remembered Helen had a husband, a stupid one to leave her alone with handsome, witty Paris, but a husband nevertheless. It struck Justin that this woman could also be married, and even if she weren't, she'd have a million suitors just like Helen did. The terrible thought dropped into his brain like a lobbed grenade, threatening to blow his hopes to smithereens. Unless, he thought, unless he won her over, took her heart, even if it started a bloody war.

'Hubby was Menelaus, the only history I really liked at school in Cyprus,' Spirou says. 'When I came here it was the Boers. Now there are new heroes whose names I can't pronounce. I'm done with heroes, man.'

'Menelaus was a *mamparra,* a fool, leaving a beautiful woman like that on her own,' I say. 'He should have professed undying love for her.'

Pain my new companion, I go to sleep with it and wake up to it. Caro talks more to her Facebook friends than to me (she has hundreds versus my dozen – a forerunner to our funerals?). She watches food programmes and soaps while I crack newspaper chess puzzles. With her I'm stumped.

'Forget about the history, did you like it?' Russ sounds frustrated.

We say as one, 'Yeah, Russ!'

'Cunning linguist you are, bru,' I add.

Not often that Dunbar grins. 'Hey, Russ, I hope Justin and Helen make out. Read us that part next time, okay?'

No Graham Greene or Martin Amis here, but they didn't have to make the leap from auditor to author at sixty. That alone gets my respect. Save the rhino, but fight for the apostrophe too. That's Russ, my friend.

*

Cal steps onto the deck as if he's never been away. 'Hey guys, good to see you again!' It's the smile of old – big and embracing. The same shock of hair with middle parting but now silver-blond, face and body a little fleshier. Still the good-looking man he always was, if anything with more gravitas: the extra pounds, the European paleness, the English accent. And his clothes: brown-grey chinos, coral T-shirt overprinted in French, beige loafers, and black diamond stud in one ear. Has he gone gay? Handshakes all round.

'Forgotten us, hey, life too good on the other side?' Spirou's dark eyes shine for his old friend.

'Yeah, tell us what you've been doing,' I say. 'Here's some tea, pot's still hot.'

Cal turns towards us, the diamond black against his pale skin. 'Well, I marked time in legal practice in Jo'burg to see what would come my way. Altogether too staid, though. Then discovered business consulting, or rather it found me, through a head hunter.' He attempts an unassuming laugh, 'It was love at first sight. Haven't looked back, been based in London doing projects all over the world...'

'Love ... you and the head hunter, ha, ha.' Bones looks bored.

'What kind of projects, Cal?' Russ asks.

'You name it. In the energy sector, financial, automotive, FMCG, mining, even aerospace.' He stretches out, facing the sun, 'Got to get back my tan.'

'Not much time for a wife and kids, I suppose,' Dunbar says.

Cal pulls an unhappy face. 'Regrettably I had to carry that baggage from Jo'burg, but it's in the past now. Two marriages, and two kids – doing their thing now in the US, thank heavens. Nah, the traditional marriage model has lost traction – there are alternatives nowadays that don't come with onerous legalities. Quite a paradigm shift, if you ask me.' His English accent is suddenly stronger.

Maybe Cal has gone gay after all. The word *alternative* has always sounded dodgy to me in the context of relationships.

'Bru, let's say I prefer plain English.' The twin furrows on Dunbar's forehead are deep, his long nose stern.

'Yeah, not this Greek ... what's he saying, Spirou?' Bones asks.

'Well, it's what Zorba – another Greek – called the full catastrophe: house, wife, and children. You know, the whole caboodle,' Spirou says.

I stare at Cal. More memories: outgrowing our surf-o-plane days to become champion junior lifesavers, Spirou in the belt race and beach sprint, Cal and I in the double ski race; attending fundraising bop sessions at the club, learning to drink, chat up girls, and fight. More girl successes for Cal than Montgomery had in World War 2, Spirou second, and me trailing. But with the bucket full how could I complain? And anyway, I was the best at fighting. At the smoky Empire snooker saloon, at the Lonsdale during Cookie Look, and at rock sessions across Durban, cops often had to come in their Dodge vans with long scorpion aerials to break up fights I had been involved in (it was the corporate straightjacket that finally subdued me). Life got even better when we were selected as pro lifeguards for the Christmas holiday – retrieving people instead of overdue surf-o-planes, collecting wages even when rain kept swimmers away and we could take turns surfing in front of the bathing area. Blistering summer sands, woolly red lifeguard costumes with shoulder straps that we wore folded down, patrolling the shoreline whistle in mouth or on skis in front of the crowd. And always the reel and lifeline laid out for us above the high water mark, belt open, ready to jump into and dash for the sea. All this time our torsos acquiring formidable V-shapes with our legs staying trim and lithe, like true watermen. Parents cast wary chaperone eyes as we strode the beaches past their daughters. Young boys watched in awe as we swam out to the shark nets to keep fit or just for the hell of it. I'd hold onto a buoy and look out for fins on the other side, and still accept Spirou's dare to swim across and stay there to the count of sixty. Then the race back to the beach. Born to be friends, Cal said.

Now this man opposite me, his eyes everywhere except on mine, laughing, slapping a back or two, nodding in agreement, using our names frequently.

'But why come back when it's so good over there?' Dunbar asks what everyone is thinking.

'Transcendent Worldwide – the company I'm with in London – sent me. SA is a gold mine for consulting, Dunbar ....' Cal chooses his words carefully. 'You see, government needs assistance playing catch-up after apartheid. There's a serious shortage of managerial skills and know-how.'

'Bullshit,' Russ's one brow shoots up. 'They've had ample time. A generation has gone by.'

'Russ, the fact remains that although they inherited a sophisticated infrastructure, it's now staffed by the untrained, and there's decay, broken processes, and unhappiness. Result: a hundred billion spent on consultants in just three years. Imagine all that low-hanging fruit ready for the picking! I come in, create a burning platform around which they mobilise the work force, and bingo, projects are born complete with performance indicators, dashboards, and score cards.'

'Hello, here we go again,' Bones says.

Spirou's dark eyes roll, 'Jesus, mercy, a *hundred billion!*'

Russ puts his cap on firmly. 'Since 1994 skills have been lost either through affirmative action or by skilled people leaving the country. Now the government needs help? Come on!'

I add my piece. 'So my tax money is funding that hundred billion?'

Cal looks me in the eye for the first time, 'It's common and accepted practice worldwide, Tom.'

'For work that highly-paid bureaucrats should be doing but can't! Or won't?' I can't let him get away with it. I know consultants. They side with factions that are likely to win then create thick reports regurgitating information already known, using fancy graphs, charts, and quotes from Chinese and American sages – knowing that only the summary will be read.

'Guys, if Transcendent doesn't do it others will,' Cal is calling it a wrap. 'I see you're not convinced. Just don't let it spoil old friendships, right?' Another engaging smile, 'Sorry, I have to go. I'm at the Hollywood, near the casino. Why don't we meet next Thursday, say at seven? Find a pub and grub, and make up for the lost years. Sounds good? Good. I'm in Pretoria until then.'

In the gents I pee with my head on my arm against the wall, feeling disappointed and sad. What did I expect from my old friend? Life does things to people, doesn't it? After twenty years Cal came back, looked, and is ready to conquer – Caesar, conquistador, wielding seductive jargon instead of the sword. And Caro accused *us* of mangling the language.

CHAPTER SEVEN
Durban

'Mr Bland, I'm afraid Hugh's been wandering around at night again knocking on ladies' doors. I've had complaints.' The sternness from Matron adds to her formidable stoutness. In her office everything brown or grey except the walls, no windows to see the sun, or the flowers in their immaculate beds. The fact that eight out of ten people in the retirement home are women seems lost on her. And that old wombs may be atwitter at the prospect of being ravished by the tall slim man that is my stepfather.

'Heaven forbid ... I mean that's not good, matron. What do you suggest?'

'Well, we can't lock him in at night. There could be consequences. There's the clinic, he could sleep there. I know you already have a day-carer. The clinic would be extra, you understand.'

'A bit heavy on top of the levy and the rates, but let me discuss it with him. I'd like to think about it.'

'By all means, Mr Bland, but please understand we can't allow this to carry on. It's disruptive to others at Golden Days.'

Yeah, old age catch-22. You have to be healthy when you arrive in order to get frail care in later years when you really need it. But if you develop dementia along the way they can't help you and no one else will take you because you're not healthy.

I walk to the annex ensuring I stay clear of the lawns, through this garden of the white-haired sitting on shaded benches, some knitting, most just staring, while in the trees around them there's vibrant birdsong. Into the building, familiar musty passage, schmaltzy pictures on the wall, razor wire visible through the windows along the sills, Hugh's door open, a breeze coming through the security gate. And next to it *Hugh's Home* ornately carved on a block of wood.

Hugh comes to the door in a tracksuit: long thin body, wispy white hair, gossamer skin, blue veins bruised in places, faded blue eyes vacant with moments of comprehension of the present and the long gone past, and little in between. Too gentle to make it to headmaster at the government school for boys where he taught English and History, but who gave me a life at the age of ten and, as time went by, his love of books. Letting everyone think I was his and Marge's – a surrogate care unconditionally given, to ease my angst about the world and who I really was.

'Hi Pops.' I put my arms around him, pressing lightly for fear of breaking something. 'Hear you've been chasing women again. Now, now ...'

'What? Me? Since Marge died I've had eyes for no one else. Maybe a cuddle here and there, yes, and a little goosing ...'

'Just don't go for Matron, okay. Come, let's sit down. Your TV screen is on the blink, Pa.'

'Bloody remote again ...'

'Give here ... there you go, you keep pressing the wrong buttons!'

'It's my eyes, my boy. How are you, Tom?'

How can I burden him with my insecurities, my searching for clues in Caro's handbag the other day, my face hot with shame but unable to stop? Then finding only little items of innocence: an appointment card with a sports massage therapist, a brush, a comb, two lipsticks, a powder compact, pen, headache pills, a pack of tissues, a bridge score card, a small battery-operated plastic fan, and her purse with cards, and photos of Franny and the twins in Hong Kong (I actually made an inventory). At first I agonised over the Dentyne gum, the bottle of Diorissimo, and the string of pearls, convincing myself later that they could be normal accessories. I marvelled at the wondrous thing that is a woman's handbag. In her gym bag I found only Reeboks and socks, black Nike tights, training vests, a towel, gym card, and some toiletries. I couldn't look Caro in the eye for days (not that we regularly exchange glances, my separate bed now a fixture in our lives). I thought about her bridge twice a week in Durban North, and the away tournaments.

It happened in companies, didn't it – men and women drawn to one another? But Caro had complained about how dull male bridge players were, and their terrible dress sense. Still it preyed on me.

'How are Caro and Franny? I'm a grandfather did you know?'

'Pa, you're a *great* grandfather. If only Marge had lived to see the twins.'

Hugh and Caro, an uneasy relationship from the beginning, with me letting it go out of a selfish fear that he might one day let slip our secret. Hugh would forget what happened hours earlier but remember things from two decades ago. His creeping dementia has become my punishment: my wish that my past should fade away in his head like the colours of a painting exposed to the sun, and that once he stops remembering my name and face I'd be safe, strangers again like the day we met.

'Pops, listen, we might have to move you, not tomorrow but soon. We have a bit of a problem but I don't want you to worry, everything will be all right.'

'Oh my, doesn't sound good ... hope I haven't done anything wrong. Should I tell Marge? No nasty surprises please, my boy. Her blood pressure is already high.'

And he takes six different medicines every day for his heart – blood thinner, tranquiliser, and other stuff – following a by-pass and the fitting of a pacemaker. His hand on the armrest is shaking now. I pull him up gently and hug him. He smells of baby powder. 'Don't worry about Marge, or the move. I'll take care of everything.'

I hold him and rock him because the world has little need for old people and sometimes even children.

*

'You paid only half the rent this time Tonderai. What's up, man?'

'Mr Tom, it's like this, I've had unplanned expenditures. Had no idea my *mbongo* – my money – would be eaten up like this. But I'll sort it out ... call you in a few days and we can meet somewhere, okay.'

Tonderai's voice becomes indistinct. What is he doing on the other end of the line? I have thoughts of a messy eviction, of good tenants difficult to find, but I stay calm. 'You're breaking our lease agreement, Tonderai. I might have to invoke clause ten on special remedy for breach, should it happen again. I'll have no choice, hope you understand.'

A little intake of breath, Tonderai's voice suddenly clear, 'Wait! Mr Tom, please ...'

'Here is what it says, to remind you: "Should the lessee default on any payment due under this lease and fail to remedy such default within ..."'

It's as though I'm outside the conversation listening in, with me sounding like a corporate type, affecting anger control and poise under stress, attempting to convey executive presence when all I want to do is knock the shit out of the man.

*

'So what does the Hollywood set you back per night, Cal?' Spirou's first sip of draught has given him a white moustache. I think of Tonderai's mouth covered with macchiato foam.

'One thousand four hundred, nothing in pounds, and really spacious – flats converted to suites. Of course I still have my place in London. ' Cal relaxed on a bar stool, top button and tie undone, sleeves of his shirt at half-mast, the lines on his grey pin-striped trousers looking pressed even after the flight.

'Why not take a furnished flat?' Bones, in baggies and T-shirt, is impressed.

'Must stay flexible ... that's consulting. Projects could be anywhere.'

TV on the wall, Sharks rugby match from last season, a line of elbows on the smooth counter, faces turned towards the screen like flowers to the sun, washed glasses upside down at the sink, fridges filled with drinks, a row of handles and beer taps, steel necks glistening with condensation, the air buzzing and punctuated by guffaws.

'How are you feeling, Bones?' I ask.

'Bloody sore down here, whatsit called ... the peri something?'

'The perineal area, it's between your balls and your arsehole.' Russ drinks from his glass as if the thought of Bones's nether regions needs washing away. 'Anyway, you can't get any balder, buddy.'

Bones turns to Cal, 'Prostrate cancer, you see ... just had radioactive wires put into the tumour. Not sure which is worse – the wires or Addington.'

'Oh boy, you don't want to go there. Gotta take your own linen, I hear,' Spirou says. If Dante lived today, Addington hospital would have a spot in his *Divine Comedy*, in *Hell*.

'You mean prostate, Bones,' I say. Years of pro lifeguarding and living with a parrot haven't helped Bones in the communication area.

'I'll take the wires anytime over the fucking finger,' Dunbar declares.

'This is all too banal,' Cal's expression seems to be saying.

'So Cal, what's your take on SA since you've been back?' Spiro asks.

'Ah, much improved wine, food pretentiously mediocre, and clothes middleclass at best.'

'Come on, you can expand on this? You're a consultant,' Russ says, fingers tapping the counter.

Cal's pauses always seem to have gravitas. He takes a sip of wine – on the rim of the glass with lips tight as if he needs to savour the nose too. No one else is having wine. He could be gay after all – every now and then a gesture, a movement.

'Guys, I've been away too long, I'm not even a citizen anymore. I've come for the projects, not the politics. Transcendent doesn't do politics, you understand. And this is my swansong. I'm calling it quits afterwards.' As Cal gets up the ends of his trousers fall neatly on his shiny shoes. 'Let's get comfortable at that table.'

It's the third time we're drinking with Cal, once at the club, twice at this pub, Cal interacting with us as a group, avoiding one-on-ones, changing subjects, steering the conversation adeptly through his knowledge of things and places, and smiling so as not to affront anyone. The feeling we once had for each other seems to have diminished. It happens over time between people. I'm looking not at an old friend but a newly-acquainted stranger. I order another round of large draughts, 'This one's on me, guys.' 'Good old Tom!' A little later Dunbar buys, then Spirou, and Cal and Russ, each one having to wrestle Bones's hand away from his pocket – funny-sad because there's nothing

in it anyway – and following it with a toast: '*Vasbyt,* bru!'
'Here's to nuking the tumour!' 'Yeah, in your peri-peri!'

A dumb thing to have on a pub wall: a clock. Who cares
about the time when beer taps are gushing, and the room is
brimming with bonhomie? Maybe I've been too hard on Cal, not
giving him time to slot back into our band of brothers. I smile at
Cal and he smiles back.

The night air is soft, with a whiff of sea. Spirou, Dunbar,
Russ and I piling into the taxi Cal ordered. Car rocks violently.
'Like old times at the drive-in!' 'Yeah, the late show!' Raucous
laughter, the driver stares ahead looking forward to his bed, too
young to know what we're laughing about. We wave at Cal and
Bones on the pavement, the one walking to his suite, the other to
his parrot.

*

I'm trying to tiptoe up the old Oregon-pine staircase (I've had
enough practice over the years, heaven knows), clutching the
railing to stop myself from falling over. I pause to quieten my
breathing, and take off my shoes. Onto the landing now, the
Persian welcoming under my feet, but God what thirst – isn't
beer supposed to be mostly water? I shuffle to my room in the
dark, something on the floor at the door. Down on my knees,
patting the carpet: a piece of paper, no, an envelope. Why get up
to switch on the light – just to see someone's name and
handwriting, ha, ha. Wait! I stumble to the kitchen, open the
envelope and let it float to the floor. To Caro's bedroom now –
dark and silent, bed made, undisturbed – then to the balcony to
find a chair and stare at the lights in the bowl of the city. What
reprieve tonight from summer's humid haze – a taste of the
season to come, of gentle offshore breezes, cream-soda surf, and
friends to share it with!

Much later I go to the kitchen for food, to find she's left me
cold roast chicken with a note to heat up the roasted vegetables:
butternut with edges deliciously blackened, scored aubergine
halves, deep burgundy beetroots, and potatoes.

Standing up, careful to load a little of each onto my fork, I
finish Caro's meal, eyes at half-mast with pleasure and pain.

CHAPTER EIGHT
Durban

(Many) years in power has changed the African National Congress from the party of Nelson Mandela's righteous revolution into just another rapacious developing-world elite. Inequality – stretched wider by a fabulously wealthy ANC-connected cabal – has increased.

— Alex Perry, 'Africa Rising', *Time Magazine*

I go into the blue-white Skype cloud, click on Franny Palmer and wait for the welcoming sounds that would reconnect me to the world after four days. Please let her be there; it's 9am in Durban, 3pm in Hong Kong.

'Dad, good to hear from you, how are you, how's Mum?' Franny in tracksuit, no make-up, freckled nose and cheekbones, ponytail hurriedly tied. Slim like Caro, not from gym but having to cope with twins and endless chores. 'Wow, Dad, you don't look well at all.'

'Thanks, it's all I want to hear. I'm glad you're sitting down, Franny.'

'Oh dear ...'

'Your mother has, well ... left me, just a letter on the carpet, no discussion, and not a word since.'

'*Your* mother, she's *ours*, Dad! She could at least have told me. When was this?'

'About four days ago.'

'Da-ad ... and you didn't call! This letter, what does it say?'

'That she feels we need a break from each other ... oh, and that the decision upset her no end. Not half as much as me, I tell you.'

'She leaves without good reason and tells you she's feeling bad. And doesn't discuss it with me, I don't like the sound of it ...'

'Grandaddy!' Liam and Josh now next to Franny. 'Look, I can touch your face,' Liam pokes at me on the screen, Josh claps his hands. Sturdy three-year-olds, carrot-coloured hair, blue eyes, square-jawed trouble (Stephen threatened to sell them to the Triads – two for the price of one).

'Hey, don't touch, it'll crack!' Franny slaps Liam's hand.

'When you coming again, Grandaddy?' Josh asks. 'Yeah, yeah, when?' Liam says.

Ninja suddenly on the keyboard, walking across it as though it's a minefield, large pointed ears and blue almond eyes deep in concentration. 'Ooh, look, a computer cat!' says Josh. 'Get off!' Franny snatches Ninja from the laptop. 'Lord, this place is too small for us.'

'Shall we talk later, Franny?'

'No, Dad, I've got questions. Give me a minute ... I'm going to shut them in their bedroom.'

'Love you Grandaddy! Hate you Mummy!'

What more can I tell Franny? Caro up and left me, staying with her parents. Don't call me I'll call you, her letter said. Back in the Old Durban Family camp which at best tolerated me all these years – James and Diana Whittington, Essenwood Road dentist and socialite respectively at the time I met Caro. I of lower Glenwood, bank teller studying part-time for my B Com (an iffy future not rooted in the professions, James once told Caro, what can one expect with a government school teacher as a father), beach type to boot, paid lifeguard whose brain would be addled by the sun in no time. And when James saw he was going to lose his daughter, insisting on Whittington-Bland as Caro's married name – a win-win for him because he got the distinguished double-barrel and blunted the Bland part in one fell swoop.

Most of last week I spent at home on my own, waiting and hoping (exacerbated by the fact that it's not really my house because James gave it to Caro for a nominal sum when he retired and moved to his townhouse in La Lucia). And now Franny stressed too. She's always been highly-strung. Maybe it was her bruising birth – twelve hours it took – Caro having insisted on the natural way, only to have her tubes tied afterwards rather than have another child.

Life in Hong Kong to the twins and the cat means constant warfare, with alliances made and broken at the drop of a hat, their bedroom a den of plotting during truces, and a battle zone when they disagree. Cooped up in Soho that is more suited to bohemian nightlife than to a family, but easy for Stephen to walk along Hollywood Road to his office in Central.

'Right, Dad, where was I ... ah yes. Don't be upset, but have you considered that she might be seeing someone?' Franny's ponytail more dishevelled and rings visible under her eyes, my news no doubt exacerbating matters.

'Another man ...'

'These things happen, Dad. After so many years together she's probably just too distressed to talk about it. Is there anyone else maybe? Think of the places she goes to.'

'Well, I thought of bridge, but my impression is those men wouldn't last five minutes on a surfboard. Her hairdresser's a woman, and so are her physiotherapist, manicurist and pedicurist, so it rules them out. Then there's the gym. She *has* been going more often, yes. And she's had eyeliner tats done, so she doesn't have to worry about showering ...'

'Tats? You don't mean tattoos?'

'Yes, your mother, at fifty-six.'

'Oh dear, what can I say. But there's no difference really between that and false nails and eyelashes, is there?'

'You know what? I don't think I'll ever understand women. How's Stephen?'

'Now that he's survived the headcount cuts he's holding on, like Ninja, except he's used up all his lives, I think. At the office at seven, back at eight if we're lucky – it's the time differences between Hong Kong and New York, and London and Frankfurt, trading on the phone.'

'At least he got a bonus ...'

'Not enough to buy in the south of the Island. We're so worried about pollution from the mainland, for the kids with their young little lungs.'

Furious cries from the bedroom, Ninja's some decibels higher.

'Their lungs sound just fine to me. A little reduction in capacity might not be a bad thing.'

'I must dash, Dad. Heaven knows who's being killed. Let me know if you find out more. I'll talk to Mummy. Love you … hey, hope you're eating properly!'

'Don't worry about me. Love you too, my precious girl. Chin up, okay.'

My news is threatening to pull loose one of Franny's anchors in life. Wish I could make things easier for her – take the twins to Disneyland on Lantau, or to Repulse Bay beach. Be a dad to her again. Let her have some time of her own. It's what I wanted for Caro (that it didn't work out doesn't matter, it was the right thing to do). Franny will probably never come back. I can't imagine Caro doing the same.

At least Franny didn't ask the question I dreaded most: 'Can you think of any other reason why she wanted to leave you?' How could I look her in the eye and say no?

I open the fridge – things in bottles, limp vegetables in trays, bread I'm trying to keep fresh, Gruyere going mouldy, a couple of bottles of Sauvignon Blanc, and a whole lot of beers.

*

On my way to the new nursing home the thought hits me: what if Caro has a thing going with her personal trainer? Dylan as her toy boy, her cub as they call it nowadays – isn't that what can happen in a marriage of many years? A spouse feeling life has passed him or her by, finding a younger, and I hate to say it, livelier and spicier partner? Grabbing the opportunity to make up for lost time? Everything points to it. Caro going to the gym every other day, her glowing skin, eyes and hair, the eyeliner tats, her waning interest in me, the manner of her parting – the letter on the carpet like a landmine in the dark. Yeah, Dylan has never had it so good: getting three hundred rand per hour three times a week from me then having fun with Caro somewhere. Or is it the other way around: Caro as his Mrs Robinson? It's killing me.

I shoot through the intersection's red light. Motorists swerve and hoot, some resorting to finger language I deem most unseemly. My hand goes up saying I'm sorry as I sit paralysed in the middle of the intersection – damned if I reverse and damned if I go forward. A lesson from my corporate life: when the going gets rough, do nothing, and nothing will befall you.

*

I'm at reception at Happy Days Nursing Home, elbow on counter filling in forms, frowning. On the walls, notices and rosters, a clock, some sun-faded flower prints, and certificates in fancy script. In the office, filing cabinets, computers, a whirring ceiling fan, and a pair of open windows staring at the park across the road: the bench against a tree, some swings, a lopsided see-saw, tibouchina shedding pink blossom, jet trails in the sky – a world left behind, never to be re-entered.

'Sister, it says nothing about the period of stay or the notice required?'

I give her a look-over: slim (a nice change), white uniform, eyes and breasts competing for first prize. She doesn't answer. My appreciative glance seems to have struck her dumb. Is she so prim?

An old lady appears from the passage in slippers and gown, head white and wispy, skin wrinkled. 'Am I sleeping here tonight, dearie? Have to fetch my things if I am.'

'Yes, Mrs Lang, like you have for six months.' Sister's firm grip on the woman's elbow, voice gentle, 'Now turn around … there we go. It's nearly time for tea and cookies.'

Perplexed green pools behind Sister's round-framed spectacles. 'You asked about notice, Mr Bland – at Happy Days?'

I bang my forehead. 'Ah, I understand. Please forgive me.' Time has no meaning when you're here to die and you can't diarise your death, unless you're planning suicide, and if you're able to plan your death you won't be here in the first place (Joseph Heller would have a field day). 'I'll take the corner room I saw last week, number fourteen. Nice light and air coming through, and no basin. He's taken to water like a duck – plugs up basins, opens taps and walks away, smiling. He should never shower alone. He'll never turn the water off.'

You see, Sister, I'm a waterman too. Wouldn't you like to come and swim with me? Your name again … ah, yes, it's on the board: Sister Amber John. No man's hands are safer in the water than mine. Brought Caro to me, one day at South Beach when a vicious rip cut a dozen swimmers from the crowd like carrots being chopped – short ways not julienned, you understand – carrying them out in its grip. And I first into the belt, pushing the pin in, swimming out with the wet weight of the line behind me. Spirou, Cal and Pete feeding it out, letting me have just enough. More lifeguards scrambling on skis and boards. Swirling sea, blue bottles caught in the currents, tentacles everywhere. Bobbing heads turned towards the beach, arms flailing as if legs clamped by octopuses, mouths taking in water. A few gulps too many and goodbye. Reached three of them, two men and a girl, gripped one in each arm and one between my legs. The girl all eyes with fear but quiet, not like the whimpering men, as if she knew I'd bring her in. Glanced at me once or twice from under my arm willing me on, my lungs rasping, my skin burning from the tentacles on my ears, neck and back as Spirou, Cal and Pete pulled us in. It's one big reason why I love the sea, Sister Amber – it delivered Caro to me, even though it asked a lot of me that day.

*

'Surf's up!' Numo squawks, gnarly claws resting on Bones's shoulder, eyes flame yellow, tail chilli red, nose and mouth a single black curve. Pigeons perched a healthy distance away this morning, sparrows twittering high on the club's roof, Spirou's water gun tucked away in his locker.

'Can't he see it's not?' Dunbar says, unimpressed.

'I thought parrots are so smart they can read barometric pressure,' Russ says.

Bones looks hurt. 'I tried to teach him the difference between an easterly and a westerly so he wouldn't wake me up every morning. I mean if it *were* a westerly I wouldn't mind.'

'Let him sleep where our boards are,' Dunbar says, 'it'll stop the pigeons crapping on them.'

'Come on, Dunbar, I can see *you* doing it. He's one of us, man!' Bones gets up. 'Gotta piss … there, Numo, you go sit with Tom. Over you go.' Numo takes off my glasses, puts them down and peck-kisses me then lowers his head to be stroked.

'Someone loves Tom,' Spirou says, dark eyes glistening.

'Bones is his life,' Russ says, 'I think he'll die for Bones. Wonder how long parrots live. Whoever's left behind won't *want* to live.'

Uninvited thoughts float in the balmy air. Who'll be the first to die? Not just Bones and Numo – I can't imagine *any* of us not coming back to this deck. Russ is down too today. Not one publisher has responded to his query letter and synopsis. Editors unavailable or in meetings, piles of manuscripts to go through, we'll contact you, was all he got. And Spirou, gentle soul – how could I not tell him about Caro? Not to ease my pain but to avoid hurting him.

Bones returns with spots of water on his baggies (or is it piss?).

'Well, what do you know, my cock also lies to the left,' Russ observes.

'Ha, ha, you guys should be so lucky,' Spirou says. It passes over Bones like a puff of cloud. With Numo on his shoulder the world's all right.

Maybe Dylan is the one with the luck. At home I'm sleeping in our double bed again but not well. It feels even emptier than the spare room, her pillows carrying her fragrance. I can't get myself to change the pillow cases, and I can't stop looking at her clothes – it's as though she left her favourites behind on purpose. I take them out, bury my nose in them and hang them up again. Her letter I don't touch, the words I know all too well. I live on takeaways, and drink on my own (a sure sign of trouble, they say). I'm having bad dreams about work with Donovan snooping around making notes. I avoid Agrippa and Precious. The worry in their eyes makes things worse. I look at myself in the mirror to see if what she's given up is really that bad: same old blue eyes, my hair still intact but now a deeper brown accentuating the flecks of grey-white, a few lines on my face, my upper body not as muscular as it used to be, but my laterals, pecs and legs still good. It's when I look at my penis that I really worry. I'm sure it used to be longer and fatter. It looks shrivelled as if it's been in the Atlantic. I'm convinced it has become smaller from underuse. And I think of Dylan again. Round and round I go. It's driving me crazy.

Dunbar breaks my thoughts: 'Tom, you say the tenant is still messing you around? With a rich father in Harare ... I don't like it. A Zanu-PF man if you ask me, in with the Mugabe crowd.'

Dunbar is the prickliest of us all. Years with 5 Reconnaissance Commando of the South African Special Forces Brigade (aka the Recces), initially at Duku-Duku camp in Natal followed by a stint in Phalaborwa in the north. Then to South West Africa for the showdown with SWAPO and their Cuban and Russian backers – as if the time in camps, training to kill then vanish ghost-like, was preparation for this cataclysmic event. It was the invasion of Angola that changed Dunbar, or so we assumed because he never talked about it. Only years later did I get an inkling of what it must have been like, not from Dunbar, but from background reporting and books: the brutality of the training, the unforgiving African bush, the unconventional nature of the conflict as well as its complexity involving an array of adversaries. Dunbar returned from the border in 1988, not talking and we not asking. We trod warily around him – there had been stories about *bosbefokte* soldiers going berserk upon their return and going on shooting rampages. Dunbar went into the security business, caught the industry boom post-1994 with crime escalating to unprecedented levels, and sold out twenty years later, financially independent. But here's the irony: he lost his family, not through crime or illness but through estrangement. Again, he didn't talk and we didn't ask. We just accepted the changed Dunbar. And so it is today: Dunbar not the same because he's carrying things he can't talk about, and he doesn't talk because whatever happened in the bush and with his family changed him. Catch-22 got even old Dunbar. We are brothers, Dunbar and I, bound by things we don't even know about each other. If it had a trillion people, the world would still be a lonely place.

Dunbar looked out for his friends and he expected the same from them. I guess it's what the bush did to him. It was never clearer to me when, one night over a board game called Risk, a player who had formed an alliance with Dunbar suddenly switched, and laughed about it. Dunbar picked him up from his chair, held him in the air with his feet dangling, and said: 'Cross me again and you leave in a body bag, my friend.' No one doubted Dunbar that night, or ever since.

I turn to Dunbar, 'Let's talk about the tenant over a beer, bru, I can't think straight now. There's something I must do first.'

CHAPTER NINE
Durban

I drive through the rows of cars parked at the gym, my heart wanting to bolt from my body. Check left, right, and left again, hands trembling only slightly less when I reach the end without spotting Caro's silver BMW 325.

I park with much manoeuvring, reluctant to leave the snug, safe cabin of the Wrangler. My lined face in the mirror watches as I smooth down my hair, clear my eyes of sleep and pinch my cheeks for colour. What for? In case I see Caro?

I'm at reception. 'Morning, I'm interested in taking out membership.' Music pumping from multiple speakers, weights thumping on the floor. Gym rats on the move everywhere.

'Of course, sir, shall I call a consultant to take you around?' Anishka on her name tag: skin the colour of almonds, long hair glowing like cabernet in a glass held to the light.

'Not now thanks. I'd like to know about your personal trainers. Maybe I should get one … better than getting a hernia from the weights on the first day, eh.' I pat my chest smiling.

The girl frowns. 'But sir, we require you to see a consultant first. The personal trainers are usually on the floor with clients.'

Reception areas can be tricky, questions and labyrinthine forms designed to put one on the back foot, flush out industrial spies, infiltrators, and imposters. Turnstiles locked, moat filled, drawbridges up. But there's no turning back now.

'No, no, I don't need to speak to a trainer. I want to know *about* them … like what qualifications they have. After all, I'd be handing over my body to them, wouldn't I?' I put on a little shiver. 'It's like going to a doctor you don't know – could be a quack and next thing you're even sicker, right?' Like Caro handing over her body to Dylan for an hour of pain in the gym followed by hours of pleasure.

Faint smile in Anishka's eyes, more people swiping their cards and pushing through the turnstile. I press home, 'Can I suggest something? You let me in to study that board about your personal trainers, and when I get back you call a consultant, deal?'

'That's fine, but please don't wander around. May I have your name please?'

I cough suddenly, slapping my chest. 'Sorry, just nerves, haven't been to gym in years. Ah, my name … this morning when I woke up it was Drake, John Drake.'

'Mr Drake,' Anishka laughing now, 'there, you can go through.'

I'm in front of the board. Photos of perfect bodies in fine poses: Dylan's jumping out at me, shorter than I expected but well-proportioned with V-shaped laterals, hillocks for pectorals, and kneecaps and ankles appearing too delicate to support the rest of him. Not a hair on him (does he or doesn't he use Nair?) except for the black mop on his head. No doubt his pubes are as luxurious. Dylan is into 'Weight Training, Functional Training, Cross-fit, and MMA.' Christ, mixed martial arts – no-holes-barred cage fighting, blood and guts stuff. And I bet with testosterone to burn.

I gaze through the glass partition. On the other side furious cycling, running, rowing and stepping, bodies of all shapes and sizes straining and sweating without going anywhere. In a separate area, Charles Atlas and Austrian Arnie wannabes with their branded gear, caps on backwards, fingerless gloves, tattoos, sockless sneakers, and iPods, carrying their water bottles from station to station, where they lift weights and grunt to the count from their buddies. To my left lies the pool – permanently on a chemical drip in ICU.

No sign of Dylan and Caro but my relief is brief. They could have come and gone. Still I linger, to contemplate this world behind brick and glass that cannot feel the westerly wind, the rhythm of the sea, the thrill of riding a wave – reasons why I've never cared for gyms. And now to be defeated by one, the irony stings. I who was so supportive, hoping the gym would make her happy and keep her lovely for me.

*

Franny calls to say Caro didn't want to talk. Franny worried about me on my own, begging me to come and stay with them. But I can't leave this place where Caro still is. I buy bread for Agrippa and Precious in the morning, and whatever else they need. For myself I can't get beyond a curry takeaway, a pizza, or a pie – a break from shopping for Caro, but also from her wonderful meals. I hate TV even more – fatuous American fare that keeps channels running twenty-four seven, as non-stick as Teflon on my brain.

Bad dreams again that clamp my heart and push my blood against arterial walls – afflictions from my corporate days emerging again like bats in the night. And long forgotten organisation charts with names and titles, sharp-edged steps to success, with lessons to tread carefully: lift the feet high so as not to stumble, and always look who's behind you.

*

Strange that I'm not dreaming about Dylan now that I've seen his face, defined as though on its own training regime, eyes too close as if someone squeezed his temples too hard at birth, small flat ears, but somehow a face that works. I don't dream about Tonderai either, although his grinning macchiato moustache still gives me the creeps. Maybe it's because I think of them during the day. I don't even try to understand it.

On any given day my intake of liquids exceeds that of solids. Trouble is most of it is booze, not tea, juice, or water. Even the steenbras and the kabeljou in the freezer from my last trip to Namibia can't tempt me. I'll give the fish to Chloe, Spirou's loving wife, hoping she'll invite me to dinner.

*

'So how's Hugh getting on, Sister? Not too much trouble I hope.'

She looks up from her paperwork, pristine all in white, a glint of afternoon sun on the rims of her glasses. 'Hello Mr Bland, nice to see you. Oh, he's just fine. Loves the monkeys though … had to stop him from feeding them. He's crazy for the cat too but it's mutual I'm happy to say. Ah yes, the hosepipe. We've had to put it well out of reach. He sprays everyone making shooting noises, never the monkeys or the cats though, strange ...'

'Maybe he takes a dim view of humanity.'

'An angry old man, a bit late for that, isn't it? Anyway, humanity shouldn't be despised, it should be helped. It certainly needs it.'

'Is that your mission in life? Anger isn't just for the young, you know. It can strike at any time.' I want to tell her just how cruelly it can happen.

'Mr Bland, are we having a philosophical discussion or an argument?' Her green eyes are full of spark, her bun battling to stay contained, like the rest of her in her uniform.

'An argument is the last thing I want to have with you. You're an angel, Sister. From the time I walked in I thought so. And I appreciate what you're doing for Dad. Let's just say I sense the potential for some stimulating discourse.'

She bites on her ballpoint. 'That would be indulgent to say the least, even if you're serious which I doubt you are. You see, I spend most of my waking time with people who can't think for themselves. So I have to do it for them, at the level of *their* needs, not that of a Socrates. Think feeding, Mr Bland, washing, and nappy-changing – for old people, not babies. Let's just say it's my calling.' She holds my gaze, then says abruptly, 'Shouldn't you go and see your father?'

'I meant to ask – apart from hosing women down, does he bother them?'

'No, he doesn't, not like you. And they actually like him.'

Sister Amber John is starchy but sensual, she changes old people's nappies, and Socrates is no stranger. If only she'd smile sometimes.

Walking down corridors now, past open doors: a man on his back on a bed, veined hands folded over his stomach, mouth open, a fan on a chair cooling his bruised legs, his twitching big toe the only sign he's alive; a woman shuffling past me in baggy jersey and pants, head moving to and fro like the pigeons at the club.

Hugh on a couch wedged between two women; more women on other couches, all of them staring at the TV in the corner.

'Hi Dad, keeping good company I see. No, no, don't get up.'

'My boy, give me a hug … there, ah, I love my hugs, nice strong ones.'

'Hey, where did you get that ring, Dad?'

'Oh, Daisy here gave it to me. Daisy, you got it at the jewellers, didn't you?'

'Don't be silly, Hugh. I got it from a Christmas cracker.' She smiles toothlessly at me, 'Sorry, I can't have my hair cut now. I'm watching a concert.' On the screen Scarlet and Rhett Butler are having a tiff.

'Dad, I got something to tell you. Can we talk in the room? It's about Caro.'

'Caro, oh, she came to see me.'

'Jesus Dad, what did she say? You know she's left me, and staying with James and Diana in La Lucia, in the townhouse by the sea.'

Milky eyes fixed on the screen, horses, soldiers and mayhem in the Deep South.

'Yes, she's by the sea, and tomorrow I'll be with her. My clothes, my boy, please get them ready. Only my best for Marge …'

How they loved each other, my stepparents, from the moment they met at Dokkies, Durban's training college for teachers, at a Saturday night 'social' in Queen Mary Avenue. Marge would relate the story forgetting, or not caring, that people had heard it many times. It was perhaps why it sounded every time as if it had happened the night before. Her eyes would go dreamy and her voice a little tremulous and Hugh wouldn't know what to say, except it was clear he felt the same way. Hugh – BA in English and History, Higher Education Diploma, senior master at a prestigious Model C school, taking his 'package' in the 1990s as part of the new affirmative action policy, never making it to headmaster. To me everything I'd hoped for in a father but never had with my own. It was why, when the matron at Hugh's previous nursing home said, 'Best that you take him away, Mr Bland, at least he'll be remembered here with most of his dignity intact', I wanted to smash the furniture in her office.

I stroke his white hair, this man who nursed *me* once upon a time with William and Biggles, Tarzan and Zane Grey to get me started, opening my eyes, my mulish ears and my clenched fists, bringing in the greats as my mind grew stronger, leaving aviators, ape-men and cowboys behind. Building model airplanes with me on weekends crafted from fragile balsa and paper, moistening the tissue to dry tightly like skin, painting the planes in the colours of the RAF or the Luftwaffe, winding up the propellers on elastic bands stretched through the fuselage before aiming for the sky.

What next for me to read? I think of *Steppenwolf*, hiding somewhere in a corner in my bookcase. Maybe it was him I heard the other night on the old floorboards, sniffing around.

*

I find myself at the gym again – I have to be the only person coming here without working out. My story to Anishka won't work again, and other than saying I'm now ready to see a consultant (which I can also do only once) I have no other ideas to get through the turnstile. And do I really want to bump into Caro? Sitting in the parking lot is a bad idea because the Wrangler is distinctive and she knows the number plate. What would I say anyway? That I can't live without her? That she can make a list of things she hates about me and I promise to change them? Maybe it's too late. The manner of her departure and the build-up to it was too measured. All I want is confirmation of my suspicions, although it seems a waste of time now that I feel so sure it's Dylan.

I wait outside the parking lot in a side street from where I can see the doors to the gym, binoculars handy to lessen the strain on my eyes on this bright morning. Got the newspaper, not to read – I wouldn't take in a thing – but as cunning camouflage. The name is Bland, Thomas Bland but spot the difference: I'm in a Jeep not an Aston Martin, and I am as monogamous as a Mute Swan (some might say as uxorious). Today with the westerly blowing I should be out on the water with my friends, not on the lookout for my wife and her personal trainer on their way to a tryst, rendezvous, *tête-à-tête*, whatever. It muscles out all other things from the mind.

Is that Caro? Brown bob, blue track pants. It's her all right – always more on the toes than on the heels, a springy kind of walk, training bag over the shoulder, cell phone to the ear. I follow her through the binoculars, past rows of cars until she disappears. I have the urge to run to the fence but can't move, wiping the sweat from my eyes. I'm confused. Why is she alone?

She returns, this time without her training bag, walks past the sliding doors of the gym to the sidewalk and waits. Minutes seem like aeons, cars stream by, and a lone gull rides the currents over the buildings. Why aren't you skimming the waves, you lovely bird? Are you lost, like me? A car stops next to Caro. She gets in, leans across the seats for an embrace. I raise the binoculars. It's Cal Ryder.

They fall from my hands. I grope for the paper, pull it over me to blot out what I'm seeing, and taste the print – it's bitter, foul. Suddenly it goes soggy around my eyes. Like a man having a heart attack my face drops onto the steering wheel.

CHAPTER TEN
Durban, Caro

The whole point about scenarios is to recognise when the chandelier in the ballroom is beginning to tremble. The way we are programmed is to stick our heads in the sand and go on enjoying the party until the lights go out.
— Clem Sunter

'Cardio today, Caro,' Dylan tells me with relish, 'treadmill and bike for the legs, arm-ergometer and rowing machine for the top. Feeling strong, I hope?'

Knowing that in two hours from now I'll be seeing Cal makes me weak in the knees. I don't need some machine to bring my heart rate up. It's already high.

'Dylan, do you mind if we do strength and stretch instead? I'm feeling a little heady.' I punch him playfully in the tummy. It's like a brick wall. He doesn't flinch.

'Slacking, hey? You've done it a few times now. How will Tom feel if the kilos come back? It's simple: less cardio, more kilos.'

I look at him in desperation. Hearing Tom's name hurts. '*Please*, Dylan.'

'Oh, all right. But just this time, okay?'

*

Listlessly I perform the mandatory number of reps with Dylan counting. I'm caught between the anticipation of seeing Cal again and surges of guilt, and I think of how it all happened, how unasked and unwished for it was. Cal a dim memory in the recesses of my brain, with no conscious thought of him at any time, then suddenly coming across him in the gym doing bench press, arteries blue against his pale skin with the effort, the old smile when he saw me, the feel of his gloved hand as he took mine. Had we known beforehand that we would meet we would have hugged, but the surprise was too great. We went to the snack bar area for a cup of tea, choosing a table in the corner as though we'd done it often. It should have been a warning to me. We talked, Cal asking about Tom only cursorily, and me not elaborating in my answers – another warning. Oh, how easy it was at that first meeting! Only afterwards did it become more difficult, telling Tom we should sleep in separate rooms, then walking out on him, my refusal to talk to Franny (was I too ashamed?). It nearly killed me doing these things, yet I did them. It's like the white water Tom sometimes talks about – too powerful to paddle against, so that he'd have to lie on his board and go with it all the way back to shore. Cal sweeps me along like that. When I'm with him words come to me from the wings, *sotto voce*, that life with Tom isn't going to get better, that this is it, and from here on there'd be only a slow downward curve. It's like a seductive stream: Cal living in London, jetting across the world to lead projects for his company, new sights, tastes, smells, and sensations, plugged into the pulse of things, far from my country that is decaying in every way imaginable. I'll be sixty in four years' time and what then? Watch more gardening and cooking programmes on TV, and ah, let's not forget the Antiques Road Show, none of them too late at night for me.

'Caro, you're not yourself today. Are you okay?' Dylan places three fingers underneath the bar to help me push it up on the last three counts.

'Sorry, coach, not my day.'

It *is* my day, just not here on this bench. It is my day away from the sameness and saneness of my existence that has become all too tedious.

*

In the shower I'm careful not to put too much soap on my new eyeliner in spite of it being permanent. Everywhere else I wash thoroughly. I would have preferred a bath; somehow it makes one feel cleaner. Fresh socks and underwear, blue track top, a few generous sprays of perfume, some lipstick, and I'm almost ready, just enough time to tell myself again if Cal hadn't re-appeared I would have gone on with Tom as before because I do still love him. How he fought his way up at the bank, from teller to sales consultant, branch manager, regional manager, assistant general manager, and finally senior manager, the two of us based in Johannesburg, and Tom away two weeks out of four in the earlier years, to the far corners of what was then called Eastern, Northern and Western Transvaal (Daddy didn't make it easy for him, saying if you can't be your own boss in a profession, the next best thing is CEO of a company, and this, of course, Tom never achieved). I love him too for his kindness – buying brooms we don't need from street vendors, paying car guards over the odds, setting up savings accounts, pension plans, and funeral policies for Agrippa and Precious, giving money to those rummaging through our black rubbish bags in the street on Wednesdays. And there's his loyalty to his friends, Dunbar, Bones, Spirou, and Russ (the fact that Cal was – is? – one of them has caused me more anguish than anything else).

But am I still *in* love with Tom? I'm not sure. Oh, he's still good to look at: hair dark brown with the fine ends going silver, nose and chin fitting his face nicely, eyes deep blue like the ocean far out, skin tanned, and a body still pretty good for his age. No, the trouble with Tom is what you can't see. It's as though his body and mind have diverged, the latter pummelled over the years by nameless apprehensions that have blunted all sense of curiosity and adventure. I find it difficult to think of him as the same man who pulled me from that killer sea and tackled his job with such steely resolve. His horizon is now circumscribed to what he can see from North Beach, with little interest as regards what's happening in the country. Tom so wants his life to be on an even keel since he's retired it's become boringly predictable, making my own stretch out in front of me like a road through the Karoo. If only he'd say 'I love you' more often. I can't even count the times on one hand. Being taken for granted is one of the worst feelings ever for a woman.

I go through the gym's sliding doors to the car park, my bag over my shoulder, cell phone to my ear checking for messages. I put my stuff in the boot and walk back, this time to the street, where a car is waiting. With my heart hammering away I slide onto the front seat and put my arms out.

As I hold Cal close I thank God that Tom doesn't know a thing.

CHAPTER ELEVEN
Hong Kong and Bali

Flight attendant in the aisle with her trolley, addressing me, 'What will you have to drink, sir?' I hold up a piece of paper on which I've scribbled, 'Two beers and some cabernet please'. Neither sylph-like nor smiling as in the airline's ads, she probably wishes the entire plane is without tongue for the long flight. It pleases me that the man next to me observes this – hopefully it will stop him jabbering in the night. Passengers packed in without an empty seat in sight. Oh, to lose myself in Patagonia, Mongolia, the Namib, or the Outback, in Uzbekistan or Kyrgyzstan where consonants outnumber vowels – any place where no one knows who I am and I can laugh at the human race like Borat.

Yet where is my baggage tagged to? To a place where seven million people live on top of each other in the sky and traffic spews fumes down below – all to get a little comfort from one of my own.

*

'Oh, Dad, I'm so sorry.' Franny's arms around me, head on my shoulder. 'I can't get over it, Mum and Cal – how terrible!' I feel the warmth of her tears on my shirt. She raises her rouge-free face, her cheeks two red anger spots. 'What are you going to do about *them*?'

I've come straight from the taxi, and am standing at the entrance to Franny's flat that's so small the lounge-dining-kitchen area needs only one air-conditioner. Wooden floor, taupe couches, scatter cushions in earthy hues, stone-coloured side lamps with cream shades, and a cherry wood dining table with the legs of the chairs in Provençal green – a taste of Caro in Hong Kong, and a stab of sorrow. Through the window, IFC2 towers above little brother IFC1, its eighty-eight floors curving inward at the top like elephant tusks. City with a can-do attitude – what would it make of me, Tom Bland, prize wuss with no idea what to do about *them*? Would it reveal that I lack backbone, the right stuff? I sidestep it. 'Where are the twins, Franny, or have you finally sold them?'

Franny laughs. 'They've been impossible knowing you're coming. They're with friends for the afternoon. I had to make time for us to talk.'

A wedge-shaped face peers at me from around the corner, watchful china-blue eyes and pointy ears. 'My usual room I take it, Franny? I could do with dragons and hobbits on the wall.' My pull bag follows me faithfully to Josh's room. The cat takes fright and disappears, tail in the air. 'A quick shower then we'll talk, okay. It's good to see you, my precious girl.'

*

We're on the small patio drinking green tea with lemon; sensation of being inside a bowl of buildings. Spring day without the sun, hubristic skyline trapped in a haze.

'Dad, you told me what happened, but I don't get it. Mummy faithful to you for God knows how long and Cal away all this time and bang, they have an affair. Just like that!'

I flinch at her choice of words and focus on a gap between the buildings to lessen the impact of steel, glass and concrete. Franny doesn't let up, 'That she did it knowing Cal is an old friend!' She shakes her head. 'Unless …' her cup stops halfway to her lips.

'Yes, Franny there *was* something, long ago, but not once in our marriage was it a problem. We made our vows in church and that was it, so I thought anyway – maybe foolishly. Then I got caught up in my career – had something to prove, you see, especially to her father, and I suppose I became complacent. These things creep up on one. And yet …'

She takes my hand. 'Talk to me, Dad, it's why you came. We can't Skype about this.'

'All that time I loved her, Franny. More than that, I was *aware* that I loved her and thought I *showed* it. Either it wasn't enough or it was the wrong kind … I won't ever know.'

'Dad, you were saying …'

'Ah, yes, we met in the ocean as you know, Mum in trouble and me rescuing her – a story told at dinner parties many times, more romantic than boy-meets-girl at party, work, or nowadays online. Cal was there, helping to pull us in. He thought she was sleek and beautiful – a mermaid from the deep – said I was lucky. What the ocean brought together everyone seemed to respect, except her father who hoped it would blow over, and when it didn't, he stopped me from coming into the house. I had to wait in the street to take Mum out. How ironic – the house I'm now living in!'

'You never told me that ...'

'There's more, Franny. James then forbade Caro to see me. She was furious, threatened to leave home. James put up the ante. He knew Cal's father well, Rupert Ryder – they belonged to the Durban Country Club, played golf together, and James was a client of Rupert's law firm. Get this, Franny, James sneakily invited Cal's family to a Sunday barbeque – he'd heard Rupert speak with pride about Cal attaining his BA and LLB and then doing articles. James thought Cal eminently more suitable for his daughter than I, a bank teller from Glenwood. Cal was Old Durban Family, Mentone Road, in the professions, one of those people who prefer to say Labuschagne and Blignaut without the guttural g.'

'That's Natal for you, Dad – putting down Afrikaans, extolling things French. It's the stuff novels are made of, wow! Now just the ending.'

Ninja sleek against my leg, then onto my lap, almond eyes trusting once more, neat oval paws folding up in rest.

'The whole world knew we were a couple. Sometimes Cal joined us, with or without a partner. At least he observed the rule of the beach not to mess with someone else's girl. Until that Sunday at James's house – Cal with his formidable charm, having had a thing about Caro from the time he saw me bring her in from the sea ...'

'Don't tell me they *dated*?'

'Yes Franny, for a while, but I'll say this: Cal made his intentions known to me. I was gutted of course, but couldn't find it in me to ditch him as a friend. In any case, Caro soon broke off the relationship and told me I was the one after all. We regarded it as an episode to put behind us.'

Too awkward to tell Franny I didn't pursue the reasons for Caro's change of heart because I was afraid I'd spill my past, confirming James's worst fears and losing Caro forever. Caro choosing me over Cal tied my tongue from then on. Only recently did I wonder if the real reason Caro came back was to assert her independence from her father. It brought more doubt: if she had *believed* that I'd get to the top and prove James wrong then I did let her down, didn't I? And what about making her think Hugh and Margery were my real parents – wasn't it even worse?

'Terrible it should come full circle after all these years, Dad.'

'Yeah, and Cal this time going behind my back like a coward, but then he's changed, Franny. I sensed it when he talked about making a killing in South Africa.'

'Why aren't you angry? You only seem sad.'

'Been through the anger, the thoughts of murder, I've had time on my own.'

'The house is in Mummy's name. What if she turfs you out?'

'I'll go and live in Bali. Surf's great and maybe some of its spirituality will rub off on me, ha, ha. Could be what I need, my girl. In fact, I'll go there on the way back.'

'It calls for another cup of tea.' Franny gets up. 'The twins will be back soon. Be prepared, they'll be around you like puppies.'

'I'd love that. And Franny ...?'

'Yes.'

'Thank you for being there for me.'

'Promise you won't do anything silly.'

'Like what?'

'You know, murder them ... or, I have to say it, do yourself harm.'

'I must admit I imagined catching them together, and with my gun on them talking about honour, friendship and God – you know, a meaningful conversation like in *Pulp Fiction* – watching them freak out.' For the first time I laugh.

'Stick to imagining, Dad, *please*! I'll get the tea.'

'A cup o' Rosie would be good, Franny.'

No point in telling her I'm experiencing missing heart beats that make me short of breath, waking me up at night as though a pillow is pressing on my face. That maybe what made Caro leave was the accumulation of many small things: the chlorine on me after a training session in the beach pool, my clothes smelling of moth balls, not being good at DIY, being around her too much, wanting her too often. I'm guilty of all these things, and more, like ending my career two notches from the top, I know that. But that's me, Thomas Bland. Maybe my surname got too much for her – a daily reminder of how unexciting life was with me.

Yeah, I'll check out Bali, have a little practice at becoming the ultimate detached man, like Axel Heyst in *Victory*.

*

To Repulse Bay beach with Franny and the twins, sun penetrating the haze at last, umbrellas bright, sand warm under our feet. Sea here a lifeless body of water, enabling buoys to be arranged in a semi-circle against sharks, not like my pulsing Indian Ocean so capricious the nets have to be placed parallel to the beach and far out. To my right, on the terraces of the Life Guard's Club, the statues of Kuan Yin and Tin Hau keeping vigil over swimmers. I think of Durban, shooting the breeze at the backline, and afterwards on the deck drinking tea and taking the mickey. And I try not to think what Caro and Cal might be doing.

Back in the flat in the evening I welcome the jostling of the twins and the cat at my feet, and Franny and Stephen avoiding the subject of why I'm here. Stephen straight from the trading floor: long-sleeved white shirt, black trousers, neatly trimmed stubble, bags under his eyes and a waxy pallor, the *Greeks* in his derivatives trading job turning his hair grey at thirty-five – *thetas, rhos, gammas* and *vegas* thirteen hours a day. Small wonder Stephen decided to buy a machine to provide him with thirty minutes of synthetic daylight every afternoon in his high-rise office.

On our plates a paella steams, cold Cloudy Bay Sauvignon Blanc canters through our systems and, underneath it all, sadness that it is our last supper.

*

Denpasar, Bali, visa on arrival, passport control, customs – long queues, dead time. Stare ahead. Think of Kuta and riding its surf. Let the fabled spirituality of this place wash over me: the gentle Balinese, temples, art, forests, and lakes. There's a book, an ode of sorts to this island – something about love, eat, and pray.

In the back of a taxi looking out: a million Mad Maxes on motorcycles, potholes that make Durban seem like paradise. I want to ask, 'How has the surf been?' but enquire instead, 'You are registered, aren't you?' Then checking the meter most of the way; beware of takes, even among the meek and gentle.

Twenty minutes to Kuta. Buildings cheek by jowl along miles of beachfront: bars, clubs, western fast-foods, clothing shops, hotels, B&Bs. Everywhere billboards, signs, posters, and flags. Line of cars moving slower than a man can walk, roofs shimmering in the sun.

Find a place to stay. Nothing with soul here it seems but that's okay. Small TV, small round table, thin brown carpet, forgettable pictures on the wall, Bible at the bedside with a lamp to read it by. I could be anywhere. My stuff fills only two drawers and a quarter of the wardrobe.

In the morning I visit sacred Uluwatu to soak up some of its celebrated spirituality, but the macaques are in control of the temple snatching bags, cameras, glasses, hats, and attacking feet that happen to wear a colour sandal they like, baring their horrible fangs. Blessed with holiness so you can't tell them to piss off, or throw things at them. On Uluwatu's organisation chart they surely are the bosses, with the staff working for *them*. George Orwell got it wrong: he should have used macaques instead of pigs.

In the evening, drinks over a calm sea at Kuta, winter approaching yet the humidity worse than a February day in Durban. Tourists and bottles of Bintang spread out on the grass, reminding me of a comment about Kuta in a travel book: 'Everything you never wanted in one hellish abyss crammed with dangerously sunburnt, semi-dressed, lager-crazed foreigners.'

I stroll back to my room, pass bars advertising tequila at a dollar a shot, shops selling wood carvings of penises, and T-shirts with messages to choose from: *Simon is Gay, Do it up the Bum, Want more Grunt F**k like a Pig, You're Fat but I'll F**k You Anyway.*

A Balinese man smiles at me, pointing to his T-shirts for sale. I look at him squarely. 'I am really sorry.'

'No problem.' His smile goes into the corners of his eyes.

'I mean I'm sorry you need to sell these things. It's not you, it's them.'

I walk a few metres, turn back. 'Where do you live, where's your house?'

'Ubud, sir, not by the sea, you been there?'

'No, but I know it makes really beautiful things.'

I walk on, ashamed to be a traveller on this earth.

CHAPTER TWELVE
Durban

If we had to share the wealth of this country, there won't be the need to build high walls because anybody (sic) will have food. So, as long as Alexandra continues to swim in a pool of blood (poverty), you will have reasons to be worried and one day they will visit you.

— Julius Malema, at the time of the launch of his Economic Freedom Fighters Party (EFF)

I'm on the balcony of the house cleaning my Smith and Wesson M&P 9mm. Brushes, handles, cloths neatly laid out on newspaper, acrid smell of Hoppe's powder solvent and gun oil, the magazine with seventeen rounds removed, including the one from the chamber. Sea air and not practising at the shooting range are enough to create nasty surprises: the gun jamming, shots going wide at a critical moment when your life is under threat. Or you want to kill yourself.

I turn the gun around, the barrel's round black eye trained on me, mesmerising like a cobra's or a great white's. A little shiver goes through me as I reinsert the magazine, I, Harry Haller,[i] Steppenwolf in a house belonging to someone else, gun loaded with lonesomeness. The Smith and Wesson a perfect fit for my hand, like a lover's shapely breast. I reach for the single cartridge still on the table, pause, and pick up my iPhone instead to read the email once more.

Dear Tom and Caro,
Lost my email addresses setting up my new laptop a few weeks ago! Felt terribly cut off here in Germany as you can imagine. It's almost a year since we left can you believe it? Missing SA in spite of the bad press – I suppose born in Africa always an

African. Having German lessons and battling to remember if a word takes der, die or das, or nominative, genitive, dative, or accusative. Then doubling up the cases because of plural! At least I can now ask for Roggenbrot or Weissbrot at the bakery, and Ken for his Bier vom Fass at the pub.

Anyway I managed to get your email address from Gerald. We're coming out in May, and Les and Annie are letting us stay at their Ballito home, how sweet of them (not sure if you've met them?). Ken and I are planning a get-together with as many of our old friends as possible, and Les and Annie have insisted we use their house for the occasion. The balcony's huge and has a built-in braai, just right for those wonderful KZN winters! Now here's the plan ...

I remember Trisha and Ken in the Taunus hills in Königstein outside Frankfurt, Ken taking the train every day to his job in the city, spooked by thoughts of retirement: being untethered from an organisation chart, drifting outside his capsule like a lost astronaut, being back in Johannesburg and living behind security gates. A daughter in Sydney and a boy in Houston – two kids in the great Diaspora of South Africa's youth. In most cases ageing parents left behind who dread becoming irrelevant to grandchildren they see maybe once a year, using Skype, WhatsApp, and Viber as proxies for hugging and reading bedtime stories.

I get up, clear the table, and forward the email to James with a covering note: 'James, please pass on to Caro.'

*

Heavy cloud, foggy rain leaving the sea unruffled, sky and horizon merging so that I can hardly see the dividing line, like snow blindness I once encountered in the Austrian Alps. I can dimly make out the next swell, Dunbar's ghostly figure paddling towards me, and the Bluff's bulk down south pushing into the ocean like a grey monster. To my right the massive arch of the Moses Mabhida stadium hanging in the sky, its tented roof supports tippexed out by the mist.

'I love it when the lady's in a mood,' Dunbar opens his arms to the water around him, 'not often it happens in winter.'

'I don't mind her moods. It's lightning that freaks me out when I'm on the water.' I scan the sky. 'Still prefer it to Bali.'

'Lightning means fewer surfers, and you should've told me you were going to Bali. Just the other day Jason mentioned another Indo island, said it was like Bali thirty years ago. A strange name – Lombok I think it was. I'll find out for you.'

Dunbar also likes it when the shark nets are removed during the sardine run and most surfers stay on land. There would be madness on the beaches, people with nets, buckets, shopping bags, even shirts and skirts scooping up the wriggly little fish churning the inshore waters.

So what if a shark takes me? Just don't let me survive minus an arm or a leg; take all of me, quickly, leave behind only the neoprene from my wetsuit and foam from my board – an honourable way to go for any waterman, no ignominious demise at the end of a long illness. A sudden, brutal death that takes people's breath away and makes headlines, for Caro and Cal to reflect upon their sins, and Sister Amber to regret not taking up my offer of deep discourse over a fillet and a bottle of cabernet. The club would hold a memorial service for me (packed, standing room only), followed by a paddle-out by my friends who'd sit in a circle and scatter my ashes (sand in my case because there'd be nothing left of me).

Dunbar looks at me. 'You got to get out of yourself, bru. Find another woman.'

Bones wanted to smash Cal up, in his fancy Hollywood Hotel suite. 'I bet it was where they did it,' he muttered. Spirou hugged me, his dark eyes moist. Russ said it was the stuff Greek tragedies were made of and that catharsis was good – it purged one of excessive emotion – and that in any case one could never trust a slim cook. Dunbar said betraying a friend was the worst thing anyone could do, brought his BSA airgun to the club and promptly shot five pigeons that had been crapping on his board. He gave the birds to Spirou in a shopping bag saying, 'For the little sparrows, and your restaurant staff to clean and take home,' and drove away as if nothing had happened.

Find another woman? The last time I found one was at South Beach, B.C. – Before Caro, ages ago. 'At sixty I don't have the foggiest where to start, Dunbar.'

'Can't help you either, bru, I'm out of it too. I hear it's pretty much on their terms, though. Only good thing is they share the bill. But I can assist with the tenant. Is he still giving you the run around?'

'I'm afraid so. Promised to pay while I was away but didn't. I'm following up tomorrow.'

Another wave rising, another exhilarating ride, then paddling back to resume the conversation and ride more waves, with no sorry or excuse me, just understanding that some things are more important than others – opium to old men of the sea.

'Don't call him,' Dunbar says, 'there are other ways to deal with people like that.'

'Oh, what's that?'

'Let's go have some beers. Think of it – no one to ask, no one to apologise to if you're late, or smashed. It's not all bad you know. You need to get out, Tom.'

*

'So, agreed we go to the flat, Tom?' Dunbar says. 'Don't warn him. You have spare keys. If he's there, we'll have a little talk, if he's not, we'll have a look around. He's out of line not paying but you want to avoid the legal route – it'll drive you to drink.'

'I'm already there, bru. I've got other stuff gnawing at me.'

Friday night, Florida Road pub, last week's Sharks game against the Brumbies on TV, frosty glasses and guffaws, waitresses scurrying, ceiling fans too languid to lift a hair.

'You must get over it, Tom. Move on.'

'My pulse is missing beats, it's scary … I'm having headaches, and I can't sleep.'

'Have you seen a doctor?'

'Yeah, I have.' A spooky sound rises up from my glass as I run a finger around the rim.

'You need another one, sir?' Rose asks.

'Make it two, thanks … large,' Dunbar says. Rose smiles and sashays back to the counter through a gauntlet of hungry glances. 'So what did he say, Tom?'

'Gave me beta blockers and told me to have as much sex as possible, ha, ha, with whom?' And with my testosterone level at twenty-two, a crying shame.

'You obviously didn't talk about Caro and Cal.'

'No self-respecting man would. Neither did I tell him of my double bind since I retired.'

The furrows above Dunbar's nose deepen with confusion.

'You see, Dunbar, everyone needs to feel *relevant*. The more relevant you feel the greater your reason to live. Now when whammies start to hit you they take away from that. First it was my job. Nice things were said at my farewell, sure, but by morning I was history, my responsibilities cancelled by a single HR email to the organisation. Then it was my wife, the constant in my life, or so I thought – bang, gone, in the space of weeks. The next thing to happen – and it's not far off, Dunbar – is that we'll get to our sell-by date, you know, like stuff in a store. Take Bones: small flat, small pension, a bike, a parrot, and cancer; no car, cell phone or internet. Of what relevance is he really, not with us of course, but to society, in their eyes? Zilch, I tell you. Soon he'll be slumped on a stained couch in a nursing home, or curled up like a cat on a bed, oblivious of the time of day. Like my old man. To remain relevant is a bugger, Dunbar.'

Dunbar nods. 'I think Spirou's lucky: a loving other half, boys that would do any father proud, the entire family involved in the business. Money and harmony; his old age should be a doddle.'

'That's why this thing with Caro is so bad, bru. These are supposed to be my golden years, *before* the fucking nursing home!'

The nursing home, gun no longer available; even if it were, the awareness and desire to end it might not be there. The gun might be picked up in the dim belief that it came from a Christmas cracker, and the wrong person could die.

Dunbar stares at the droplets crawling down his frosty glass. 'Think about it. You still have the sea, and you have friends, real friends. You're not alone. The deck, however small, is where we're *something,* where we are relevant, to use your word. What's outside doesn't do it for me anymore anyway.' He pushes a lip into the foam. 'I'm not good talking about stuff like that. Just accept that Cal is no longer part of our deck. He's on his own now.'

Dunbar's past is always with him, and mine with me, creating new layers even now, like calluses from years of surfing and cataracts from too much sun, here to stay, a part of who we are. The lines Dunbar and I drew for ourselves long ago only we can cross. Or live with.

My hearing now dulled as if I'm in an aircraft descending too fast, the chatter around me just a hum, the necks of beer taps like ducks on the move on the counter, Rose our redeemer slaloming between tables carrying more tall glasses. Please, don't let them fall or spill.

'Sorry, sir, I have to ask you to put out your cigarette,' Rose says to a man at the next table. 'Smoking's not allowed.'

'A fag when I drink,' he said, 'and after a good *pomp.* Isn't that right, boys!' Sweat glistens on his thick neck.

'Sir, please, I don't make the rules.'

Red-streaked eyes taking her in. 'You're a smasher, Rose, I'll say that.' He throws the cigarette onto the floor and grinds it with his heel. 'You owe me one, petal.'

I look at him. There are bad guys in this world who kill and rape, steal public funds and investors' money. It's in the papers daily. Then there are the betrayers of friendship, and the boorish, who lack *ubuntu* – humanity to others – with no laws to convict them for that. I've had my fill of all of them. The man catches my stare and holds it.

'He's not worth it, bru,' Dunbar says, 'just as Cal isn't.'

Oh yeah? For how long have I suffered men like that, I, Thomas Bland, writer of company mission statements, defender of corporate values, singer off the same hymn sheets, even while the knives were out?

Dunbar suddenly decides to open up. 'You're not alone, you know. My wife also took off, but for different reasons. It started when I went to the border. That I had no choice was immaterial – I thought it was the right thing to do, fighting what P.W. Botha called the "total onslaught" against our country. It was also the adventure, the challenge to survive not only the Cubans and the might of Russia but also the bush. A terrible thought came to me, bru, while I was there, and here's the irony: that a threat of a different kind was building up back home, one that got worse with each trip.'

Dunbar now forward on his elbows, grey eyes intense. 'It wasn't another man. It was something unexpected, starting with my eldest daughter of all people. I can't say in hindsight I should have seen it coming because I didn't. After P.W. Botha gave the world the finger and declared a state of emergency, 1986 it was, she left for England – partly at her mother's insistence – fell in love with a Brit, left-leaning as it turned out, and married him. From there this thing spread to my other daughter who'd also gone over and finally to my wife. I had no chance, it was three against one. You see, Tom, the world was changing fast. It believed we had no moral right to be in South-West, killing freedom fighters on behalf of a discredited apartheid government and calling them terrorists. From the start we couldn't win, but I didn't see it, just as Ian Smith didn't when he said he'd maintain white rule in Rhodesia for a thousand years. In faraway England my daughters felt embarrassment at first, then moral outrage at the fact that their father was part of an elite killing brigade, betraying me doubly by talking about it when the information was secret. Instead of absence making the heart grow fonder my wife grew into a stranger. My brief visits became so stressful I wanted to blow my brains out, and hers – by then, you see, I was also beginning to doubt the government's reason for being in Angola.'

'Jeez, Dunbar, that's grim – as if the fighting wasn't enough.'

'You know what? I ended up fighting in that goddamn bush not for my country but for *me*. So I could live. And that's what stopped me from killing myself, and her, if you get it ...'

'You never talked about it with her, or made up?'

'Too much water under the bridge or too many bridges destroyed ... fuck it, whatever.' Dunbar is withdrawing again, a tortoise going back into its shell.

'Hey, petal, come and sit on my knee, got something to tell you,' the big man says to Rose swishing by carrying more draughts. 'She hasn't got it for you, Dennis!' another man says. 'Watch me, pal,' Dennis says.

As Rose hurries back with a tray full of empties, Dennis stretches out catching her apron with one hand like a fielder in the slips. For a few seconds she manages to keep her tray aloft. Then it crashes down scattering glass everywhere, Dennis still not letting go of his quarry's apron as though his pride depends on it. 'Playing hard to get, hey, petal?' Dennis laughs. 'Boys, firm treatment is what they like, nothing limp-handed!'

I'm on my feet, take two strides to where Dennis is sitting, chop down on the arm holding the apron, and bring a knee up into Dennis' jaw with a cracking sound. As Dennis falls backwards, I upend the table throwing more glass onto the floor, and his pals. I grab Rose by the arm and lead her to the counter. 'Get behind it, and stay there,' I tell her.

I turn to see his friends coming for me. '*Moer die ou ballie,*' says one. 'Yeah, the old guy's crying to be fucked up,' says another. Patrons head for the room's perimeters, Dennis lies motionless in the middle, Dunbar sips on his draught, an ad on TV extols the virtues of Mercedes-Benz, and boots crunch on shards of glass as the men advance.

For a moment I'm at Smuggler's again – standing behind the sailors going for Dunbar, warning him that one has a knife, tripping the man at the crucial moment. Tonight Dunbar is at the back, signalling he'll take care of the men on the left. Trust Dunbar to do the selection, leaving the beefy ones for me. The exit beckons metres away. I shake off the idea. Too late anyhow, I can see the reds of their eyes; burly men, and as mad as hell. One man hears Dunbar, turns around and walks into Dunbar's fist. Blood spurts from his nose. He howls as he bends down. I grab a barstool by its backrest. From my side-on position the swing arcs wide, too wide, the legs sweeping bottles, glasses, spoons, cutting boards and lemon slices from the counter. People scream and duck, more stuff on the floor.

Momentum carries my faithful barstool onward, hitting the semi-circle of men from the right, flattening the first two. I swing it again, from the other side, and hit more flesh. In my mind it's Donovan and Jack at the office. They had it coming for a long time.

Dunbar, standing over the whimpering men, smiles his biggest smile ever. 'Good going but I think we'd better vamoose.'

As we dash into a side street off Florida Road a *soupçon* of the control I used to feel in my days as a lifeguard runs through me. Not nearly enough to call a meal, you understand, but sufficient to make me feel amped.

CHAPTER THIRTEEN
Durban

It is not alarmist to state that the middle ground in South Africa is coming under increasing threat. The EFF's militant demands and popularity indicate that there are a number of people out there who want to break the system, despite the consequences.
— Max du Preez, *The Mercury*

'Another minute and he'll be ready,' Sister Amber John says brushing Hugh's fine, unruly hair. 'Don't forget the wheelchair, Mr Bland, and please watch his hip, it's still bruised from his fall. Remember to tell doctor we put oil into Hugh's ears two days ago, so the wax should come out easily. And then there's the general check-up.'

Sister Amber should be modelling nurses' attire today: uniform as white and crisp as Antarctica, tight belt emphasising her fullness (I'm reminded of Botticelli), sheer stockings, and black shoes with bows, hair in a bun, a few loose strands holding out the promise of it all coming down one day.

'I'll get a wheelchair from the shopping centre, Sister, don't worry, and the lifts are on the level where I park.'

She pinches Hugh's pallid cheeks for a bit of colour. 'Be good now, straight to the doctor's rooms, okay.'

Heaving Hugh into the Wrangler, stage by stage, one leg after the other, clip on the seatbelt and stroke his face before shutting the door. 'Well done, Dad.' Relief all round; Hugh staring through the windscreen.

'If I promise not to do wheelies with him will you have dinner with me?'

'Oh, oh, Mr Bland ...' Surprise, a moment's thawing in her green eyes, all too quickly overtaken by alarm. 'Durban's so small, even though you've told me about Mrs Bland. And I don't think it's a good idea with me working here. You'd better go now, you'll be late.'

*

I park the Jeep in a spot for the disabled; shades of things to come. And when I can no longer drive who will take *me* to the doctor?

I lock the doors. 'Dad, I'm going to get a wheelchair, back in a jiff. Now you just relax. I'm leaving the music on for you. You're okay, Dad?'

Hugh nods after a pause. Talking less nowadays, not even about Marge, and foregoes his daily walk too often, getting weaker – an un-virtuous cycle where the mind is no longer stronger than the body. They say a folic acid tablet a day keeps dementia away. I must get some.

Into the shopping centre with Hugh clutching the wheelchair and squinting. Maybe too much light and colour and movement for him, like a frightened mole suddenly outside its dark hole.

Down a long corridor, fewer people now.

'Hey, Dad, you want do a wheelie, for old time's sake?'

'No, no wee! I've done one.'

'A wheelie ... like on your bike, remember?'

'Ah, yes, yes my boy.'

'Okay, keep your feet on the rests ... that's it. Now hold tight!'

Brakes off, weight onto the big back wheels, front raised just enough to get a little speed; startled faces, a few smiles, a speechless security guard. For my old man, a last bit of pleasure to make up for the tasteless, overcooked food and lack of sex. I hear him laugh for the first time in God knows how long. I feel a little wild again, trying not to be niggled by the knowledge that if I can't score with Sister John – even through Hugh – how in heaven will I fare with strangers? Easy for Dunbar to say I should move on and find someone else, but I've never been good at seduction. Cal was always the Valentino amongst us.

*

I arrive at the club to find Spiro with an arm around a distraught Bones. 'What's wrong, bru? Please don't tell me the cancer's back.'

Look at Jimmy Osborne – doctor said they'd nuked his cancer. Six months later it returned; by Christmas he was dead. Bones's PSA reading came down from sixteen to five thanks to his treatment. His hope is to get it to below four. Maybe it isn't to be.

Spirou answers for Bones. 'Numo's dead, Tom, he died this morning.'

Bones had only Numo – co-hobbiting in his little flat he said until Russ corrected him. Bones is beating cancer but has lost a feathered friend.

Spirou adds, 'Feral cat, we think, got into the flat while Bones was buying bread at the café. The cat must've pawed at him through the bars of the cage … didn't kill him though.'

'He actually died of a heart attack later, can you believe it,' Russ says, 'didn't think it happened to birds.' He pauses. 'Why not, come to think of it. They must experience shock like we do, and the heart's just a pump, isn't it?'

'Hey, Russ, cut out the biology lesson,' Dunbar says.

'Where's Numo now?' I ask.

'In a pot, so *nothing* can get at him. The cat could come back.' Bones looks on the verge of tears.

'A pot that goes on the stove or one that goes under the bed?' Sometimes Russ can't help it.

Spirou gives Russ a swarthy, unshaven look. Spirou not well – stomach pains and not eating everything that's put in front of him as he usually does. And depressed, not sure which came first, the pains or the depression.

'Got no place to bury him, I live in a bloody flat! And until I can think of something, that's where he stays – with the lid *on*,' Bones says. A blustery southerly is roughing up the water. Below us a man with a horned headdress rears up on a rickshaw; big uneven wheels and feather duster tops, ankle beads and bells sounding off, all of it jarring today.

'No worries,' I say to Bones, 'we'll give him a decent burial in my garden, with something permanent on top to mark the spot.' Caro's garden to be exact, but nothing a quiet word with Agrippa won't fix. As a proud Zulu male he's been feeling aggrieved on my behalf. I change the subject, 'Hey Russ, any news from the publishers?' No good everyone moping.

'No.' Russ's attempt at looking unconcerned fails. 'It's still early days, and anyway, I'm sending it to others. Did you know *Catch-22* and *A Catcher in the Rye* were rejected a number of times, and Harry Potter – something like seven times before Bloomsbury took it!'

It's a miff day when you can't surf, or live in peace with your pet, or get a book out with your name on it. Or be with your wife of many years. When the universe is out to get you and you're just an ant anyway, buying anything more than food feels like overcapitalising. I mean, what good is a life-time guarantee on a machine when you're sixty?

'Why not publish it yourself, Russ, as an e-book? It's the future, man. Some have even made the New York Times bestseller list – after many rejections from agents and publishers.'

'Dunno, call me old-fashioned but I like to crack open a book, feel and smell the paper, have it by my bedside with a bookmark sticking out. And when I'm through with it, find a spot in my book case so I can *see* it when I walk by. Nah, I'll take print over pixels anytime.'

'Anyway, bru,' Spirou says, '*we* like it, don't we? And you've not even read us the sexy bits.' He suddenly flinches. 'Argh, my breakfast is heavy in me.'

On my way home, on a banner on the wall of a police station: 'Kill crime, before crime kills you.' And I wonder: is it for the police to act on? Or is it a message for me, Citizen Bland, to become a vigilante with a gun? Whatever, the strong words disturb me. There's violence in me, yes, ever since I can remember – a kind of emotional magma that builds up and needs to blast its lid off every once in a while. I must have a fault line going through me. The fact that I went back to the pub, owned up and paid R2 457 for the damage didn't take away the satisfaction I felt when I caused it. What made me feel even better was that Rose rooted for me, telling the owner that for months Dennis had been an unmitigated menace.

*

Dunbar and I going north on the M4 in his Land Rover, our boards on the roof in case the surf is good at uMhlanga.

'I'd like to see his eyes when he explains why he can't or won't pay his rent – this dude whose daddy spoils him so,' Dunbar says.

'Don't lean on him too much, Dunbar, let him explain. But he's verbose. The Gettysburg address would be no more than a warmup for him at two-hundred-and-seventy words.'

The rebellious rhythm and lyrics of *Wooly Bully* by Sam the Sham fill the Landy's cabin – Dunbar's favourite compilation. Waiting now for the saxophone bit that sends shivers down the spine, even after all this time.

We're on the uMhlanga off-ramp now, over the M4 and along Lighthouse Road towards the sea. 'Better not park in the grounds,' I tell Dunbar, 'find a spot in Lagoon Road. It's quick from there.'

Upmarket houses, flats and shops, the red top of the lighthouse now visible as we walk towards the shoreline and take in the ocean smell. To our right a tower of glass and steel, its curved balconies staring vacantly out to sea on this quiet mid-week day. My spare remote allows us in through two security gates to a bank of lifts. The numbers zigzag as we ride up to the twenty-fourth floor. I glance into the mirror. 'Jeez, I'm looking old, these bright lights don't help I suppose. It's why I like pubs, Dunbar, kinder on the lines.'

'Being sober doesn't help either, bru.'

Down the passage, to Tonderai's door, Dunbar's eyes frosty as I knock. My friend bleak at the best of times – a man you want with you in the trenches and in dark alleys. The day Dunbar fails a friend the Pope will wear an earring.

I knock again. Wait a while. Dunbar nods. I insert the key and go in, antennae up for any sound or movement. But it's Caro who greets me with her furnishings: taupe suede couch and chairs with scatter cushions in metallic bronze and silver; mahogany tables on the side, in the centre and in the dining area; cream ceramic lamps with silk shades, mirrors on the wall, hurricane lamps with cream candles and Vanity Fair and Tatler on the table (we didn't know then it would be a single male tenant) – all of it Caro's except the wood-sculpted animals and assegais Tonderai brought with him, a Caro making a statement that she's still young and with it. Yup, her eyeliner tats would fit in well here.

We walk through the flat – bed unmade, clothes on the floor, wardrobe open, a toothpaste tube without top, dishes in the sink, papers on the desk. Saving the day is the view – a sweeping vista lifting the soul above the sloppiness.

'Shoes for Africa,' Dunbar says. 'The man only *has* two feet!'

'Shades of Imelda, she of the Philippines, remember? Let's check out the place. Tough luck if he walks in.'

'Yeah, for him.'

'What have we here ...' I stare at a bank statement in the name of T. Manyika. 'Fifty-five grand coming in, from daddy I presume, a fortune. He's single, for crying out loud! Debits for internet, fuel, satellite TV, and yes, EFTs towards rent and utilities – but never the whole amount, see this, always short, and I think I know why. It's these frequent ATM withdrawals, no wonder he's on overdraft! What on earth is he spending it on?'

'Well I never,' Dunbar says.

We drive out in silence, all thoughts of surfing dispelled. 'This could be tricky,' Dunbar says. 'Maybe he's a gambling man.'

'I'm entitled to enter the flat as the landlord, although strictly I should pre-arrange it. Do we tell him or don't we? It *was* lying open, Dunbar.'

The Landy is about to take the onramp when I see it. 'Whoa, slow down! I think it was him going down the road ... drives a BMW 3-series, silver. Give it five minutes and go back, park inside this time, yes? In for a penny in for a pound, bru.'

*

As the door opens Dunbar puts a foot in to stop it from closing again. Surprise and shock registering on Tonderai's face: 'Ah, Mister Tom, an unexpected visit, come in, come in. I'm Tonderai Manyika.' He puts a hand out to Dunbar and winces as Dunbar shakes it.

'This is Dunbar, Tonderai. Yeah, we were checking out the surf and decided a little visit would be appropriate seeing you've been avoiding me. Or should I say evading?'

'Neither, Mr Tom, and a prior message on my *chimbeva* would have been civil. Anyway, now that you're here, and your friend – sorry, his name escapes me – can I get you something to drink? Tea, apple juice ...' He looks at his Rolex. 'Ah, it's after twelve, perhaps a cold Corona with lime? Not every day you come, Mister Tom. Please, do sit down.'

Unfazed youth of the man, more like misplaced moxie; tight white jeans, leather belt with the Argentinian flag logoed on it, blue Dockers T-shirt, heavy watch and, incongruously on the other wrist, a bracelet of bronze guitar string wrapped in black and gold wire with a blue crystal. Tonderai sees Dunbar staring at it, minces his way to the drinks cabinet as if the bracelet gives him no choice but to walk in an affected manner. A man unlikely to want to fight, yet carrying an air of foreboding without being aware of it – a mule loaded with premonition.

'Nothing for us, thanks, but we'll take a seat and hear why you're behind on your rent,' I say evenly.

Tonderai on a couch with his beer, the sun's brightness behind him and in my eyes; he smiles. 'Expenses, expenses, Mr Tom, I had no idea living away from home was so costly. If it's not this, it's that. Mostly things that can't be avoided, like dentist bills, and my *vhuzhi*, my car, playing up, leaving me stranded twice in as many weeks, the last time needing to be towed. That alone was a thousand bucks!' He raises a thin-wristed hand. 'I can only apologise once again for this state of affairs. I'm thinking of asking my father for a raise, ha, ha … Or maybe I should move to a place where the rent isn't so high, hey, Mr Tom?'

'Are you saying fifty-five grand a month isn't enough, with rent and utilities less than half of that?'

'I told you I had unforeseen expenses.' Tonderai registers no surprise that I know.

'Is that why you've been drawing big amounts of cash – to pay the dentist and the garage?

Tonderai's sudden cough makes his eyes water. 'Sorry, it's the lime. Yes, I hate credit cards – they're debt traps.'

'Come on, Tonderai, carrying so much cash in a country like ours is like wearing a suicide vest. Why do it, man, when you don't have to.'

Tonderai glances at Dunbar as if checking his role in all of this – hoping perhaps that Dunbar is just a surfing buddy. Dunbar says nothing, slides his dark glasses over his eyes and leans back.

Tonderai gets up speaking fast as he paces, 'It's like this, Mr Tom, a young man on his own for the first time, far away from home. Looked after financially, yes, but living with loneliness that's bigger than any allowance, you understand, sitting in paradise on his own night after night watching TV.' He rakes a few fingers through his knotty hair. 'So what happens? He gets women, Mr Tom, plenty of them, because he's hungry. Not in the streets or strange hotel rooms where it's dangerous, but phoning like he's ordering pizza, delivered to the door, so all he has to do is pay, eat, and throw the boxes away. So there you have it, Mr Tom, the reason he visits the *madziros*, the ATMs, by day, is to pay for the Margaritas at night. There's nothing like eating pizza and pussy to while the night away.'

I'm still trying to reconcile the image with the man when Dunbar is on his feet, lifting Tonderai up by his blue T-shirt, pulling it horribly out of shape and squeezing the body inside. Tonderai gasps, his pencil moustache up against Dunbar's face, the big man's words barely audible: 'Listen, cuz, if you haven't paid by the end of the month, I'll be back. And if you're not in, I'll be out there waiting for you.' He turns to me, 'Time to go, bru.'

*

That night I have a dream:
'Hello, hello, can you speak up please, the line's bad.'
'It's Elvis, Tom.'
'Oh, yes, Elvis! You said you'd call. How's the tour going?'
'Awesome reception, man, they can't seem to get enough.'
'I know, I know, the Free State is starved of live entertainment. Good shows all go to Cape Town and Johannesburg. Even Durban gets missed. Hey, Elvis, what's your number? Let me call you, you shouldn't have to pay. Yes, right, 83 at the end? Now repeat it please. Sorry, there are digits missing, Elvis.'
'Bloemfontein, Tom ... 695683.'
'Not enough digits, Elvis ... never mind, I'll pay you back when I see you. Now tell me more ...'
'Better than Memphis, and the women even hotter, but the power outages – twice last night, guitar dead in my hands, mike gone, my hips frozen, people yelling! Oh, man, but we'll talk more, Tom.'

Around me a sea of admiring faces, Sister Amber's among them. She comes up to me. We kiss. Her glasses instantly steam up. I remove them and look deeply into her eyes.

I wake up smiling. I'm taking charge of my life again. Dunbar's music compilation just needs less heartbreak hotel and more woolly bully.

CHAPTER FOURTEEN
Durban, Amber

'Sister Amber, is that you? The line's so bad.'

'Yes, speaking. Goodness, it's four in the morning! Has anything happened?'

'Sister, it is Maria here. You should come please. The lady in room nine, you know, bed fourteen in the corner … she's in a bad way.'

'Just a moment, let me think … mm … you mean Mrs Pringle? What's wrong, Maria?'

'Stroke we think. She fell, and then had another one.' Maria sounds matter-of-fact, as if it was Rufus the dog. I would rather she be hysterical and know the person's name. How often have I told them not to think of people as numbers, but to know each one by his or her name? That's what looking after the frail is all about, the last bit of dignity they have left – to be referred to and addressed by their proper names. All else has been stripped away.

'You called the doctor?'

'He's coming.'

'I'll get there as soon as I can, Maria. You know what to do in the meantime, right?'

*

Streets ghostly at this pre-dawn hour, their lights casting an unhealthy hue over the city; beggars huddled up on pavements and in entrances to buildings, in blankets or coats if they're fortunate, in cardboard if they're not; most of humanity still in bed in the last stages of REM sleep, when eyes move frantically and dreams happen and, thank heavens, paralysis of the body sets in lest they move about and harm themselves. My REM sleep and my dreams exciting for me too, sometimes frightening, never boring, so different from my working day which, although deeply satisfying, I can't exactly say is filled with thrills and variety.

I suppose it's why I like scary movies. I check the latest showings for them. I even take out DVDs. In the cinema my heart pounds, my face I'm sure pulls this way and that from sheer nervousness. Just as well everyone is looking at the screen and it's dark. At home I'm safe watching. I can shout, get up for a drink or a tissue, or switch off. But here's the thing: I won't watch third rate stuff, like *Scary Movie 6*, and *Ogre of the Suburbs 2*. A girl must have standards, some IQ in a story even when its main purpose is to see how far it can push up your heart rate and blood pressure while you're sitting down.

Not that my fussiness with movies has helped me with men. I've had some real rotters. Take Boris, manager of a hotel on the beachfront. There he was dealing with the public yet hating them. You'd never say so when you met him. Immaculately dressed, clean-shaven (people with beards have something to hide, he said – oh, the irony!), big smile, and an almost old-fashioned politeness – opening doors for me, walking on my outside on pavements, pouring my water in restaurants, kissing my hand. And paying me compliments, about how I looked, my good conversation – it never stopped. But, behind it all lurked a resolute misanthropist. I could tell by the way he muttered when someone drove too slowly, or stopped for an orange traffic light; his impatience with people getting in his way in shopping centres, parents not controlling their children, and salespeople calling him after hours. He sounded as if he hated them all. Yet at the hotel he was Mr Nice Guy. Maybe it stressed him out having to be nice, acting out of character all day long. It would be like me working with old people but secretly wanting them all dead (stories about nurses and doctors quietly killing patients fascinate even as they horrify me). I had to accept that Boris could never love anyone, including me.

David took the cake. On the surface so nice, going around the suburbs trimming and felling trees. Owned the company, said he'd never be out of work because his money grew on trees – as they grew and dropped pesky leaves in great bundles, or blocked views, especially of the sea, or became dangerous (falling onto cars, houses and people), his men would scale them like squirrels using ropes and saws and do whatever was necessary. The trees would grow, and he'd be called in again after a few years. His work was like one big annuity. He seemed kind and considerate and said he was crazy about me. Told me his wife had died a few years back. It was all quite flattering, sort of swept me off my feet. Until one evening at his Westville home when he asked, 'Are you in for some fun?' and poured white powder from a packet onto the glass table top. I didn't fully register until he took out a credit card to make two neat lines, each as long and thick as a middle finger, and proceeded to snort an entire line using a rolled-up hundred rand note. I wanted to leave straightaway, but he had locked the doors. He just leaned back waiting for the stuff to take effect, watching me with this weird expression. I threatened to scream if he didn't let me out. To cut a long story short, I grabbed a chair, smashed the lounge window and ran into the garden yelling. I remember well his words as I climbed onto a wheelbarrow laden with compost bags to scale the wall, spikes ripping my clothes and right arm: 'If you say anything to anyone, I'll come for you.'

I was too frightened to find out if it was naïve optimism or thwarted expectations about the human race that had made Boris and David so dysfunctional. It made me wary of men to the point where I wondered if Alastair would have revealed another side to him had he not died so young.

And now Tom Bland: first thing about him is that he's a dreamer too, sometimes doing it while he's standing in front of me – the faraway expression, the little smile not meant for others, jaw set in tense mode one minute, opening in a laugh the next, and at times looking so vulnerable, if one can say that about a man who strides around as if he's thirty-something. On the surface he seems a regular guy: married for ages, now separated, a banker before he retired (a conservative lot I gather), and a father he dotes on (I like that very much). But I also heard some bankers are rogues who lose obscene amounts of money and bring banks down. And what is doing wheelies in a shopping centre with an old man if not irresponsible? (He said he did it out of love for Hugh.) And asking me to dinner, not once but a few times, with that look in his eye? All pointing to male hormones, I'd say, exceeding their normal range by quite a margin.

*

Mrs Pringle is deceased. I don't have to be told that by the doctor. I've never been able to get used to death coming my way often, not like other sisters I know. It takes away a life but also a little part of me. And always the question: did I do enough for that person?

I go to the ladies room, and don't like what I see in the mirror: a pallid face, wilted eyes, too many loose strands of hair and, oh dear, one of my maroon epaulettes with green bar all skew – not how someone with a quarter century's general nursing and midwifery experience should appear in the workplace.

In the office I get ready to do the rounds: say hello, find out who was sick in the night, see to their needs, if necessary phone a doctor, and afterwards dispense medicine from carefully labelled ice cream containers so that each person gets the right medication at the right time: yellow stickers for the morning, black for the evening – a routine that comforts everyone, patients and carers alike, especially when someone has died. People may arrive believing in heaven, but once here never seem to refer to it again. It is the daily visits, the meals, and the arms around them that bring them comfort and succour.

CHAPTER FIFTEEN
Durban

I'm listening to my friend Spirou and all I want to do is put my hands over my ears. Like when I was a boy and tried to block out my mother's screams. It didn't work because our house was small, with some rooms separated by board instead of brick. My father used every beating, whether aimed at my mother or me, as a warning to both of us. It didn't help my little sister, who came into the world dead after an assault on my mother who was then eight months pregnant. Only later, in the corporate world, did the word *leverage* remind me of the methods my father used to instil fear in us.

Cancer of the pancreas, Spirou is saying matter-of-factly, as if he's announcing a trip to his hometown, Paphos. My mind races, I've heard of people getting lung, breast, and prostate cancer, but the pancreas? I'm not even sure exactly where it is and what it does. Please God let it be like tonsils or appendixes – things that at the first sign of trouble can be operated on and removed. I'm too frightened to find out more, but here on the deck, on this beautiful winter day, the boys hanging on Spirou's words, I know I'm the exception.

'Where the hell is it, bru?'

'How important is it, can they cut it out?'

'Can they nuke it like Bones's prostate?'

'Anything to do with your stomach pains, and why you haven't been eating properly?'

'One at a time, guys,' Spirou says, sipping his tea. 'It sits below the stomach, is about fifteen centimetres long, produces enzymes that help with digestion, and hormones like insulin to regulate sugar metabolism ... the doc's words, don't ask me to explain. Let's wait for the final test results.' He looks at the ocean where a westerly is shaping the waves after a bad north-easterly – two prevailing winds affecting the mood of sea and surfer alike, from wayward to welcoming in a matter of days, sometimes hours, as though they operate on some cosmic pendulum.

'Sea's *kiff*, I'm going out,' Spirou says.

I can see Spirou's not keen to answer more questions. Doesn't want to alarm us and, being Spirou, always thinking tomorrow will be better. It is his nature. The terrible thought comes to me that he might not make our fishing trip to Terrace Bay on the Skeleton Coast. I count the months: nine to go.

We follow Spirou to where our boards stand upright in their racks as they have been for decades. I can't imagine a gap appearing in our row all of a sudden.

*

In between waves Dunbar says quietly, 'It's upset me too ... another fucking whammy, bru. You must start enjoying your life. Sitting on the deck isn't going to help, and maybe Spirou will pull through, I mean look at Bones ...'

Further out, ships at anchor waiting to enter the harbour, bows into the wind. At the bathing area flags flapping in the direction of uMhlanga.

'I know ... gotta psyche myself up for it, Dunbar. Just a small matter first that needs my attention – it's kind of standing in the way.'

*

Saturday evening, strings of red tail lights ahead of me on the freeway, motorists happy that both dawn and work are a long way off, fun the objective until then. Except for me, holding the steering wheel tightly, eyes fixed on the road, mind many miles ahead. In my black shoes, black jeans, and black polar neck jersey, the only silver lining on me is my hair.

Past uMhlanga and King Shaka, fewer lights and cars now, the sugarcane hills on my left smooth dark humps, the night filled with stars, a jet's lights puncturing the sky as it comes in on its final approach. Wouldn't it be nice to take off to some exotic place? But is there a Bali left in this world that isn't overrun? Keep on driving.

Tongaat Plaza, attendants in booths taking money like automatons, toll arm rising and falling with hardly a pause, and me shooting through as though I'm a racehorse in the July Handicap.

Off-ramp to Ballito, over the freeway, past shopping centres and commercial buildings, houses on the way down to the sea, lights struggling to be seen in the thick growth, enclave of wealth and privilege. I check the streets on my left and right, looking for a T-junction, and Minerva. Aha, both ahead. Left into Minerva, peering at numbers in the badly lit street, all the way to the end, shit. Shaking a little now; why not just turn around and forget about it all?

I find it – a convoluted extension called Minerva South off Hawkins. It portends poorly for my mission, sapping my confidence. I think of the Navy Seals helicopter crashing at Bin Laden's compound. But they still killed him, didn't they?

I don't have to check the number – cars parked on both sides of the street tell me it's the house I'm looking for. The road runs parallel to the sea on a hill about five hundred metres up. I open my window, see the white of the surf far below and take in deep breaths to still my nerves.

I park well away from the house, a monstrosity of glass and concrete on the upper side of the street, with a sweeping balcony. I walk slowly to the gate, people milling on the balcony, chatter filling the night like a tower of Babel. Car guard pointing two middle fingers at his eyes to show he'll be watching my car. I press the intercom under an ornate canopy.

Eternity, then a bright female voice: 'Halloo.'

'Oh, hi, I'm John, for Ken and Trisha's party. Sorry I'm late. You're not Annie, are you?' I roll out the names. What's a little fiction on a mission like this?

'Yes, I am. Do come in. Would you mind closing the door after you?'

'Sure, thanks Annie.'

Up the garden path – on the one side angels with faces raised heavenward, on the other grinning gnomes as if to say this is where the fun is. Faith and fantasy, where does reason fit in? I might ask the same of me. Bougainvillea purple, rose and pink, a double door opening to a smiling Annie.

'Pleased to meet you,' she holds out her hand. About Caro's age, blonde, figure that loves food, and weathered features sadly to be forgotten by morning like an indifferent movie.

I smile. 'I haven't seen Ken and Trisha for years ... good of you to hold the party.' I follow her up an imposing staircase. Pictures and mirrors almost wall to wall; dark, heavy furniture, floral carpets and curtains – not Caro's style. Caro haunting me, chose me long ago, made me her own then coolly chose another. I have to break her spell.

Long table with hurricane lamps, bowls of salad, potatoes warm in their jackets, wine cold in their coolers, condiments to spice up the night, plates and utensils, serviettes held down by salt and pepper grinders. Hiss of coals from the juices of meat, heady aromas and, in a large group of people, Caro and Cal.

I see them side-on, leaning against the balustrades of shining nautical wire. I notice such detail only because my mind is so clear and sharp. Like the day I saw them embracing. Except tonight I don't want to hide my face.

'Ken and Trisha are over there,' Annie says. 'If you'll excuse me, I have to get the food ready. Help yourself to grog ... beers are in that container. Enjoy ...'

Nothing for me, thanks. Need my hands to be free and steady. Voices hustle for attention, no one managing to finish a sentence. Yeah, neither the meek nor those who listen will inherit the earth. I walk towards them, Ken the first to notice me. He looks as if he's been told he has to retire. Then, 'Oh my God, it's *you!*' Trisha's hand goes to her mouth. Voices fade, Caro and Cal speechless. It's an understatement to say I have everyone's attention.

'Yup, thought I'd drop in for old time's sake. How's Frankfurt, Ken, still working I take it? And Trisha ... conquered your *der, die* and *das*? It's a bugger isn't it, makes Afrikaans a doddle.'

'Tom, how can you do this?' Caro in cashmere with a cowl neck and three-quarter sleeves, neat fitting black slacks, and high-heeled court shoes, face pale, eyes dark and distressed. My heart goes head over heels again, stronger than any bitterness I feel, sucker.

'I know about you and Cal, that's how. In any case, weren't we both invited, by mutual friends?'

Caro flinches but Cal keeps his cool. 'Hang on, the invite was transferred to me, by default, everyone knows,' he says, 'so why don't you make a quiet exit, Tom. No hard feelings buddy.

It's just the way it happened. No good after all this time drilling down into whys and wherefores. Either all three of us are to blame – in equal proportion it has to be said, a balanced scorecard – or no one. Triangles of the heart can get awfully complicated you know.'

It pains me to see him looking so good: fleshiness gone around the face and neck, light winter tan, shock of hair, diamond stud in the ear, all of it giving him a bohemian, entrepreneurial air, Branson versus Bland. More like a soap opera on the balcony with Cal pontificating about love and betrayal in consulting lingo. I don't interrupt, letting his silvery tongue seal his fate. A hollow man hanging himself, you understand.

'Far from me to contradict you, Cal. Evermore the consultant I see. No, I've not come to claim my wife. I'm done with her. I am here to get an apology from you as the instigator in this affair, and for you to give it like the man we know you are.'

'You're delusional, Tom. I was the catalyst, not the cause. You're not her type, never have been. Get the hell out of here, before I lose it.'

'Tom, please,' Caro is pleading now.

Ken takes my arm, 'For everyone's sake, please go. I'm asking as an old friend.'

'Yeah, vamoose,' Cal says. 'You're gate crashing, man. Don't you remember what we used to do with gate crashers?' Cal waving his alpha-male dong around, territory claimed and woman won. Not all the acquired manners of man and veneers of civilisation can hide that fact.

A chorus of support for Cal erupts, everyone wanting to eat and drink and have fun. I take two steps back, slip a hand under my jersey and pull the gun from my belt. I see his eyes go wide as he stares at the squat snout.

'Drinks on the floor, hands on the head, *now*, I said *now!*' I wave the gun. A few just drop their drinks, shards and red wine over the pale tiles, looking like the aftermath of a bomb explosion.

Caro crying, 'It's his gun, from under our bed … God, what's happened?'

Annie whimpering, 'In *my* house, do I really deserve it? And he said he was John.'

Cal's jaw goes tight. His eyes shifty like a rat's.

'Shut up everyone. And don't move! My quarrel is with *him*, don't make it yours. Cal, listen, I want you on your knees, and once there, to say the following: "I Cal Ryder am sorry for fucking up Tom's life, for betraying his friendship and for stealing his wife. I am a despicable human being." Oh, and also, "I apologise for my greed, for plundering the country of my birth."'

'You're raving mad if you think …'

'Putting a bullet in your brain would be a pleasure, cuz.' I line up his head in my sights.

Caro, softly, 'Tom, don't. Please don't. It'll be cold-blooded murder, in front of these people. You know what it means.'

'You think I came all this way not realising that? Yeah, you thought I'd accept it meekly, didn't you? Cal, I'm waiting …'

Cal, seeing the look in my eyes, drops to his knees. Something in his neck starts to twitch. 'Please, I'm sorry for what I've done, just don't kill me! I'll come to the club, say sorry to the guys. I'll go back to England! I'll put an apology in the paper. Just don't shoot, Tom…'

I look for signs of remorse, *any* sign, but sense only fear. 'I, I, I – it's all you can think of, you pathetic, blabbering idiot,' I say and pull the trigger.

Cal is hit in the face. He screams as he brings his hands up. Everybody's screaming.

The hot water with red dye I put into Spirou's pistol must've stayed pretty warm after all. I was worried it might not.

CHAPTER SIXTEEN
Durban

There has been a definite increase in the incidence of mental-health illnesses (in South Africa). This is due to the environment we live in becoming more threatening in general ... it must be noted that we live with a baseline of anxiety far greater than most other nations.
— Durban psychologist Shaquir Salduker, *The Mercury*

'The man who shot Cal Ryder,' Spirou grins. 'So you did it, bru.'
'Yeah, he had it coming,' Russ says.
At the club we're waxing our boards, affixing leashes, putting on surf caps, hiding locker keys.
'So what happened afterwards,' Dunbar wants to know.
'Well, I melted away while they were still in shock thinking it was blood on his face. Amazingly no one stopped me. I was at the street gate when I heard someone laugh, then someone else. By the time I got to the car a lot of people were laughing, some a bit hysterically.'
'Jeez,' Bones says, 'talk about losing face, Cal I mean.'
'Yeah, here's the thing: Cal wanted to lay charges of *crimen injura* but Caro talked him out of it ... told him it would get into the papers and he'd be humiliated even more. I think it was more to save her old fart of a father from embarrassment.'
'How come you know all this?' Russ's bushy eyebrows pull together.
'She called me later that night, had a real go at me, wanted nothing to do with me ever again. Made noises about the house ... that I should move out. You guys don't know my wife – once

she was mad at me for not loving a Nat Geo doccie on sloths.' I shrug. 'Who knows where I'll be sleeping soon.'

'Don't feel bad about Cal. He came at you low and from behind, like a fucking horsefly, but you delivered the last sting.' Russ is all cut up, as if he was the aggrieved party.

'Atta, Russ. Hey, how's the book going?'

'It's not, got another rejection. It said, "A little too much *deus ex machine*; an ending of contrived Greek cheerfulness doesn't fit the modern novel". At least they got the Greek connection.'

'You and Cal with your *larney* language.' Bones looks pained.

Dunbar chimes in, 'Stick to surfing, bru'.

'Hang on, Shakespeare used it in *The Winter's Tale* and in *As You Like It*,' I inform them, 'and what about Monty's *Life of Brian*, with the space ship just happening to pass by, and *Lord of the Flies*, when the officer appears at the end to save the kids? In all of these works the *deus ex machine* is present.'

One publisher told Russ he used too many well-worn phrases, to which Russ responded: 'With Shakespeare having invented most of them, please understand it's difficult for me to find new ones.'

Today a false sense of summer emanates from the warm north-westerly, smoothing the sea and creating a respectable wave. It's all that matters.

'Let's go,' I say. 'Hey, Bones, why wax the front of your board when you don't hang five anymore? It's like putting shaving cream on your nose.'

We limber up on the beach, bodies as recalcitrant as the crankshafts of old cars, neither elegant nor eager, and prone to knocking and rattling once started. We stretch our arms, arch our backs, and make attempts at squatting.

'Good practice for hole-in-the-ground toilets,' Bones says.

'Yeah, like we had in Paphos,' Spirou says, going extra low.

Then out in the rip along the pier, to the backline, where we sit facing the sea so as not to miss any sets, in between solving the problems of South Africa, the world, and the heart. 'You don't still love her, bru, after what she's done?' Spirou asks.

'Love? Love's nothing but a cauldron of chemicals,' Russ says, 'fading in potency over time.'

'Yeah, like a rainbow,' Dunbar adds, 'you think it's real when in fact it's just an illusion.'

Bones says, 'The only two things that are real are sex and surfing. And if you have difficulty with the one you can still do the other.'

'You want us to guess which is which with you?' Dunbar wants to know.

'Tom, you're not saying anything,' Spirou says. 'You still love her, don't you?'

Spirou isn't mocking me at all, merely stating what they all suspect. And why does Russ pull love down when he writes about it like a moonstruck teenager? He's either a typical author – creating characters who say things he doesn't really believe himself – or he's a vulnerable human being who's hiding his real feelings. I know where I'd put my money.

*

In the car park Spirou is packing away his gear in his boot, and I can't help saying, 'Looking yellow again, bru. You're holding back, aren't you? How bad is it really?'

Spirou in a muffled voice, 'It's not good, is all I can say.'

'Talk to me.'

'Come and sit in the car.'

Jan Pretorius on duty – traffic warden, keeper of keys, car guard all at once, *tonfa* swinging from his wrist. Overweight metro cop checking licence disks, sweating in the winter sun, little book and pen in hand. No peace for sober, surf-loving people.

'Okay, I'm listening.'

'The head and the tail of the pancreas show tumours. It has spread to the liver and stomach, and they're worried about the lungs. Surgery is out because it's so advanced. That's the trouble with this cancer – you often don't know you have it until it's really bad.' Spirou's eyes a matt black today, the sparkle gone.

'What now, my friend?'

'A lot of chemo – more to improve quality of life, they say, than to cure the cancer.' He stares through the windscreen like a blind man not taking in anything. 'I don't get it and I'm not sure I want to.'

'You've told Chloe and the boys?'

'Yeah, and I think I'll tell my attorney too. You know ... get my things in order.'

This man like a brother, physique like a Greek god's once upon a time, belying a gentle, un-conniving heart. 'If you don't have treatment, Spirou, how long ...?'

'Six months, maybe longer, they can't really say.'

I try to banish the image of the tomato that's been in my kitchen far too long (like most of the food I buy with good intention): the lesion that has spread its black, grey and white ugliness on something that was once lustrous and healthy.

To lose dear friends for reasons I cannot understand is hard enough. Harder still is that I feel no forgiveness for Cal, and find myself in two minds about God – that he is letting Spirou go, a man with unquestioning faith all his life.

*

I look at my tablet, coughing nervously as I read: 'Dating local women in your area. Prepare yourself to meet a new woman every day. We currently have more women than men. Please do not be overwhelmed if you receive a large number of dating requests. Please do not date more than one woman at a time.'

Ha, ha, some problem. But what quality, that is the question. Fortunately this website (I found fifteen when I Googled 'dating online South Africa') doesn't require me to give my name, email address, or age at this stage. I can peek before registering.

I fill in the fields: 'I am male', 'Looking for women' (that I should have to say so after stating my gender shocks me), 'Age 50-60' (Caro lookalikes would be good), 'Area: Berea, Durban'. I press 'Search'. A bevy of smiling faces comes up, each with name, age, and short self-description. They seem to view themselves in similar light, as if they're from the same batch of cloned babies: fun-loving, easy going, appreciating the simple things in life, living life to the fullest, looking for someone to make them laugh, looking for someone special, appreciating honesty and trust; soft-hearted, flexible, intelligent, hard-working, and sensitive. And then one romantic soul who said, 'I love dancing to the music of the universe.' Zonked out on something; doesn't she *know* about the universe? At this point in the game it's about putting one's best foot forward. Kids and messy divorces are revealed later. I shudder, relieved that not one of them takes my fancy.

I have a dilemma: if I go for younger women disclosing my age and posting a picture of myself I'd probably receive no approaches. If I lie about my age, submit an old photo and make it to the first meeting I'd probably be rejected. Ah, how uncomplicated the beaches of my youth: what you saw you either liked or you didn't and you decided to pursue or pass long before a word was even said. Or you lay in wait on the wall at North Beach in front of the club, hair combed and skin oiled, holding a copy of *Romeo and Juliet* or *Hamlet* as a come-on. The real world of sun, sea and sand beats cyberspace hands down. I'm a waterman, for Christ's sake, not a cybernaut.

What about a hybrid approach, seeking out younger women and disclosing my age but showing a picture of me on an awesome wave, my face a bit fuzzy? I fetch a cold beer and go to work in an improved frame of mind, not quite confident, more like feeling less freaked out about having to hunt again after forty years. The spectre of rejection looms over me once more, but what the hell, I've lost love and friendship, and could lose Spirou. We have only so much time left on earth.

*

I can't walk past my computer without checking emails, my heart sprinting as I wait for Outlook to open. I put out three feelers ten days ago via the website's messaging system, saying, 'I saw your profile and it appears we have some things in common. Have a look at mine and if you're interested, send me a message.' I've heard nothing. Neither have I had approaches (as I was led to believe). It's been like an extended run of piss-poor fishing. Maybe my profile comes across as too bland. Yeah, Bland-like. Maybe I'm targeting them too young. I mean, why would someone in her forties go for a man of sixty? Unless it's for his money, or security, neither of which I can offer even though they don't know it yet. These women want toy boys, don't they? I might have to set my sights lower by going for a higher age group. Going from single to mingle is a game to which I'm not very partial.

*

At last, a bite: an approach from a woman called Tamara. After some emails and phone calls I still can't get a proper fix on her but agree to meet (her suggestion). Tom and Tamara – at least the names have nice alliteration (regrettably, so do Caro and Cal). Any morning, for coffee, I say. She replies Monday would be good, because she's a hairdresser. I check the meaning of her name on the internet. It means 'date palm' in Hebrew, and also refers to a 'well rounded' person, but what if she's actually a misandrist with psychopathic tendencies, a Jacqui the Ripper trawling the internet?

I put on smart casual clothes and a lot of aftershave, and make sure I get there fifteen minutes early, choosing a table in the quietest section of the café in Musgrave Centre. Anand the waiter finds me. 'Hey, Mr Tom, nice to see you again, how's Mrs Tom, long time no see.' He has a Clark Gable sleekness and insouciance.

'Hello, Anand. Actually, I'm here for a business meeting. I'll have an apple juice while I wait, thank you, no ice.'

'No ice but cold, I know.'

Her photo was of a golden-haired Tamara. Walking towards me on the dot of eleven is a transformed woman: hair charcoal black, spiky ends the hot colour of ember, dragon tattoo in black, yellow, and green jumping out at me from a sinewy shoulder as I pull her chair out for her; small smile, glacier-green orbs for eyes. She could have come from a page by Stieg Larsson.

I'm rattled in a shopping centre in broad daylight. In the dark with her I'd be too afraid to sleep, assuming I survived the sex act: a male praying mantis offered unbridled pleasure at the female's leisure and bidding, followed by swift, certain death. Three-and-a-half billion women on earth and I have to be sent this one. Schopenhauer was right– the universe doesn't care a shit about humans.

Anand takes our order and disappears. A tetchy clock inside me starts ticking.

*

This thing isn't working for me in spite of the website bragging about how many people it has brought together. A few times I've had to cut short email exchanges, saying things like 'you clearly haven't read my profile properly', or 'regrettably I don't think we're suited,' sometimes adding 'I'm an atheist' (I'm not actually; I vacillate between agnosticism – which reveals my tendency to fence-sit – and flashes of faith). I've spent a lot of time at the coffee shop, and I'd hate to think how much money. When I add it all up I might as well have rented a little office at the centre, if nothing for the privacy, considering my various experiences. Take Jasmine, who revealed a disconnect not apparent in her emails: rather solid physically but emotionally very fragile, saying sorry far too often, in a loud voice to boot – a victim of her own doing. And Mara who, as I got up having paid the bill, said, 'Do you have to go now, please don't.' If one coffee did that what would making love to her do? The mind doesn't want to go there. Bernie seemed bouncy in her emails and on the phone, as if she was on top of the world, but during our second meeting burst into tears, saying everyone was out to get her: her ex-husband, the landlord, and the taxman. Anand cast concerned glances at me during these encounters, obviously wanting to know how things were going but mercifully refraining from asking (I have the same thing at home with Agrippa and Precious).

In Caro's empty house, sitting on the balcony staring out at the city and harbour lights, I reflect, who am I to judge these people? I am as fucked up as they are, in ways I cannot even describe.

*

I want to ask Sister Amber again if she'd have dinner with me. I think of her often. But when I get to the nursing home she seems to have given herself more wholly to caring for the frail and helpless. Holy would be more apt – a medical nun in white, dedicating her life to Hippocrates. Doesn't she see what she looks like in the mirror *sometimes*? What a woman she is? I suspect she'd look great pregnant (you just know some women would; I mean, Caro looked better un-pregnant, as if she didn't embrace the whole thing). But Hugh's worsening condition makes me feel guilty about having such thoughts. He has to wear nappies now, the silences are longer and so are the stares, his memory is short-circuiting, he's like a handsome, washed-up shell in the sun, life inside shrivelling. The only animation he shows is rocking backwards and forwards in his chair, and calling out Marge's name, the latter accompanied by pulling at his clothes, as if he's expecting a visit from her and wants to look his best. I had a quiet panic attack last time I was there, certain that my chaotic stream of dreams and mind-wandering during the day were indicative of my own creeping dementia. I should do a course in mindfulness to help me cope with the stresses of over-connectivity, and anxiety about simply being alive.

I tell Hugh over and over that I love him. If only he would show a little determination not to let go – like a drowning person would with a lifeguard. But I am the one clinging to him as he drifts away.

I'm not sure he knows who I am anymore. And with the realisation that my secret is safer than ever my guilt rises to new heights.

*

On the deck again, in my world, with my friends and the ocean, and Dunbar asking: 'Isn't the deadline today, Tom?'

'I know, but let's give him until tomorrow. Fair is fair.'

'He either doesn't have the money or he's playing games, paying us back for dropping in on him like that.' Dunbar's soft voice doesn't go with his lava eyes today. Dunbar takes things personally.

Sunday, people milling about in the club, some new faces who do not know who we are, what stories we have about monster seas, daring rescues, and lost comrades. Cyclists, skate boarders, joggers, and strollers on the promenade – a last day in the sun before the weekly grind commences again. On the sand, nippers with long skinny legs racing in their red tops and black caps as purposefully as migrating buck.

Yeah, Tonderai, I'm going to have to hand you over to my attorney. Legal processes are my worst. They consume time, money and emotion. I'm dreading the day I get a letter from Cal's father's law firm saying Caro wants a divorce. Bet she can't wait to change her name back to Whittington.

CHAPTER SEVENTEEN
Durban

What the government is seeing and responding to is just surface mass, the real trouble lies beneath, the growing discontent that must be addressed sooner rather than later. The clock is ticking...
— Ellis Mnyandu, Editor, *Business Report*

I'm in a supermarket pushing a trolley, in black jeans and Crocs, white T-shirt with 'Jeep 1941' on the front, hair slicked down, on this mid-week day one of only a few men shopping.

An attractive blonde browses in the dairy section, nipples visible through her bra and blouse in the refrigerated air. My trolley promptly runs into an old woman's heels. 'Oh, damn, so sorry lady, are you all right?'

'Look where you're going for heaven's sake! I sincerely hope you don't drive like that, young man.'

I love that. 'I'm really sorry. Can I help at all?'

'Yes, give me and my heels a wide berth please. And no more swearing. Goodbye.'

The blonde woman smiles at me. 'Having a hard time?'

'Not at all, it's trolleys that have a bloody mind of their own. I'm sure it's happened to you.'

'Trolleys are no different from normal, healthy children. They have to be managed. You're not in your comfort zone, are you?'

'Wrong, I've been doing the shopping for years. I know my way around here.'

'Wow lucky wife, or what?'

'I can't see any expiry date on this milk. Can you find it?'

She leans over; wafts of woody, spicy fragrance. 'Here it is. Five days to go. You'll be okay.'

She watches as I put five milks into my trolley. 'Oh, are you a baby?' Her blue eyes tease me.

This isn't going remotely the way I wanted, nothing about my morning is. Thought I'd give up the high-tech, low-touch online dating stuff and go for the low-tech, high-touch store environment. The beach won't work at my age. I'd be seen as freaky, even dangerous. Shops are kinder. Products offer all kinds of opportunities to strike up a conversation. Asking for help on sell-by dates is just one. On the downside, women don't exactly have men on their minds when they're shopping for meals.

I buy my things and go into the queue, watching women ahead of me succumb to chocolate bars and sweets piled within easy reach – a gauntlet of temptation from which there seems no way out. Oh, to be Cadbury man – taken home, tucked away until husbands are at work and then wantonly consumed.

'The store has impulse buying down to an art, hasn't it? I'm watching to see if you'll throw a sweetie in your trolley,' a woman behind me says.

I turn around. She's a stunner except for the prominent cleft in her chin that gives her a strong, resolute look – General Patten in silky black pants. Good God, is there more abuse coming my way, with me trapped in this queue? Maybe I should give up women altogether. Enter monkhood in a Thai monastery, where compassion and gentleness forbid even insect spray (on second thoughts mosquitoes deserve death – they have no redeeming features; ants, although a nuisance in the kitchen, at least have awesome work ethic).

'Are you all right,' she says.

'Yes, yes, sorry, I was far away.'

We talk and for once I'm glad the queue is long. There's no ring on her finger. As we move to the front I invite her for coffee the next day. It seems to come naturally. Maybe it's all the practice.

'I'll have to think about it.'

'Why not, unless you're otherwise engaged, or there's someone in your life?'

'As a matter of fact, I am, and there is. Write your name and number on your slip and I'll let you know.' Unlike the blonde woman she isn't mocking me.

Behind me in the queue a voice says loudly, 'First he crashes his trolley into me, now he's holding everyone up. And he swears. What next!'

*

'So tell me, Tom,' she says over coffee, 'what do you really like?' Her name is Zoe Roth (Zoh-wee, she pronounced it for me), and she's recently divorced from a man who found it necessary to run off with a woman thirty years younger – an office romance. She isn't bitter, just battling with her self-esteem. Not that she says so – she has a quiet pride – it's the bruising in her eyes.

'Well, I'm a surfer, and my passion is riding waves with nice shoulders.' Hers are pretty cool – like a model's in her white halter-neck top – dark brown hair short enough not to spoil the lines.

'I can't stand men who aren't passionate about *something*, even if it is surfing. And when you're not surfing?'

'Fishing and I also love books, all kinds of books. Especially those with rust spots – they're like old friends. I also like good food and wine.' How trite it sounds!

Her tawny eyes seem to agree. 'Sure, sure, but what about the small things – don't you think they say more about a person?'

'Oh, okay. Well, I like to pop washed-up blue-bottles and fallen jacaranda blossoms under my heel. I love the smell of the first peach of the season, it tells me summer's here. And the aroma of grated ginger, it beats joss sticks anytime.'

'That's better. You're quite different, you know.'

'If you mean it in a good way please tell my wife. It's your turn now.'

'What I *don't* like are bank queues, call centres, politicians, phonies, and the pious. The last three are all the same anyway. Oh, and trying to pick up watermelon pips from the kitchen floor with your fingers ...'

'And people tweeting what they had for bloody breakfast ...'

'Plump litchis with small pips are something else.' She studies me. 'Your eyes too, if I may say so, they're velvety blue, like the sea in Croatia. I went there, on a yacht, in happier days.'

Zoe says she's fifty-two, with a son playing rugby for a French club, and another writing copy for a London advertising agency, a stock-broking husband who made enough money to buy her a flat in Norfolk Road off Musgrave and pay her alimony so she won't have to work and he can fuck his thirty-year-old bimbo whenever the urge takes him, 'There for him every night like an inflatable Barbie', she says. Zoe has travelled the world, and now feels stuck in Durban.

Talking to her about what turns us on and off is balsam for my lonesomeness. The cleft in her chin suddenly looks sexy, like Sandra Bullock's. She almost crackles with the need to be touched. I feel a hint of a hard-on for the first time in months (an involuntary one, I should explain).

When I pay the bill and we agree to have dinner on Saturday I'm shaking a little. The fact that she hasn't said a word about the person she's seeing merely adds to my excitement.

*

'He's paid the whole lot, Dunbar, I can't believe it.'

'He couldn't take the pressure. It's called intimidation and it beats the law, in this country anyway.'

'I would've put money on it he wasn't going to pay. He was seriously in the red. Remember his bank statement? Maybe daddy paid. Have you told me everything, bru?'

Dunbar's measured tone causes me to slow down. We're riding bikes along the promenade to uShaka, Dunbar and I next to each other, the others having stopped to check the surf at Wedge beach. It's a day on the cusp of spring, carrying with it the prospect of another summer.

'Well, I figured he had to crack at some point, and that you wouldn't agree with my methods. So I went solo, waited for him one morning in the car park, and when he opened his car door pinned him ...'

'For Christ's sake, that's assault ...'

'Hold it! I didn't touch him. It was his door that did it. Anyway, I made it known what would happen if he didn't oblige. Then I squeezed him for good measure, using the door not my hands of course. He couldn't even shout. But the money came, didn't it, like an ATM when you press on it.' He laughs. 'What can I say, you sorted it, but how did you leave him? 'A little bruised, nothing broken you understand, no blood, just his promise to pay. He really gets my goat. I've a feeling he owes others.' Dunbar still waging his bush war, special ops warrior looking out for his comrades.

Palm trees making little bows in the breeze, patterned promenade and grassy banks, three women in tights and sneakers talking faster than they are walking, a beggar eating dry bread with pigeons watching, Mynahs mock-diving a hapless grey cat, the old clock on the South Beach tower still stuck on 9:30. And the West Street pier, the Lido, Scotty's photo shop, the Little Top – all still there in my mind's eye, like lost limbs imagined.

Past Addington Hospital's bricked bleakness, where I was born as if meant for the sea. My mother could see the surf from her ward (so she said) but I had to wait nearly ten years to set eyes on it because of what happened, a sight I would never forget: water stretching so far I couldn't see where it ended, breaking and thundering at the shore as if warning land to keep a distance, deep and mysterious unlike anything I'd known, with a smell that made me want to open my nostrils wide like a horse's, and above all, free.

So much happening when all I want is for my days to pass peacefully, stretching out time as though it were a giant elastic band. Not this train of insalubrious events that feels as if it's heading for derailment somewhere down the line.

*

On the deck, spoons clink in cups above the deep drone of the sea.

'I fear our fishing trip may be too far off for Spirou. The ride to uShaka tired him,' I say.

'Yeah, and on flat ground too,' Bones says. 'First time he's skipped his tea.'

Silence as we sip, our thoughts gathered under the umbrella; southerly puffing, making the surf lumpy.

'We should go before Christmas,' Dunbar says. 'Not the best time for fishing on the Skeleton Coast but hey, it's for him.'

'Well then, when?' Russ asks.

'I say the sooner the better. Let me check the accommodation at Terrace, and talk to Spirou.' I glance at Bones. 'What's the matter, bru? It's not the end of the world.'

'I can't go.'

'What do you mean you can't go?' Russ pats down his hair.

'What I said.' Bones looks everywhere except at us. 'Guys, I don't have the cash, simple and *klaar*. You go.'

More silence.

'Listen, bru, we're in it together. Spirou wouldn't want it any other way. We'll make a plan, okay. We're not going without you.' I stand up, 'Board meeting over, guys.'

*

I'm on my balcony, executive pad and pencil in hand, studying my handiwork: 'Dinner menu for Zoe.' Below it blank – writer's block, Russ would say. For this first date I'm taking no chances. For a start, it has to be at home. What if one of Caro's friends sees us or, God forbid, Caro herself? And the food has to be a success. No good if halfway through I have to order takeaways. Yeah, go for the simple and tasty, not a Caro-like triumph that could leave egg on my face. Ah – pencil poised – how about beetroot carpaccio with chevin cheese and just-cooked sugar-snap peas as the starter? Then a chicken in the Weber (fail-safe), and jacket potatoes and a nice salad – did Caro not say how good I was at dressing salads (even though it was in the context of how badly I dressed myself)? And I know my cabs.

I write down my menu like a possessed Michelin chef and stick it on the fridge with a magnet.

*

Strange after all these months to have someone to talk to in this big house, on the balcony tonight, so that the shooting star no longer seems to be on a lonesome path to destruction but racing through the sky in sheer exuberance. Zoe's fragrance wafting my way on the north-easterly breeze, and down in the garden frogs smelling summer in the air. Birds and children and old people already in bed, lovers not yet. In the road the sound of testosterone engines, the deadly embrace of traffic lights and lampposts on this Saturday night far from their minds. Soft side-lighting throughout the house (Caro hated brightly lit restaurants and homes). Zoe's face and shoulders are suffused in it now and my brain in cabernet, so that I no longer see the purple bruising in her eyes, or feel old longings.

*

Thinking back on it, it was why I felt no surprise when she took my hand and led me into the house. It was when we stood next to the bed that Caro and I had slept in for all those years, and Zoe proceeded to lie down, that I knew I couldn't. Zoe bathed in Caro's soft lighting was one thing. Zoe and I *amore sitis uniti*, united in love, in Caro's bed was another. The realisation was like a firm tap from a doctor's little hammer, rendering my member useless. Not even going to the spare room would have brought it back to life.

CHAPTER EIGHTEEN
Durban

South Africa's most valuable asset, stability, is under threat from daily protests, many of them violent, in townships and squatter camps. Just in the past 10 years at least 43 service delivery protesters have been killed by police.
— Max du Preez, *The Mercury*

When someone like Dunbar asks, 'how was your evening?' the boys pick up on it like sharks smelling blood: 'Hey, Tom, back in the saddle again!' 'Atta-boy, making up for lost time!'

They can be out of line, these friends of mine, and sometimes a little sharp, but never a stab in the back, only rooting for one another, and understanding that what makes one's years golden are the small victories. It's why we talk about surfing and sex, and hardly ever about death and religion. Religion can be toxic to friendships. I mean, if someone says earth is only six thousand years old, or Big Bang and evolution are plots to undermine faith, how can I let that pass? On matters of God the deck, like Hollywood, minds its Ps and Qs. And politics, well, who cares, as long as surfing isn't taxed or the sea nationalised.

'Let's just say the food was a symphony of flavours.'

'You don't sound so sure, bru,' Dunbar says.

'Why, was there music while you did it?' Bones asks.

'What do you mean *did it*?'

'Well, you know ... fracking.'

Bones uses the word when he's treading cautiously; howls of laughter.

'Frigging is a more apt euphemism,' Russ says.

'Yeah, Bones, it was more like Bolero,' I say, irritated as hell, 'you know, music that makes you think of committing suicide. Listen, it was my first real date with her! I'm working on it.'

But I think it could be the end of Zoe. I tried to tell her it wasn't her, that it was me because Caro had probably cast a spell on the house to stop me from making love to anyone else. Zoe remained convinced that *she* was the problem – had her husband not also pulled away from her suddenly? (I wanted to ask about the person she was seeing but the moment didn't seem right). We parted amicably enough but I could see disappointment in her eyes, mixed with, strangely, defiance rather than hurt. Was she angry with me, or herself? I didn't know what to make of it, except to say the lady didn't strike me as one of life's helpless victims.

*

I'm overwhelmed by a sense of things falling apart: Spirou's health, my life (was there ever not a question mark over it?), the very earth I'm standing on (polar vortexes gripping countries in arctic conditions while the earth's temperature rises – you explain that – earthquakes and tsunamis, ever stronger cyclones and hurricanes, ever larger areas of the world being flooded, droughts and wildfires, volcanoes springing to life), the increasing number of failed and near-failed states, protests turning into uprisings and bloodshed, the deepening divide between the moneyed and the desperate. And South Africa not spared – an escalation in civil unrest, with police sometimes killing marchers, and always two sides to the story (the unthinkable happening in a country where apartheid has been dead for a quarter of a century). Acts of God and acts of man speaking of a distressing disconnect between God and man, and man and man, crushing faith and bringing out the Darwin in each of us. Stuff you, I'm all right Jack, we say – except for Dunbar, Spirou, Bones, and Russ of course, and a few days later Zoe, just as I am enjoying a takeaway and a bit of Nat Geo on TV.

'Hello surfer boy, what are you doing?'

'Watching TV, it's my only free night this week.' I have the grace to laugh. 'And you?'

'Thinking I'd like to have you to dinner – at my place where there are no ghosts. Will you come?'

'You're not cross then?'
'I wasn't cross, just frustrated.'
'Can I bring anything? Oh, when?'
'You seem very busy.'
'Touché.'
'Tomorrow night, okay?'

As I eat my lukewarm food I reflect that maybe my feeble murmurations are being picked up by the universe after all.

*

I park the Jeep in sight of the man guarding the street – a coated figure on a chair beneath a yellow street lamp, no one else out. South African cities are not places for walking about at night. I take a deep breath and enter the lobby with two bottles of cab. No others invited, come in jeans, T-shirt, and no socks, she said.

Zoe opens the door, her fragrance escaping like an excited pet, in high heels, shimmery black trousers and a thin-strapped burgundy top. She takes me by the hand, 'Come right in. Here, let me take those bottles. You shouldn't have.'

Apartment on the top floor, beech parquet flooring offset by darker furniture, open dining and lounge area, the far corner all glass from ceiling to floor. No balcony or porch so that the terrain seems to drop off sharply to an awesome view of the city. A decaying CBD to be sure, coming into its own at night when twinkling lights mask all lesions and warts.

*

Meal over, second bottle almost finished, lipstick freshly applied, perfume and expectations filling the air. The meal, alas, nothing like Caro's – a lot of it sourced externally I could tell – but I'm starved for company, not food.

'Where do you go now, Tom? You seem to be at some sort of crossroad?'

'Until last summer I had my life mapped out. Now I have no idea. At twenty it might be exciting – one's life about to unfold and all that – now it's just unnerving.'

'Snap, I could say the same about me.'

'That saves me the question.'

'But then doesn't it make you want to do things you wouldn't otherwise, Tom? Suddenly this freedom – not the kind one enjoys at twenty but at fifty, kids and spouse gone, health still good, and just *knowing* so much more. Wow!'

'Mm … I've done things lately that corporate types would definitely give a miss. Exciting, sure, but unsettling. Courage withers with age, Zoe, like muscle. Lonesomeness creeps in, and with it fear. Seven billion people on this earth and you know how many friends I have? Four! I don't count those on Facebook who say, "David suggests you like David".'

She holds her ground. 'I've been telling myself now that I have my freedom back I must use it, there'll never be a better time. Anyway, what things have you been doing?'

I spend the next fifteen minutes telling her about taking Hugh on a high-speed ride in a wheelchair in the shopping centre, the fight in the bar and the mayhem, how I shot Cal with Spirou's water pistol when I really wanted to kill him with my .38 Special, *after* a long *Pulp Fiction* kind of conversation with him and Caro.

Zoe seems entranced, leans over and kisses me, wipes the lipstick off me with a serviette. She needn't have bothered. Her mouth is on mine again, now with more purpose, putting her desert even further down in the gratification stakes.

'And you, Zoe,' I finally manage to ask, 'I want to hear more about you.' She doesn't answer, takes me by the hand and leads me to the bedroom. This time I'm overcome not by Caro's ghost but an intoxicating readiness as she removes her clothes piece by piece. I hear my hoarse voice: 'Sorry Zoe, your status, I have to ask …'

She looks puzzled. 'It's on my page … ah, of course, I haven't sent you a friend request yet.' She laughs.

'No, no, I mean … you know.' Oh Lord, spectre of the hammer tapping me again.

She's almost naked now, and giggles. 'Now I see! No, I don't have HIV-Aids. I've not had a man since my husband left. Snap again? Somehow I think so.'

'Yes, but Zoe, you said in the supermarket you were seeing someone.'

'Would I be here like this if it were serious? Come on!'

I take off my clothes, too far gone. She said she was fifty-two when she could easily have claimed forty-nine. That's honesty. In this immaculate room our clothes are flung every which way. She lies down on the bed. 'Now that we've screened each other why don't you make love to me, just as you are, without a condom ... you are so beautiful.'

*

In the cold light of day I reflect: two people suffering from esteem deficit syndrome, endeavouring to top things up a little for a few hours. It matters not. I'll take happiness where I find it, even if it proves to be transient or delusional. Like cocaine or Ecstasy or heroin. Up one day, down the next. Why did I think retirement would be different just because there would be no Donovans? Donovans don't ever go away, they're like tax returns.

Flashes of memory of Zoe naked: breasts disproportionately full compared to the rest of her (if they are fake the doc did a good job), slender shoulders, a ridge around her tummy from two sons, nice legs, lush pubic hair (dark brown – a case of matching collar and cuffs – does she use colourant to stop the greying?). Why had her husband dumped her – was she too passive, maybe she couldn't come (nothing more dispiriting to a man who does his best), was she off sex altogether? All of this had gone through my head. How wrong I was. She was like a Christmas cracker waiting to be pulled to reveal its little treasures, going off with a bang within minutes of my entering her (not that I could have lasted any longer). Soon she wanted more, this time showing me just how much she knew. She wouldn't let me go. We slept in each other's arms and I thought what an arsehole her husband was.

*

I do a double take the next day when I see it is Caro texting me (does she know about Zoe? Is there no escape?).

Tom i've been thinking. as much as i love daddy and mummy i can't be around them forever. i need my home back, and all my things. can i ask that u make other arrangements please?

    Caro, i know it's your house and u must take it back if u insist, but fair is fair, u ran off with Cal so i want not less than a month

    good god a month! i don't think i can take my parents another day sorry, no dice, make that a calendar month

i'll just arrive and change all the locks and then what?

i'll burn the house down and go to South America. hey, why don't u get the boyfriend to help out?

that's not funny Tom

actually it's not, sorry

Long break.

Caro are u there?

okay, Tom, one calendar month but that's all understand

How to explain to my friends that my wife wants to go back to the house but without me in it? And Bones who'll worry about not being able to visit Numo's little grave – I'll have to assure him it is safe because it's under a protected Milkwood.

Bloody Cal's lawyer father probably advised her to ensconce herself in the house before instituting divorce proceedings. Would the final humiliation be Cal moving in, sitting on the balcony I sat on for thirty-seven years, and sleeping in my bed?

*

For the first time since retiring a deadline looms that I haven't set myself. It's like having to get used to a suit and tie again, and it brings back memories of the meetings I used to attend, the cabals playing the blaming game in corridors and toilets. Meetings for everything: exco, manco, ops, strategy, HR, IT, projects, you name it, with unilateral decisions as rare as Karkloof Blue butterflies.

Living in the house is a daily reminder that I have to leave, probably for good. I'm at the crossroads I've been dreading. Zoe said I should move in with her. I'm there so often anyway, lost in her arms and her world of sensuous pleasures. I've gone from too much beer with my friends to too much wine with Zoe (most nights we polish off two bottles). I frequently skip early morning surfing. The boys take the piss (with not inconsiderable envy) when I pass cryptic comments as to where I've been. When I do manage to get to the beach, I find it difficult getting through the white water after just a few waves. They don't judge me, they're happy for me. Doesn't every old dog want his friends to say when he's gone, 'Ah, at least he had a good innings'? I pray it's not a dread disease that kills me but a sudden hearty on a mountain bike or, more sublime, while on the job.

*

I'm not moving in with Zoe. I want to take it one step at a time. Some strange things are happening, stuff one only reads about, or imagines. No complaints, you understand – what's happening is mind-blowing. Makes me think my time with Zoe has been mere preparation (it explains for instance why the TV is in the bedroom not the lounge). Can't see it being Caro's scene though – she's too upper crust – except I've known Caro to be pretty abandoned in bed (doubt besets me once more: she may have left me not because she didn't want these things but because she couldn't imagine doing them *with me*; now that I'm deep into it with Zoe I suspect anyone can be a secret, guilt-ridden sex addict just as there are compulsive chocolate eaters tormented by their habit).

The first few times in bed with Zoe were conventional in that we made love in the missionary position. Matters progressed from there in breath-taking fashion. She got me to do it in so many different ways that I started making notes before 1 lost track (like with Caro's creations in the kitchen). In the doggy position she asked me to slap her buttocks, so hard it made *me* wince. She sucked my nipples bringing tears to my eyes, and I in turn left vampire marks on her neck. We tied each other up in every imaginable manner (once, in the mirror, I looked like a naked Houdini about to be put into a crate). We licked port, liqueurs, yogurt, ice cream, and peanut butter off each other depending on how hungry we were. She put on porn movies and fed me high-cocoa chocolate and Viagra to get me going again when I got tired. It was a new act of some sort every time – a Kamasutran repertoire from this woman who could have been any university student's mother. I was beginning to think the reason her husband left her was because he'd been worked to the bone in bed. With his bimbo he could take time out and get her to watch soaps while he slept.

I was on a new-found path of pleasure with new milestones to look forward to, new sensations, and new adventures (she asked if I'd consider a penis piercing, to which I initially replied, 'I don't wear jewellery', then changed it to 'maybe'). I had been a monk for months with my only bed companions a squadron of mosquitoes before I found carnal enlightenment. I was zonked on Zoe.

*

At the nursing home I can't look Sister Amber in the eye. If she knew just a fraction of what I have been doing (it's a phobia of mine that others might see in my eyes what's going on in my head, like Zoe and I pythoning so you can hardly make out whose limbs belong to whom). Sister Amber cares for the elderly with the zeal of a Sister Teresa while I'm on a hedonistic trip of Roman proportions. One side-effect is that it makes me more aware of Sister Amber's femaleness – fecund, ripe as in a tree heavy with summer fruit. I feel the craving kicking in as I look at her. If it isn't a sign of sexual addiction I don't know what is.

'My goodness you're losing weight, Mr Bland. Not surprising, I suppose, in the absence of Mrs Bland's cooking.' She looks at me more closely. 'There's something else though ... never mind, perhaps it's because you haven't been here in a while.' Her disapproval comes like bullets, enough to kill me, Caro, and a stadium full of people.

I nod vigorously to allay suspicion. 'I'm afraid it's take-away most nights. The kitchen upsets me, reminds me of her too much.'

'No, I don't mean that. Can't really explain ... your eyes are brighter, and you certainly don't walk as if you're starved.' She gives a little laugh. 'Nothing personal, but a prowler in a movie I saw the other day had a similar look – it was scary but so exciting. Don't know why I see movies like that, being a woman on my own.'

Ah Sister Amber, so you do have complexes in need of therapy after all. 'Oh dear, Sister, I'd rather you think of me as a boy scout, you know, prepared and ready to do good whenever and wherever the opportunity arises.' What if she knows I've crossed the line from prowler to predator?

Gone is the proud man of old. Hugh now a little human heap, sleeping most of the time – on his bed or draped over the couch – having his meals brought to him, having everything done for him, back to being an infant. I can only watch with grief and apprehension, knowing that most of us will end up that way, the lucky ones departing quickly.

I leave the nursing home feeling somewhat absolved from the reprobate life I have fallen into. Aren't Zoe and I simply reducing our psychological deficits, albeit in exceedingly pleasant ways (licentious, some would say), and dispelling our nightmares and fears of the unknown?

*

I begin to wonder if Zoe and I will ever reach some kind of sexual plateau – a comfort zone in lovemaking where the trembling and shaking before the act diminish and predictability takes over.

I'm thinking this very thing one night at her place when the buzzer goes. Whoever it is timed it well because we're just finishing our lemon cheesecake (bought, of course – I've resigned myself to certain trade-offs with Zoe, notably in the culinary department).

'Expecting anyone?' I look at my watch. It's fifteen past eight.

'Oh, forgot to tell you a friend called the other day and that I made arrangements.'

'Oh?' We aren't exactly turned out for visitors, Zoe in her burgundy silk gown, and I in T-shirt and shorts – foreplay attire, predictable and arousing. But it assumes no door buzzers going off.

Zoe gets up and opens the door without asking who it is. 'Lola, come in, good to see you, honey.'

'And you, darling, about time!'

Arm in arm they saunter to where I'm standing next to my chair. 'Tom, this is Lola, a dear friend. Lola, Tom.' No explanation about who I am. As far as I'm aware, my relationship with Zoe is un-clarified as yet to the outside world, but me being with Zoe like this has just changed the status quo.

Lola is about six years younger than Zoe: tight black jeans, high-heeled sandals, a pea-green E.T. shirt with 'Talk to the

Hand' on it, the innocent face of the world's favourite extra-terrestrial at odds with her full figure.

'Nice to meet you,' she says looking as if she means it. We appraise each other, Zoe watching with interest. Like a lioness from another territory Lola has appeared, to be appraised by the resident male while the resident female looks on without a snarl. It doesn't happen like that in the bush. Something's up.

'The pleasure's mine,' I say, meaning it too. I pour her a glass of cab and top up mine and Zoe's. 'Shall we sit down?' My face feels flushed as I lead the way to the lounge. The air feels thick with things unsaid. I have to suppress the urge to pull my head back and rumble like a lion.

*

The mystery of the person Zoe had been seeing was finally solved. Zoe went to great pains to explain how she had sought solace in another woman's arms after being rejected by her husband (he had come to represent all men). It was that or abstinence which, she said, was 'unnatural and unhealthy – if priests had trouble how was I going to win?' It was after meeting me in the supermarket that she thought she might give men a go again. Flattered, I asked, 'Why me, Zoe?' To which she replied, 'There was something so vulnerable about you. You seemed different, incapable of doing what my husband had done to me. Besides, you seemed to be in pretty good shape.'

That first night I couldn't believe I was in bed with Zoe and Lola on either side of me. I, Tom Bland, senior manager turned senior citizen, edges blunted in smooth conformity to company ethos. Nobody would have believed it. I floated above it momentarily, looking down at Tom who was frowning as if he didn't know what to do next. Zoe and Lola giggling as they playfully discarded their clothes, touching Tom here and there as if he were some prized possession. If symmetry was a racehorse and asymmetry a donkey, Lola was the former with her braided mane, beguiling eyelashes, slender neck and finely tapered flanks. They undressed him while he watched another threesome on the TV screen to give him courage for the challenge ahead, and later, when he was spent, carried on without him until they collapsed on top of each other like exhausted cats.

*

In the weeks that follow it dawns on me that being involved in a threesome means Zoe and I can survive without each other. She's a free spirit badly in need of nourishment at a point in her life, and I, although not nearly as free, equally wilted from lack of affection. We understand that we can burn out, even destroy each other. It keeps jealousy and possessiveness at bay, makes our time fun and satisfying. Most of all, my foray into wantonness is doing wonders to lessen my uxorious feelings for Caro – whatever freedoms I've gained through Zoe go towards reducing my emotional dependence on my wife. It isn't that I don't still love Caro. It's more a case of not allowing it to get me down. Cal would say my personal scorecard is becoming more balanced (even he is weighing on me less than before).

I'm having the time of my life, with only a passing thought that maybe it is how the Romans lost their empire – eating, drinking, and fornicating in feasting halls while the barbarians were massing at the gates.

*

It is all upended one morning by an event both unexpected and brutal. It's as if the force has been looking down at me and frowning – a kind of cosmic justice at play to punish me for my hedonistic ways. What else can it be, when life suddenly turns into a Rottweiler in your street, going for you just as you're skipping down it on a nice sunny day?

I'm sleeping late, Zoe in my arms, curtains drawn, the 'do not disturb' sign on the door, cell phones off. It doesn't help that the sky is like pewter or that Zoe was particularly amorous last night. Hunger pangs make me get up. In the kitchen, waiting for the toast to pop, I switch on my cell phone: missed calls from Spirou, the club secretary, and others I don't recognise, SMSs from Spirou and Russ asking me to get to the club ASAP, nothing from Bones or Dunbar but then Bones doesn't own a phone and Dunbar hates them. Has something happened to Caro or Cal – an accident, murder, suicide (Cal killing himself? I can't see it), Franny in trouble?

I call Spirou and listen. I go to Zoe and tell her I have to go out and not to expect me back today. Sorry, can't talk now, no breakfast for me, thanks. I won't be able to keep any of it down anyway.

CHAPTER NINETEEN
Durban

With over one thousand cars per month taken forcibly in South Africa, it has become the carjacking capital of the world – 1064 at last count, and rising.
— Crime Stats SA

R uss, Spirou, and Bones are waiting for me at the police station, a patchwork of drab, low-slung buildings, the South African flag on the pole the only clearly defined element, and today a weathervane telling of a gentle southwesterly.

Spirou silently shakes my hand, Bones more distressed than the day Numo died, and Russ with one eye tearful, the other dry and cold. We go into the building in single file, I in front.

Inside the charge office: counter dark and shiny from the rubbing of many elbows, photos on the wall of police top brass, a poster on the rights of women and children (who are they kidding?), pictures and descriptions of missing persons, a helpline poster for alcoholics and addicts, an HIV-Aids educational poster, and a prominent board with the words, *We are committed to quality service. Are we delivering? We welcome your suggestions.*

The perspiring, overweight cop is slow in making eye-contact. 'Yes, can I help? I'm Sergeant Naidoo.'

'Tom Bland. The carjacking at Addington this morning, Sergeant, the police apparently contacted our club and Mr Spirou here from numbers found on Mr Dunbar's phone. Can you tell us what happened, please?'

'Oh, yes, Mr Bland, we also tried you, a few times.' He's saying if you don't answer your phone it's not our problem. 'Are you any relation to the deceased? Is anyone here family?'

'No, we are friends.'

'We normally notify next-of-kin first but haven't been able to trace his family.'

'His daughters are in the UK, and I think his wife too – all estranged. He never talked about his family. He was a loner, Sergeant. We were all he had. That's why our numbers were the only ones on his phone.'

Sergeant Naidoo frowns, not sure what to do.

'Where's he now?' Bones asks.

'In the mortuary – post-mortem to be done an' all, wash and clean, ID.'

'If you can't find family members to ID him we can save you the trouble, Sergeant,' Russ says.

The Sergeant thinking, a police radio crackling somewhere, a teary female cop on the phone sharing boyfriend troubles, shouting from the bowels of the building.

'I'll let you know. But you can go and see the deceased … Gale Street mortuary, two blocks south of Moore, on the left. I write the address for you. Remember Gale is one way.'

'Were there any witnesses?' Spirou says.

'Yes, a man on a balcony overlooking the street. Not happy about facing the carjackers in court in case we catch them.'

'Well then Sergeant, he shouldn't have any worries, should he?' Russ says.

Sergeant Naidoo doesn't like Russ's comment but then he had a pained expression right from the start like that of a piles sufferer.

'So what did he see?' Spirou asks.

'It's what he heard – two gunshots he thinks, and glass shattering. Then looks out and sees this *raven ou* at the door of a vehicle double-parked, another guy behind him, both with guns. They pull the driver out, dump him in the street and drive away, one of them in the deceased's car, the other in a vehicle that was parked behind it. Both cars facing south, he said, towards uShaka. Oh, and the guys had something over their faces. Nobody saw what happened before the shots.'

Dunbar was probably looking at the sea with the Land Rover idling. When the westerly blew Dunbar would stop at all the surf spots on the way from his home in Durban North: Country Club, Snake Park, Bay of Plenty, North Beach, New

Pier and Wedge, down to Addington. It was a ritual he loved, and he'd give feedback to everyone on the deck, especially on a big day when many surfers preferred the more protected south. Dunbar's reports were better than anything on the web.

'Did he fight them?' Bones's eyes shine hopefully. Dunbar was his hero, all but invincible.

'The witness didn't know.' Sergeant Naidoo glances at his watch, taps his ballpoint on the counter. 'I can see this is paining you all. A detective will be assigned to the case but there's so much of carjacking every month …' The Durban Indian slang slips off him as his eyes roll upwards. 'Not easy to catch them. Not like most murders that involve people who know each other. These guys don't care who's behind the wheel, it's the car they want, ordered by a syndicate usually. Like a shopping list, you understand.'

I draw myself up. 'He may be a statistic, Sergeant, but he was a friend, one of a kind. And please spare us the prospect of his murderers not being caught.'

Dunbar fought a brutal bush war in inhospitable terrain, overcame post-traumatic stress disorder only to be killed on a magnificent day by a couple of mindless men.

*

The mortuary official leads us down a grey passage to the refrigerated rooms. Inside, aisles and shelves like a supermarket's except they're filled with cream-coloured shrouds. No choice in the merchandise, and nothing to mask the smell of the unclaimed: sweet, ripe and stomach-heaving. The man takes us to where Dunbar lies and unzips his shroud. It might as well be a bag containing a surfboard for all he cares. Dunbar's once powerful aura is gone, sucked from him as if by some malign thing, making it difficult to believe his soul could escape to anywhere that's peaceful. And when Hugh's time comes? Please let him at least look serene in death.

A bullet had gone into the back of Dunbar's head, another through his face from the side. I doubt he had a chance to fight back.

*

I'm tossing and turning tonight thinking about Dunbar's last moments, the terrible realisation that I was asleep in Zoe's arms when it happened, away from it and the troubles of the world.

Hurricanes more powerful than ever rising from the Atlantic in blind fury, uninterested whether it's an island in the way or the mighty bulk of the United States responsible for infinitely more greenhouse gases. Floods across India more destructive even than those in Uttarakhand in 2013, with large parts of the country underwater and thousands killed or missing. Humans joining in earth's madness: public squares in capitals now de rigueur for staging protests against governments illegitimate or elected, with protesters the sacrificial prerequisites. And in Durban, a place smaller than a grain of sand in the scheme of the cosmos, a human being is shot for a piece of steel on wheels while communing with nature. The planet seems angrier and crazier than ever. I can only hope Dunbar's death was quick even if it wasn't merciful.

A mosquito is buzzing around me. I've tried to kill it three times. One of my attempts resulted in the soap shooting from its dish, and the dish dangling by its wall connection terminally damaged (I hate toxic vapours and lotions, and nets over the bed).

This time I'm lucky – I see it inside the toilet bowl, dark with my blood against the white. I slam the lid down and flush the toilet.

*

A reporter from the local paper comes to see me on the advice of the club secretary, young – mid-twenties – and eager for information on Chris Dunbar the person. I can tell she's been to the police because she doesn't want to know anything about the carjacking, which suits me. Not that talking about Dunbar does; Dunbar was never easy as a person which makes him difficult to talk about. But I'm taking the opportunity to present him in the best light possible to make up for some of the injustice he has suffered. So I talk to her about him representing his country on numerous occasions in lifesaving and water polo, his years as club captain then chairman, and the role model he was to adult members and nippers alike. I tiptoe over his time in the SADF Special Force and the killing fields up north that today would be all over YouTube, Twitter and Facebook. Why? Because Dunbar did his duty, never complaining about the psychological war he fought with himself and his family. And because right up to the end Dunbar hadn't been redeemed, and I doubt he would be in death – he was a lost soul. What is dismaying is that the newspaper sent a cub to write about an icon – how can she ever understand the true meaning of her own words?

She leaves me with a renewed sense of the creeping irrelevancy I told Dunbar about. Dead or alive, the five of us are no longer of any consequence. We're like the Battle of Britain or the Boer War about which kids of today have no idea and care even less. When you get to this stage in life you're history. I think I'll refuse a post-mortem when I die.

*

'Zoe, it's me, sorry I haven't called. My friend Dunbar was killed by carjackers ... he was estranged from his family so I've been helping out where I can. Hope you understand.'

'Tom! Yes, I saw it in the newspaper, they quoted you. It's why I didn't phone either, figured you needed time to yourself. Is there anything I can do?'

'Sweet as always, but no thanks, I'm just not looking forward to the cremation.'

'Yes, you have to be there for him, I understand.' Pause, then: 'I sense there's something else ...'

'It's bothering me that I wasn't there for him, Zoe. I know I couldn't have stopped it. It's where I was when he was shot and when the calls came.'

'Say it – in bed with me.'

'Yes.'

'So? Don't beat yourself up, Tom. You deserved it and all the other times. You needed it as much as I did. We're good for each other. Why take any blame? You took it with your wife as well, you know.'

'I'm sorry but I think it's best if we don't see each other for a while. I don't want to associate being in bed with you, with Dunbar. It sounds crazy but that's how I feel.'

Sigh. 'I suppose it wouldn't be a happy threesome, would it? You're vulnerable, for a man anyway. But that's what I like about you. There.'

'Oh?'

'Yes, you helped me to take control of my life again, and you must admit we had fun.'

'Loads, Zoe, loads. It's the stuff men can only dream of.'

'Can you keep the door open, so I can come in again sometime?'

'Yes, I will. Zoe, I'll see you, okay? Thanks for everything.'

'You'll be all right, don't worry.'

'From my very own therapist, Doctor Zoe.'

We laugh.

*

Have to move out of the house today, don't know what to take and what to leave, unhappy to hire a truck if there's the slightest chance of returning. Hope that the thing with Cal will blow over and Caro will want me back. What a *wuss* I am.

I needn't have fretted. Apart from my books, my stuff amounts to a pitiful heap enabling me to get all of it into the Jeep, stacked to the roof, rendering my rear view mirror useless. I leave hundreds of books behind, with a terse note to Caro not to give them to the SPCA for fundraising.

I explain to Agrippa and Precious that I'll be away for an indefinite period, and that Caro is coming back as it is her house, and that things will go on as before except without me. 'When,' they ask, 'when will you come back?' I say nothing, shake their hands. They cry and I nearly do too.

I drive away without a last glance at the house I shared with Caro for so many years. Down to the beach to a modest furnished flat where I can sit on the balcony and look at the sea all day if I want to, see the surf upon waking so I don't have to check webcams and SMSs, or get into my car.

I'm talking up my situation big time, I know. It's as though the force is having a good laugh as it hands me this twisted version of my dreams, a pale resemblance of all I hoped for.

*

So many files on Detective Warrant Officer Harrisunker's desk his elbows can barely find wood, his cup of tea relegated to the window sill, his computer on a separate stand. Whereas the sergeant is rotund the detective is gaunt, his tight shirt and narrow tie and trousers not helping. It's as if his body desperately needs a uniform to fill it out.

I stare at him, hoping that behind the chaos is an investigating officer determined to find Dunbar's murderers. 'I'm Tom Bland, Warrant Officer, and I've come to see you about the Chris Dunbar case.' What I really want to say is: 'Why haven't you called me, you haven't called once?' But I bite my lip, a legacy of my corporate days.

Harrisunker looks up – God, he has rings under his eyes too. 'Dunbar? Just remind me again when it happened?'

'Ten days ago exactly. Sergeant Naidoo told me the docket was with you.'

The detective rummages through a pile of documents without saying a word, then, 'Okay, here it is.' Long pause. 'No vehicle satellite tracking in the car, according to your statement, right?' He makes it sound like an accusation. Against Dunbar, fuck that. Millions of citizens having to compensate for the state's lack of political will to fight this and other crime scourges by installing all kinds of expensive equipment in cars, homes and offices.

'A docket was opened over a week ago, Warrant Officer. A call from you would have been nice. Someone died, you know, in very brutal fashion.'

Sigh. 'Mr Bland, we can only do what we can. The docket has also been sent to our Durban North cluster, so it's not only me on the case.'

'Please understand I've no idea if I should be hopeful about the killers being caught. You don't have to answer this, but would you mind telling me just how many other dockets you have?'

Harrisunker grasps the opportunity to unburden himself as if it were a lifeline. He lowers his voice, 'I'll tell you, Mr Bland – one-hundred-and-fifty at various stages of investigation an' all, every one remaining active until closed, that's the idea anyway. And basically I'm on my own.'

'I see, and ...'

'In between I have to attend court sessions, fetch suspects who've been out on bail, and do paperwork ... it never stops.' He waves at his files. 'Even if I find the suspects in Mr Dunbar's case, I've got forty-eight hours to lay a charge otherwise I have to release them.' Talking about all his dockets seems to drain him and he hasn't even got to Dunbar.

I stay a while longer, waiting for him to pull himself together and say something like 'don't you worry, we'll get those bastards', but nothing comes. I make my way through the warren of red-bricked passages and cramped offices to where I left the Wrangler, glad to be out in the fresh air.

*

In my small flat my Face Book page is bombarding me with pictures of women in provocative poses and words like, 'Everyone likes to have one more, see how easy it is', 'What every guy needs', 'Are you brave enough?' Even my news feed is getting in on the act. It gives me the creeps – it's as if the whole world knows I've been trawling for women. Hell, can my friends see this stuff too on my page? If so, Caro can, all because I tried to find a bit of company which didn't work out anyway. It seems my every move is tracked by some company. George Orwell had it right; he just didn't think it would be the Big Brothers of business. I've had a gutful of passwords, I must have hundreds. Soon I'll need one to surf and make love.

A sense of dislocation and isolation draws me to *Steppenwolf* lying among my books in the bedroom. I morbidly turn the pages imagining that I, Tom Bland, but in truth Harry Haller, am wandering the streets of the city caught between my man-half and my wolf-half, losing myself in sensual pleasures before the need to kill overtakes me. I have the eerie realisation that the first part – the nice part – I've already done with Zoe.

Nothing like a bottle of cab to counter such depressing thoughts; soon it leaves me with only the funny side of Tom and Harry to chuckle over. I might even buy a nice flat on the beachfront – can't spend the rest of my life in rented spaces then go to a nursing home, can I? Another voice says wait, hang loose and see what the wind brings. Am I not talking things up again, leaving the door open in case I return to the house?

I laugh into the mirror as I brush my teeth – foam all over my chin, mint on the nose. What a shame not to take the flavours of cabernet into my sleep. What did Jerome say in *Three Men in a Boat?*

Throw the lumber over, man! Let your boat of life be light, packed with only what you need – a homely home and simple pleasures, one or two friends worth the name, someone to love and someone to love you ... enough to eat and enough to wear, and a little more than enough to drink.

*

Dunbar's memorial service at the club, Russ the MC, Spirou, Bones and I and at least four hundred other people paying tribute in the main hall adjoining the coffee shop, the table in front covered by white cloth, vase on top containing two proteas with stems crossed, more flowers in a huge pot on the floor, babies in mothers' arms or on blankets on the floor, some gurgling, some crying as if caught up in the general grief, ceiling lights bright and hot. On a side wall, sepia pictures of teams in quaint, shoulder-strap costumes; on the back wall the Honours Board with names of life members, club captains, chairmen, and meritorious award recipients, Dunbar's name appearing in each category.

Reassuring words about Dunbar having gone to a better place – may he rest in peace – Bones saying he'll cherish his friend's memory until he dies, and that he'll miss even Dunbar's knuckle-punches because they meant you were okay. Spirou reads 1 Corinthians 15: 54-56: *When the perishable has been clothed with the imperishable, and the mortal with immortality, then the saying that is written will come true: 'Death has been swallowed up in victory.' O death, where is your victory? Oh death, where is your sting?* In a halting voice he explains that by dying for us, Christ took away our sins and therefore the sting of death, so we shouldn't fear death.

Maybe because of Spirou's passion and conviction a party atmosphere erupts afterwards, an air of celebration displacing the mournfulness that was there at the beginning.

*

The day dawns to say goodbye to Dunbar.

Surfers on their boards paddling out in the rip to form a floating circle beyond the break on the Dairy side of the pier, a day as Dunbar would have liked it – a warm northerly land breeze combining with the early rays of the sun to make the sea a thing of beauty: sparkling, pulsing with life at the same time welcoming to those who do not live in it. And Dunbar a small pile of grey ash.

Now the riders holding hands in union with one another and with Dunbar, closing and tightening the circle, a few words of remembrance from me, inviting others to do the same, sentiments floating like outstretched wings over the sea. Then silence as I paddle into the centre with a plastic bag around my neck, open it and toss Dunbar's ashes onto the water; hoots and whistles and slapping of boards, flowers raining into the circle.

We briefly point our boards to the sky before returning slowly to shore, looking over our shoulders hoping for a good wave that would get us there in style. There is something infra dig about a surfer paddling all the way in.

CHAPTER TWENTY
Durban

For every 100 violent crimes reported to the police in South Africa (murder, rape, and aggravated robbery), in only 6 cases had the perpetrators been convicted after more than two years.
— Institute of Security Studies, quoting from research done by the South African Law Commission

The symptoms did not alarm anyone at first. Hugh was just more sleepy than usual, didn't want to eat, and felt a little dizzy. The nursing staff added him to the list of those to be watched more closely – their default mode when faced with silent, animal-like stoicism curled up on beds, backs to the world. It was when Hugh fell, bruising his already bad hip and had to be confined to bed that matters took an ugly turn. He started coughing up green stuff, sputum the doctor called it. The bubbling and rattling noises in Hugh's lungs meant inflammation of the sacs, he said. It can happen slowly or suddenly, and unfortunately it's the latter, your father's defences have been weakened by his heart condition allowing bacteria in. In the days that followed Hugh could hardly breathe, the infection spreading from his lungs to his bloodstream, with the antibiotics fighting a losing battle.

I'm left one morning holding an emaciated body, and a dilemma: Hugh afraid of fire all his life but graveyards in Durban overflowing as a consequence of HIV-Aids, and bodies being buried on top of each other in the same grave. Rather than have Hugh sandwiched between strangers, I have him cremated and put in an urn, stored in my cupboard, ready to leave at short notice in keeping with my uprooted life. The urn is made of hessian – not metal or bronze – in blue, yellow, and pink with pleasing curves and a lid.

Tears flow down Sister Amber's cheeks when I pay my last visit. 'Oh, Mister Bland, I'm so sorry, I know he meant so much to you. And now you're really on your own.'

On my own like Sister Amber, except she never complains. Maybe it's ultimately what life is about. 'You have a charity, Sister?'

'I have too many.'

'Well, I'll leave it to you to ask one of them to fetch his furniture and stuff, they can have it. I'll take his few personal things of course.'

I shake her hand. It's cool and firm. 'Thank you for everything you did for him.'

'He was a nice man, it wasn't difficult.' She smiles between crying.

Breathes there a woman with tears so becoming?

*

Tonderai's voice has a high, petulant pitch to it. 'Mister Tom, I'm sorry to tell you I have no hot water, not since this morning, switches are falling off the plugs, and my clothes have spots on them, like measles or something. Just now I'll catch it! It's got to be from the cupboards.'

'Whoa! Take it easy, it sounds as if you're under siege. Have you called any suppliers on the list I gave you?'

Short silence, then, 'I was hoping you'd sort it out, as the landlord.'

'You need the geyser man and the electrician. In the meantime switch off the geyser. Your clothes probably have mould – from cupboards not being aired. A damp cloth will remove it. Then hang the clothes in the sun for a day and voila, you'll be able to go clubbing again.'

'But I don't know how to switch off the geyser, and I can't stay in all day waiting for suppliers, Mister Tom, got things to do in the *tonaz* with my *mafellas*, my co-investors, you see.'

Probably never had to fix a thing in daddy's house in Harare, and what investors with whose money? With Tonderai more goes out than comes in.

'Okay, I'll come and have a look. I'll let myself in.'

'Thank you Mister Tom, I'll put sugar and *katidza* out for you, milk's in the fridge, just help yourself.'

*

I'm in the flat: geyser fine, no leaks, probably the element or the thermostat; plug switches falling off due to poor quality; spots on Tonderai's clothes indeed mould.

I check the rest of the apartment: rust on the wires on the balcony, two light bulbs defective; toilets, taps and showers okay, some marks on the floor and the carpets. General untidiness throughout, things lying about, dirty kitchen cloths, dusty surfaces. I go past Tonderai's desk, papers everywhere, one with 'Land Rover light green' scrawled on it and an ND registration number. I pick it up, and freeze. It's Dunbar's.

*

'So why would the tenant have Mr Dunbar's car details? I don't like it,' I say to Harrisunker.

In the detective's office there's nothing – no pictures, photos, or windows – to look at during moments of reflection except disorder. His neck seems to have given up trying to follow my pacing around. He waves at the empty chair again. 'Mr Bland, please, it's easier for us both.'

I grip the back of the chair, ignoring him. 'I know he and Dunbar had an altercation, two actually, one inside the flat and one in the parking area. But why make a note of the car? It doesn't prove anything about the carjack, I know, but can't you run a check on the man?'

'I'll need full names an' all.'

'Here you are, his ID too – it's all in the lease agreement.'

'Ah, Zimbabwean ... sure we can check our records, but if there are no criminal offences and he came into the country illegally as so many do, he won't show up in Home Affairs' records either.'

'Start with the police then. Hope you're not saying I should join the queues at Home Affairs. It'll make my day.'

Harrisunker looks at the documents piled on his desk and sighs. 'Okay, I'll call them. But the episode in the car park was assault, *finish and klaar*. I suspect Mr Manyika made a note of the car because he wanted to lay a charge against Mr Dunbar.'

'Oh?'

'He needed only the person's name and registration and make of the car. The police would get the rest – address, ID an' all.'

'If he's here illegally it's unlikely he'll go to a police station. So it means some detective work, starting with a police check. *If* he's here legally and *if* he laid a charge he would have gone to the uMhlanga station, right?'

My fingers do a quick tap dance on the chair before I walk out, leaving the question hanging over Harrisunker.

*

I'm sleeping badly again, Tonderai, Dunbar and Harrisunker in my dreams, actors coming and going on a stage. No cause to run or scream or fight, just the knowledge that something bad is going to happen to Dunbar and I can't stop it. Tape is stuck over my mouth so I can't warn him (later I wonder why I couldn't write down a warning on a piece of paper and give it to him). All I can do is to wait for it to happen: the shots, the blood, Dunbar on the tarmac, the westerly rustling up blue waves at the break line. When I wake up I take deep breaths and drink some water, then read to tire my eyes for sleep and more dreams, my subconscious carrying on where I left off, an un-virtuous cycle leaving me exhausted by morning, the feeling a few weeks ago of taking back control of my life all gone. I'm nothing more than a grain of sand again, tossed about by the wind.

*

When I tell the boys about my discovery in the flat I get mixed reactions.

'Pity Dunbar didn't fuck him up proper,' Bones says darkly, 'broken his fingers so he couldn't write anything.'

'It was assault though,' Spirou says. 'I mean, Dunbar could have got the same result by just looking at Tonderai. Dunbar was that kind of *oke*.'

'Maybe the detective has a point,' Russ says. 'Everything you've told me makes me think your tenant didn't have the balls to do any more than lay a charge. He's a whinger, and that's what whingers would do.'

'Let's see what Harrisunker finds out.' I say. 'We can't all four go to his office. He'll freak out.'

Spirou has deteriorated. He's thin now, this man who once carried muscle with such symmetry and grace he could have sat for painters and sculptors. Dogs' noses go dry with illness. Spirou's eyes lose their shine. I keep my voice light, 'Hope you've all made up your traces and you've got line on your reels.

Bones, if you forget your passport we'll leave you behind. More fish for us, ha-ha.'

Time is catching up with us far too quickly.

*

Harrisunker phones *me* for a change. Maybe he can't stand my pacing and talking at the same time in his office.

'Mr Bland, I've got some news. Can you talk?'

I pull up on the side of the road. 'I'm listening.'

'First, there's no record of any criminal offence on his part. I then phoned Home Affairs and yes, he's on their system. It turns out he's well connected ...'

'What do you mean?'

'His family has influence here through his father's business interests – obviously it got him good political connections. Put them together – money and politics – and it opens all kinds of doors.'

'So he's legit.''

'Very much so, he didn't slip across the border, nor did he come "on holiday" – coming as a tourist then applying for political asylum. He was kind of ushered into the country if you know what I mean.' Harrisunker sounds like a man who's just cleared his desk of another pesky job.

'Clean as a whistle then.'

'I'm afraid so.'

'Any assault charges against Mr Dunbar?'

'No record of it at the uMhlanga station.'

'So we have no idea why the tenant took down Mr Dunbar's car details?'

'Mr Bland, please understand there's nothing more we can do. For all we know, Mr Manyika wanted to give it to the guards at the gate so they wouldn't allow Mr Dunbar in again. There's no reason to suspect foul play.'

Yeah, Tonderai more like royal game, an untouchable in the eyes of the ruling party. I should be relieved – a high-rent tenant squeaky clean – but for reasons I can't explain it feels like bad news. I have to move on, let it go. I can do no more now than chivvy up Harrisunker on Dunbar's murder docket that's still open.

CHAPTER TWENTY-ONE
Skeleton Coast, Namibia

'Thanks for asking if I slept all right.' Bones stumbles from the B&B towards me in the dark, Spirou waiting next to the rented Toyota double cab. 'Well, I didn't. Jeez, the snoring! Then the alarm, *his*,' he points at Russ just emerging, 'makes like a frigging rooster, loud I tell you.' He rubs his eyes. 'Eight more times I gotta hear it, gotta be bad for the brain.'

'Come on, the sun got to it long ago, bru,' Russ says, 'and what's with the pissing in the night – like a leaking bucket? Anyway, show me a man over sixty who doesn't snore. You want a heart-shaped chocolate on your pillow every night to say sorry?' Russ on his way to the Toyota intent on bringing order to the chaos inside: luggage, provisions, bait, fish boxes, rods, and equipment for our braais – our barbeques – crammed into the boot following our arrival at Walvis Bay the previous afternoon.

'Hush it, guys. It's five-thirty, everyone's asleep,' Spirou says.

In the cold air our breaths turn into little white clouds. The town of Henties Bay seems to crouch even lower on the sand this morning in an effort to dodge the draught from the Atlantic. Good for staying over, provided it's on the way to somewhere else, an untidy, haphazard sprawl of bleak brick buildings checked only by the sea on one side. Henties is about fishing, not stylish architecture or cuisine, or sartorial elegance: Russ's beanie stretched down into his neck, Bones's black surf cap warming his bald head, Spirou a Michelin man in his anorak, and I in my vintage 90s grey and blue Adidas tracksuit.

'Who's got the breakfast packs?' Bones perks up at the thought of food.

'They're behind the front seats,' Russ says.

'Let's vamoose,' I start up the car. 'Ugab gate by seven-thirty then breakfast at the South West Seal wreck, okay.'

It feels a little strange to have taken over from Dunbar as leader without a word being said or a board meeting held. We're all missing Dunbar but seem unable to articulate it. Maybe this was my problem, not telling Caro how much she meant to me. More than just how good the sex was. It's a problem surfers seem to have, not saying or showing how they really feel, hiding behind the macho and the funny sides of life. Like none of us hugging Spirou, or Bones attempting to crack jokes as the hot desert air threw the small jet around outside Walvis and his knuckles went white on the armrests. And me not telling anyone that I'm scared of the dark, ever since my real father made me sleep in a room with the bulbs removed and the door locked because I told him I hated him, and never telling my bride Caro about it because other fears got in the way, like losing her. So what happened? I bloody well lost her.

*

Driving north on the salt road, dense fog, lights and windscreen wipers on, no cars to pass, not a single tree, just the occasional marker erected by anglers at the side of the road: a stick or a stone, a beer bottle, a small pyramid of pebbles. And quaint signs of fishing spots that conjure up fabulous catches, like *Sarah se gat, Bamboesgat, Skilpadgat, Doep se gat, Bakleigat, Kastele, Ronde Klip, Blare*. Other signs say simply *Mile 62, 72, 87, 98, 100, 108, or 110* to denote distance from Swakopmund, because without them you wouldn't know where you were and you might as well be on another planet. I never tire of the landscape, its hostility and harshness to humans its saving grace – no people to mess it up.

Only at Mile 100 does the sun begin to burn off the fog, revealing endless lichen-covered gravel plains in white, green, and orange-red, weird welwitschia plants growing their Medusa heads in the barren ground, and pink salt pans. And still the road flat and straight, under no obligation to change course for anything.

At the South West Seal wreck, reduced to wood art in the sand, we have breakfast: eggs grey from over boiling, processed cheese and meat like rubber, rolls from yesterday, and flowery apples, but spirits undimmed as we look at the sea and think of all the fish in it. We drive on. Brown, black and grey hills scarred by old four-by-four tracks – man's mindless markings on earth's natural canvas.

At the Ugab our hearts race at the sight of the gate with its skull and crossbones, a reminder that there's nothing Disney-like about the Skeleton Coast's macabre entrance. If it looks deadly, it *is* – the coastal strip a graveyard for a thousand ships, some still rusting, and countless animal bones bleached white in the sun.

As we slowly cross the wide, dry river bed, I think of death's omnipresence on the other side. It never fails to awe and excite me.

*

Spirou's question doesn't quite catch me offside but it jars in this pristine wilderness. 'What now, bru, after your last visit to that detective? Can't we demand someone sharper? In the private sector he'd be dead wood.' Spirou still hasn't accepted Dunbar's fate in the same way he's accepted his own. He has meticulously put his affairs in order; justice for Dunbar is the one thing outstanding, and out of his control.

There's a yawn in Bones's voice, 'What's new? It pisses me off.'

'Tom, you'll be following up with this dude forever,' Russ says. '*He* never calls *you*. On the other hand, how do you find murderers whose only motive is to get the car not the man? These are syndicates run like a business.'

'Yeah, pity we have to go to cops to solve crimes,' I say. 'They're good for certifying documents though, and giving case numbers for insurance purposes *after* you've been robbed.'

Graded dirt road, low-lying bare hills, gravel now dotted with small green mounds like islands in a grey-brown sea. A sandy patch causes me to slow down. 'I went back to the flat, you know, to do some maintenance, and saw this strange name in one of Tonderai's doodles, next to Dunbar's car details. I either missed it the first time, or it's new.'

The Toyota takes a hump too fast and Bones and Russ hit their heads against the roof. 'Hey man, you wanna kill what cells I got left!' Bones says.

'Yeah, we'll have a zombie on the way back,' Russ says. 'I can see the headline: "Author trumps science by proving that in just seven days cell phones can kill brain cells".' Russ ebullient about his book; he's self-publishing it on Kindle.

'Never mind the bullshit,' Spirou says, 'what name was it?'

'Dragut.'

'Dragut? Now where have I heard that name?' Russ frowns.

'I Googled it – he was an infamous corsair at the time of the Ottoman Empire of Suleiman the Great, four hundred and fifty years ago.'

Russ bangs his head, this time with the palm of his hand. 'Got it, didn't he nearly change the outcome of the great siege of Malta?'

'That's the one.'

'So?' Spirou says, 'I don't get it.'

'Neither do I to be honest, but seeing that name so close to Dunbar's particulars gave me the creeps.'

*

At Bones's plaintive insistence we have another pee break, our streams of urine telling of an abating southwester and, I suspect, advancing age; windbreakers, jerseys and headgear in the car, faces raised to the sun; eerie grey-white rocks, an awesome silence, a sky bigger than anything we've seen and me feeling smaller than ever. In the distance, white Everest-like dunes have replaced the apricot ones of Walvis Bay. Bleak can be so beautiful.

Back in the car Russ says suddenly, 'The name Dragut, bru. I know it's a long shot, but here's what I think: Dragut was Suleiman's man so he had to be Muslim, right? But I've not heard of any Durban Muslims called Dragut, it's too foreign. And which foreigners are to be found in Durban that could be Muslim? Not Zimbabwean, Congolese, or Malawian, perhaps Tanzanian or Somalian but my guess is Nigerian. It's known that some operate on the wrong side of the law ...'

It's as if a little of the big silence from outside has crept into the Toyota. I'm barely registering Torra Bay on the left, where every December and January visitors from South Africa erect what looks like a Bedouin camp – huge tents on the sand complete with carpets, big enough to house entire families. A *vis-en-kuier* fest if ever there was one, and thankfully one of only two spots where humans are allowed in the park. I'm thinking about what Russ said: perhaps an unfair perception about

Nigerians but nevertheless some basis to it judging by my experience at the bank and by newspaper reports.

'If you're right it's a whole different ballgame,' Bones says.

'Good one, Russ, but let's park the thought. We can't let these things spoil our trip, right?' I want to get off the subject.

We know Terrace Bay is close when we see a four-by-four coming our way, front bristling with rods standing up like giant insect antennae, and in the distance the manmade mound behind the camp with its sloping back like a hyena's. Four Hemingways full of the fever of fishing and the great outdoors, the Namib on our right, the Atlantic on our left and our cares behind us.

*

But not for long – this might be a place of death, but did the ships and the people perish because the sea and the sand planned it? No, they *succumbed*. Dunbar on the other hand was *murdered* – a big difference. Man has always spent more time on scheming and conniving than having sex I think, although with Rasputin it was probably three-quarters sex. Machiavelli, Goebbels, the CIA, Donovan, Cal Ryder – all shafting people left, right and centre, including my wife. Not my favourite, homo sapiens (with some exceptions of course). Now perhaps Tonderai is plotting, but how will I ever know? I got it so dreadfully wrong with Dylan the personal trainer it was cringe-making. The more I ponder on it the more convinced I am that Harrisunker isn't going to provide the answer – undertrained, underpaid, overworked, and maybe on the take. He's as much a victim in my beloved country as Dunbar was.

CHAPTER TWENTY-TWO
Terrace Bay, Namibia

The ritual of the first morning at Terrace Bay makes us forget about Tonderai and Dragut. Finding a deep channel where the water isn't too still, wrapping the sardine in newspaper to thaw, checking reels and traces and readying bait boards, knives, scissors and cotton; the sun just up over the dunes behind us throwing four shadows across the pebbled bank.

I cast my six ounce sinker into the sweet spot my eye selected and, rod tucked into my waist holder and finger on the line, I take in what's around me: potpourri smell of old kelp and redbait, garlands of weed, gnarled driftwood, a small, dried-out shark with mouth open in a Munch-like scream; the sound of pebbles flung onto the banks by the incoming tide, only to be pulled down again with a deep, melodious rumble; a black-back jackal on its haunches nearby, sniffing at the smell of sardine blood; gulls sitting with chests into the breeze, waiting to swoop on morsels before the jackal does; a new-dead seal exhibiting a massive bite to the neck, its eyes already pecked out. Nature at its rawest and most beautiful, calming instead of disturbing, not death but life's rhythm I'm seeing, the endless cycle all things pass through, revealing the unknown in a manner both harsh and poetic. And paradoxically, to be feared less – no one out to get me, Thomas Bland, because here I don't matter. Only in the city is my existence exaggerated, making me feel bigger than I really am or deserve, and bringing on the unknowns; darkness as bad, artificial light always at the ready to dispel it and, forgotten in all the stress, how lovely true night can be.

On this strewn shore wedged between the Namib and the Atlantic, it is Dali's inspired images that come to me, not Dante's horrors.

*

Bountiful day drawing to a close, nine fish in the bin in the back of the Toyota: four kob, two steenbras, two blacktail, and a galjoen, having returned to the sea an assortment of undersized edibles, four barbel, a sand shark, and a spotty of over thirty kilos that nearly defeated Russ. Spirou held out well on the uneven pebble banks, with only nuts, two bananas, and biltong to keep him going. Spirou doesn't want to let us down and we don't fuss over him, treating him as we've always done, letting him clamber down the bank with the bucket to fetch new water, and not offering to carry his stuff to the car or gut his fish at the cleaning station. Greek pride is strong.

Evening: seven fish in the freezer, two in the oven of the camp's kitchen, and we in the pub, Tafel lagers in hand, watching the sun set over the ocean in hues of orange, pink, and mauve as if at an orchestrated light show. Later at the table, Sauvignon Blanc and chips with our kob, the wonderful day our main conversation, and Bones offering an awkward thanks for paying for his trip. 'Here's to you for getting me here, guys.'

'*Yamas!*' Spirou lifts his glass, 'No sweat, bru.'

Russ and I join in, Russ adding, 'Rooster wakeup call notwithstanding.'

The irony hits me as Spirou toasts 'our health'. Later, in our shared bungalow, I am re-reading my rust-spotted copy of *Catch-22* (Yossarian really speaking to me this time), and Spirou his Bible, nine-thirty feeling like midnight, the only sound the crashing of the sea, no cars, sirens, dogs, or TV.

'Remember the time you stored our red-bait in a plastic bottle, Spirou?'

He laughs, 'Yeah, with the top on, so it would go grey and smelly – the way galjoen like it.'

'And when I opened it two days later it exploded all over me. Not even two showers could remove the smell.'

'Those were the days, eh.' He places the Bible open on his chest. 'Are you going to run the name Dragut by that detective?'

'I'll see when I get back … depressing how little action there's been.'

'Tom, it gets me that Dunbar is dead and life just carries on. We owe it to him, right?' Spirou sits up. 'And those guys are sure to kill more motorists. I know it's a long shot, bru, but have you thought of the Zimbabwean mafia? They have all kinds of interests in SA and maybe Tonderai's old man has friends among them?'

'It's a long shot lumbering Harrisunker with this, but I promise I'll do what I can.' I change the subject: 'Did Chloe and the boys mind you coming this time? I mean under the circumstances.'

'No, they said it would do me good.'

'I hope it does. I thought the fishing might be hard on you. How are you feeling?'

'I'm okay ... really. Had to come one more time, it means everything to me.'

'Good, just know that you're not alone, bru.'

'I do know.' He lies back and carries on reading the Bible.

I sense he's thinking it is God who will walk with him. I meant us, his friends, and his family. As with his toast, I keep my thoughts to myself. At least he seems happy to be here. What puzzles me is how emphatic he is about Dunbar, but then he must be feeling strongly about most things these days. The knowledge that you're dying can't be easy to live with.

Spirou goes to sleep with his Bible on his chest. I take it away gently, switch off his reading light, then mine, and wish I could feel God as he does and fall asleep as easily.

*

The good conditions continue into the second and third day: the cool onshore wind on our left cheeks; the sea alive but not coming at you in long, powerful white lines; high water for much of the day, kob taking the bait with little foreplay, and steenbras not as coy as usual; yells and whoops, scrambling down the banks to help bring the fat ones up, high fives, bright eyes – days that give life a glow and a lift. Even Spirou is casting with more vigour. At lunchtime we make a fire inside a discarded wheel rim, and grill some blacktail and galjoen, the succulent flesh unadorned except for salt and lemon juice, and tasting better than anything in a restaurant anywhere. Then we wipe our mouths and throw our lines in again.

Fourth day, dense fog, driving with the lights on to a spot twenty kilometres south, baiting up with cold fingers, casting into the wind; by mid-morning the fog burnt off and the southwester beginning to push, the Atlantic like a giant air-conditioner turning the air even colder. By lunchtime I'm wearing a vest, three T-shirts, a thick jersey and a track-suit top, sunglasses abandoned, the strap of my cap tightened to the maximum. In the afternoon, sinkers battle to fly straight, lines billow, and the fish go off the bite. Four figures immobile on the pebble-strewn bank, as if believing that any unnecessary movement attracts more wind. On the plain behind us gulls rock in the southwester on thin legs, breasts bearing the brunt – but fishermen mean morsels, whatever the weather.

The next day the wind comes off the sea again, air freezing, more layers of clothing, Russ's beanie and Bones' surf cap suddenly cool accessories for the Skeleton Coast. A nasty current now, sinkers roll northward catching bunches of sea weed and pulling rod tips down with a dead weight like a shark's. Sometimes barbel reach the bait first, sucking on it before swallowing it and, once on land, become a menace, dorsal fins ready to stab anyone who miscalculates.

Spirou no longer putting on fresh bait, just sitting hunched up on the bank, his rod between his knees. Then on the back seat of the car for long periods, eyes closed, as though his mood has swung three-hundred-and-sixty degrees with the weather and the grey sea.

*

I wake up the next morning before my alarm goes off, unusual considering the deep sleep following nine hours of fishing. I lie still and listen: loud pissing next door, coughing, the toilet flushing, and water bubbling through slow-draining pipes. Bones pre-empting Russ's rooster call? Totally dark, curtains drawn, no sound now, not even Spirou breathing. I notice it in passing, without registering alarm – the Skeleton Coast is not a place where you lock doors and cars at night. I listen more intently: absolute silence except for the sea's drone. Why am I not hearing Spirou breathe? He's not in the bathroom – I would have heard him. In that moment, even though I can't see or hear a thing, I know I'm alone.

Reach for the light, and stare at Spirou's empty bed. Rush to the bathroom, waste of time. Run outside, the car is not where I parked it.

*

Tobias the manager driving the camp's Land Cruiser, I next to him, Bones in the back. Of the country's dominant Ovambo tribe, his face is as weather-beaten as this coast. He has a right hip that drags a little (the cold makes it worse he tells me; was he on the other side in Dunbar's war?), dark, attentive eyes, silvery hair, brown jersey, khaki trousers tucked into his boots, and pride in his job (I find out later he's named after a Finnish missionary).

'Have you tried his cell phone?' Tobias asks.

'It's still next to his bed, Toby.'

'Well, maybe he went for a quick throw-in before breakfast,' Bones offers.

To the shoreline first closest to the camp for signs of the Toyota, then south to the better known fishing holes, *Police Bay, As se Gat,* and *Dekka Bay,* the car shaking on the corrugated road, stones shooting away from the tyres. And Russ and Petrus – the sergeant from the local police station – making their way in another vehicle to the northern boundary beyond the airstrip.

Nothing but a grim sea, and our hopes dashed by a four-by-four and two rods in the lee of *Dekka Bay* to escape the wind.

'Why would he do something like this, Mr Bland? What do you think?'

I don't answer straightaway, then, 'I don't know, it's a surprise to me. I'd rather not speculate.' I'm flooded with all kinds of thoughts, some hopeful, most awful, but I intend protecting my friend's privacy for as long as possible. Bones thankfully zips up.

Inland briefly to meet up with the main road south, turn off to the sea again, and drive slowly along the shore. No trees or hills, only small mounds with low shrub where no car can hide – a barrenness I bless today.

Back onto the main road, this time all the way to *Students Bay* and the southern boundary of the permitted fishing area. We see nothing. A radio message from Sergeant Petrus says no sighting at his end either, and that he wants to drive another ten kilometres beyond the northern boundary, just in case.

Tobias interrupts him. 'No further, Petrus, we might need you at Terrace. The Möwe guys can check that stretch.'

Möwe – eighty kilometres north, in the heart of the Skeleton Coast, on a road out of bounds to the public. My heart is pounding now, Bones's eyes register shock – a kind of disbelief that a man and a car can disappear in a place where disappearing takes some doing.

'Maybe he's driven back to Walvis,' Bones says, 'to catch the afternoon plane to Jo'burg.'

Tobias nods. 'I'll call the airport, also Möwe, the Ugab gate, and the police in Walvis. That's a big area we're covering, with not many roads, thank the Lord.'

'You're a star, Toby,' I tell him.

On the way back to the camp I look at the gravel plains and the dunes and for the first time their desolateness holds no beauty, only foreboding.

In the bungalow I check Spirou's bag. In it are his wallet and plane ticket.

CHAPTER TWENTY-THREE
Terrace Bay, Namibia

'He must've taken his anorak because I can't find it,' Bones says.

'No note either,' Russ shakes his head.

We're going through Russ's stuff while we await news from Möwe and the Ugab. I've not phoned Chloe yet. It's not even two hours since I woke up. I want to say something more to her than just Spirou has disappeared. Spirou – rock of his family and his family everything to him. I'm dreading the call.

'Maybe he drowned,' says Russ.

'Not him, he reads the sea and handles himself too well in the water.' Am I clutching at straws?

Bones puts a disturbing spin on it, 'Spirou couldn't drown himself if he tried. I mean, he's been programmed all his life *not* to drown.'

It's the first time anyone is saying it: that Spirou might have *wanted* to die. 'So no note is a good sign, yes?' I say and ask at the same time.

The Skeleton Coast in a mood today to add to the bones scattered everywhere: wind whining through the half-closed windows, the sea in a foam-flecked froth, thick moist cloud over the coast, and inland a desert where only creatures that have adapted over millions of years can survive.

*

Toby reports that the Möwe search party did not find anything. The official at the Ugab gate also phones: no sign of the Toyota Hilux. One hundred and sixty kilometres on a gravel road at an average speed of eighty an hour – enough time for Spirou to have reached it by now. I pray silently: let him still be on this way, delayed by a puncture, a small mishap, perhaps a stop or two to take in the beauty of this land for the last time before dying in the arms of his family. I suppose I'm talking things up again – he has no wallet or plane ticket, and he'd never up and go like that without saying a word.

The thought hits me. If he didn't drown but still wanted to end it all, there is another place he could have gone to, except it probably features bottom of the list in terms of ways you could kill yourself.

*

Three kilometres south of the camp we turn left at the 'Dune Drive' sign and ascend a knoll. A thick carpet of sand has formed at the apex from three days of wind, its depth unknown. The Land Cruiser in four-by-four mode now, treacle-like sand tugging at the tyres. I hold my breath. We break free. A forbidding, hilly, gravelly landscape – colour swathes in camel, oak and pewter, thickly textured as in an impasto painting.

Then I see it: in the shallow valley below us near the path to the dunes, a solitary vehicle parked. In a voice that doesn't sound like my own I tell Toby it could be ours. I train my binoculars on it. 'Yes, it is.'

Toby slaps the steering wheel. 'Now to find him, he can't be far but we must be quick.'

I remember coming here on our first visit long ago and walking these stately dunes, a soul experience second only to surfing for us. I'm hoping it's just that for Spirou today. Otherwise it's the unthinkable.

*

The Toyota Hilux isn't locked, keys in the ignition. I don't like it. We start running up the ridge towards the first dune rising beyond it like a mountain, our shoes gripping on the brown gravel, slipping on the sandy parts, Russ way out in front, Bones last. Five hundred metres to the base of the dune and we are breathing like marathon men. I look for footprints. Only animal tracks lower down, probably jackal and hyena. Russ doesn't stop. He's on the giant dune now getting smaller and smaller, the sky above him a brilliant, windswept blue. My quads and lungs are burning. I reach the summit, the Namib stretching out in great undulating waves of sand, rooftop of the world, untouched and unconquered since creation. And we, so tiny in this grand scheme of things, searching frantically for one of our own.

Russ standing on the inland edge of the dune now, his lower legs obscured in a fine spray of sand from the wind, holding Spirou's anorak in the air as though it's a flag to plant on behalf of his country for reaching the summit.

*

Two days later we find the body.

Spirou must've gone too close to the edge of the leeward side of the dune causing tons of sand to cascade down with him in it, Toby said, explaining that sand builds up on the windward side, from the very wind that tormented us, packing the grains together tightly and creating a long slope that can be walked on without danger; but the shorter leeward side, the 'slip face' he calls it, becomes steeper and steeper, until it takes as little as a human body to set off an avalanche. He left unsaid whether it was an accident or intentional on Spirou's part. None of us wanted to go there, not until we found a note saying so. If it was suicide Spirou must've known how dunes work. But then Spirou was a meticulous man.

It was too late to call in E-Med Rescue 24 or International SOS as Spirou would not have survived his massive sand burial. And how would one get earthmoving equipment to the spot? Toby and Petrus got a work force to go up with spades, avoiding danger by walking around to the next dune and descending on its hard side to get to the base of the avalanche. 'Needle in a haystack,' Russ said.

We were lucky to find him, and I was the first to hold him, brushing away the sand from his face and hair, looking at him with dry eyes and a chest full of tears. His features were composed as if in peaceful sleep, and his body wasn't broken. At least his death was not an ugly sight.

Dunbar once talked about the three dreaded fingers in life: the cricket umpire's, the doctor's on your prostate and, the most dreaded of all, the finger of fate singling you out.

*

I phone Chloe and tell her I think he went to the dunes for the utter peace and strength it would give him, that he'd been before and thought it a most soulful place. Easy in the dark to miscalculate just how close the edge is, I say. Chloe listens quietly, thanks me in a halting voice, and chooses not to go where angels fear to tread.

I delay my return flight to arrange for Spirou's body to be delivered to his family, for a proper Greek funeral, so that he can be anointed with oil and dust, and have blessings bestowed on him and fish served at his Makaria, and be mourned by people in black.

You see, my friend could not have put me in a more difficult position with his plea to do right by Dunbar – a plea that somehow turned into a promise on my part – and then stuffing his suicide letter deep into my bag which I found only when I was packing my things. Spirou would most certainly be denied a decent burial if it ever came to light that he killed himself.

CHAPTER TWENTY-FOUR
Durban

I can predict when South Africa's 'Tunisia Day' will arrive. The year will be 2020, give or take a couple of years. Tunisia Day is when the masses rise against the powers that be, as happened in Tunisia.
— Moeletsi Mbeki, in an article in *Business Day*

Sunday afternoon, I'm watching Bill Murray in a movie that's as scary as hades, and he's paired with a bombshell young actress. Come on, it doesn't happen like that in real life. If he *was* Bill Murray in the movie then maybe, but he's not, he's some reluctant hero with a fictional name. I'll see any movie featuring Bill Murray but this guy is a bit of a *wuss*.

But wait, the movie is over and who do I see getting up four rows in front of me but Sister Amber. She sees me and smiles. Now and then real life springs a nice surprise.

'What's a good girl like you doing watching a movie like that?' I ask.

She comes up the steps. I've never seen her in anything but white, and imagine her to be in drab colours when she's not in uniform. So I stare at her: jersey bright like a Joseph coat, tight black jeans that follow her shape, and dainty black leather shoes. Not for the first time I wonder about her age – forty-something?

'I don't know why, I told you, and I haven't asked a shrink,' she says. I'm close to her now. She still doesn't wear perfume, just her woman smell, and looking younger, eyes livelier behind her round glasses.

I hold the cinema door open for her. 'Would you like a snack? Note I'm not saying dinner because you'll say no.' I'm using as few words as possible, like Bill Murray who seems to say so much with just his face and eyes.

She wrings her hands. No cigarette-holding, heavy-lidded Bogart girl our Sister Amber. 'Oh, Mr Bland, I don't know.'

'Look, I've no connection with the nursing home anymore. It's okay, really. Hell, at this rate you'll see me next when I check in as an inmate. By then I'll be slobbering, and I might not know who you are.'

The stop sign in her eyes changes to yield and I press on. 'So it's a yes. I know a nice place.'

*

Crispy ciabattas with grilled chicken strips, avocado, and mayonnaise, and I'm telling Sister Amber about Spirou: 'The funeral was last week, people from all over, then a memorial service at the club and a paddle out for him, with us throwing flowers not ashes because Greeks believe in proper burials.'

I told everyone at the funeral it had been an accident. Bones and Russ did not contradict me. Chloe said nothing, just held me tightly when I said goodbye. At the club, the gaps in the row of surfboards are already filled by strangers, like two tooth implants.

Sister Amber's eyes go moist. 'How terrible, to be buried in sand like that, and coming after your father and the murder of your friend. I see people dying all the time but one expects it at the nursing home.'

'Anyway, enough of funerals and farewell speeches, I want to know about you. What have you been doing?'

She toys with her half-empty glass of soda and lemon. 'Oh, nothing much, my work takes up a lot of my time, you know.'

She might as well be from Helsinki her skin is so pale. Does she even have a bathing suit? 'Summer will be here soon. Do you ever go to the beach?'

'God no, I'm petrified of the sea. Water, fire, and I suppose now sand, are things I'm nervous of.'

'And life – how frightened are you of it?' I want her to get out of herself, go places with me.

Sister Amber looks me in the eye and says, 'With respect, Mr Bland, perhaps you should worry about yourself first. I think I'd better be going.'

Not a Hollywood ending for me.

*

In my flat I read Spirou's letter again.

My friend,
What I'm about to ask will be hard on you but if there was any
hope I wouldn't be asking.
I don't care for my own suffering, but I do care seeing my family
suffer as they watch me die. I see it in their eyes every day, and
in yours.
If you haven't already sussed it out I've gone to the dunes. You
may or may not find my anorak, or me. Don't worry. There are
worse places to be buried, with only the desert wind around you
(the one with the name that sounds like a wind – soo-oo-oopwa, I
think Russ said).
You may wonder how I can do this being of the Greek faith.
Well, God gave me reason too. I first heard about the Stoics at
school in Paphos. One of their beliefs (the teacher didn't say
much because the Church didn't like it, so I read about it) is that
when life isn't worth living anymore, the right thing to do is to
take your life. Unfortunately the world is only slowly coming
back to that idea (after two thousand three hundred years!).
Right now it's still too difficult and not everyone will understand.
Life is sacred, yes, but at any price?
Please keep this letter to yourself. Why cause my family
more suffering, even embarrassment? I guess it's best if you also
don't tell Russ or Bones. This way everyone will remember me
when I was still walking and doing things, not a bedridden
skeleton. I have faith that God will understand (you will, I know).
Remember the good times, bru!
Just don't forget Dunbar.
Spirou

The letter is another secret I have to keep. I hide it but its
presence is everywhere in my small flat. I consider cutting it up
into tiny pieces but I know it will bring me neither peace nor
absolution.

*

I'm assailed by dreams of Dunbar and Spirou, different versions
that go something like this: they are walking towards me in
heavy grey coats as if it's freezing, but I can't see what I'm
wearing and I'm not feeling cold. In fact I'm sweating because
they don't smile or say anything and I know what they want. I'm

relieved when I wake up, until I remember the burden that has been placed on me. I also dream about Zoe and Sister Amber, and I wake up pathetically happy that they're not together (heaven knows what Zoe would do to Sister Amber). My silliest dream is of Donovan and me travelling the country performing stand-up comedy acts (unfunny to me, but the audiences seem to like it).

*

Tonderai giving trouble with the rent, once more falling behind, making me think I should sell my stake and appoint a rental agent to manage the lease so I can get him out of my life. Then I realise my true motivation: I'd be able to step back and leave Dunbar's case to Harrisunker and the SAPS, and not pursue the link between Tonderai and Dunbar that increasingly seems tenuous. In short, the easy way out.

A morning after a night of dreams – the city awakening with a drone, the sun a blood orange about to cut itself loose from the horizon and light up the grey sea. And I make my decision. Harrisunker won't crack it, not with the abysmal arrest and conviction rates in this country, Dunbar will remain a statistic, and I'll wonder about it for the rest of my life from a position on the side, as I've done with God and so many other things.

Zoe phones to ask how I am, it's been a long time she says, and don't forget big boy, my door is still open. I say it's great to hear from you, Zoe, things have been a bit hectic my side, we'll talk again, look after yourself. Zoe will be all right, she's claimed back her life from that arsehole husband of hers.

I send an email to the other three members of our property syndicate asking if they're interested in buying my share. It's for personal reasons I say, I'm on my own now, and perhaps it's time to leave Durban (it is how I feel; too many chapters have closed on me). I state what I think is a fair price.

I'm feeling better already. The transfer of my shares in the closed corporation should take a couple of weeks – some documents to sign and forward to the registrar of companies, and bingo, Tonderai will be out of my life. The short period during which I'll still have access to the flat could be the spur for doing *something* about Dunbar – a new deadline of sorts. The word 'dead' makes me wary, there's been too much of it lately.

*

I rent a grey Astra for the week and park it in the street next to the flat, the car facing the M4 so that I can follow Tonderai when he drives out. I wait for a day, no Tonderai. Empty water bottles, polystyrene containers, and used paper towelling on the backseat. I go to a nearby hotel to pee and get John Thomas pinched in my zip in my hurry to get back. Secret agent work surely sucks: more surveillance than sex, watching for hours from cars or via sophisticated equipment that takes the edge off the final pounce, if there's one. Not like the movies at all.

Roger from our syndicate phones to say they're interested but could I look at the price again, the market's gone soft with the political uncertainty. I say when has there not been political uncertainty in this country, and things carry on, don't they? I don't say at a diminishing level – a slow eating away like borer in a Berea house. But I reduce my price to get the sale.

I see Tonderai the second day but not in his car. He walks to the shopping centre and comes back carrying stuff. Sitting like this is more tiring than surfing. Last time I waited in a car for something to happen was when I saw Caro and Cal kissing. That night I toss and turn.

Roger says we have a deal. He'd get the legal process going if I could appoint a letting agent to take over. He's aware of the outstanding rent but not that I'm stalking the tenant.

On the third day Tonderai comes out with two dudes who arrived an hour earlier in a Mercedes S class which I thought nothing of except that one was big with a bald bullet head. I train my binoculars on him. His skull sort of shines in the sun, and I realise it's a combination of sweat and earrings, Big Man type, like Idi Amin. He waves a finger in Tonderai's face before driving off with his mate. Tonderai follows in his small BMW. I wait a few seconds before firing up the Astra, way down the pecking order.

Onto the M4 south towards Durban, a few kilometres later taking the Ann Abor off-ramp down to The Promenade, the street closest to the sea, narrow with only dune bush separating it from the beach, houses a messy mixture of old and new. The Merc enters the driveway of a pseudo Tuscan mansion with Tonderai stopping on the verge. I nip into a small public parking area so as not to be conspicuous. Tonderai and the men disappear into the house. Ships out at anchor, fishing rods standing up at the water's edge, the sea a beckoning blue, gulls low over it on the lookout. How long since I've been in the sea?

Thirty minutes later Tonderai emerges with a black rubbish bag, Idi by his side. It can't be heavy, judging by the way he's carrying it. Tonderai gets into his BMW and places the bag on the passenger seat. As he pulls off the big man shakes an admonishing finger at him again. It's no fond goodbye.

My throat is parched, my body aches in unfamiliar places.

Back on the M4 to Durban, left into Argyle then first right into Sylvester Ntuli, staying with it all the way to where it changes to Mahatma Ghandi. I've never understood why the old Point Road, notorious for its lowlife, should have been renamed after a moral icon. It was in Point Road that I tripped the sailor in the pub going for Dunbar with a knife. It's as though I'm here for Dunbar again today, seeking his final approval.

How the stretch between Anton Lambede and Rutherford has decayed! Buildings with dark holes that were once doors, interior lighting gone, paint flaking from walls, grubby curtains and plastic sheeting flapping from windows; pawn shops, massage parlours, liquor stores, and dodgy clubs.

Near Mulberry Lane we slow down (the only explanation I have for a name like that in this fucked-up part of town is that it was given long ago – like a baby named Goodness at birth who then becomes a serial killer). Men on the pavement beckoning me – they ignore Tonderai even though he has the fancy car. One comes to my window, another stands half in front of the Astra. Tonderai stops, takes the black rubbish bag to a bin on the pavement, throws it inside and pulls off. I'm happy to vamoose, checking my mirror to see that no one is coming after me. I see a man removing the bag and disappearing into a building. It could not have taken more than thirty seconds.

A few blocks further Tonderai stops again, gets out and heads for Rutherford Street. I park a decent distance away and run to catch up. Around the corner a hair dresser, cell phone shop, cafe, steel gates and graffiti, some ailing palms with tops more brown than green. Just over the hill South Beach – my world of yesterday, of Spirou and Cal and Caro, and eternal youth. I slow down, get my breath back. Halfway up the hill Tonderai enters a building, Breakers Town Lodge it says (did I really expect the apostrophe, and in the right place?). A man stands watch, unwelcoming like the drab, dim foyer.

I stop. 'Any action around here, I'm looking for some.'

'Why ask me?' he says. Bulging T-shirt and jeans, stomach protruding over his belt, I want to suggest braces but it might not go down well.

'Look, I'm from outta town, and they tell me the Point is the place.'

'Are you a cop, man?' He's rocking on his sneakers now, and I fear his bulk might cause him to topple over. He sounds foreign. Congolese, Ibo?

'A cop, me?' I laugh. 'Yeah, young and eager and wanting to clean up this world, that's me! Actually, I'm a businessman from Port Elizabeth on a conference at the ICC, all frigging week. Finished this afternoon, want to get my mind right, if you know what I mean.' I smile at him.

He doesn't return the charm offensive and looks at my fawn chinos, long-sleeved blue shirt and black office shoes. 'Blow it you mean. What you looking for – girls, sugars, rock?'

Girls I know, deadly drugs I don't want to know. With drugs it's pay and leave, with a girl I can stay and find out more. 'I need a woman, only the best but not now, must clean up and pack first, back at eight. What you got, and how much?' I take out my wallet bulging with blue hundreds.

I get the first smile, not a friendly one but a step in the right direction. 'And who am I doing business with on this nice day?' He tips his cap back.

'James, James Bland.' It has a nice ring to it, not quite Bond but it will do.

He gives me high fives. 'Me I'm Onochie. It's three-fifty for a couple o' hours – upfront. My girls they from thirty to thirteen, anything under that and God will punish us as sure as there's a heaven.'

I stare at him, how screwed-up can people get? 'Okay, here's one-fifty for you, the three-fifty you get later. But I get the best, right?'

'Sharp-sharp, man, mmm … Jim.'

I wave a finger, 'Never Jim or Jimmy, Onochie, James it is.'

CHAPTER TWENTY-FIVE
Durban

As sex work is illegal in South Africa, the police do whatever they want with us, and that leaves us in a vulnerable situation where anyone just takes advantage. People who are involved in crime, like robbers, drug dealers, take advantage of that situation.
— Sex worker quoted by the Sex Workers' Education and Advocacy Taskforce (SWEAT), South Africa's leading sex worker human rights organisation

Just before 8pm, as I walk towards Breakers Town Lodge, I receive an SMS: *Feeling bad about the other day didn't mean to say those things. Please forgive me. Amber.* I'm already full of adrenaline but I can feel the extra rush it gives me, distracting me from my mission.

I switch the phone off and walk on. I'm in Gillespie Street, having come via the beach road to avoid Ghandi's gauntlet, but even here decay has taken its toll. Everywhere I look the night has a hard, coarse face. I can't hear my own footfall my heart is pounding so much. As I round the corner and go down Rutherford, Onochie is there, rocking on his sneakers.

'*Kèdú* James, *nnô*, welcome! Come inside.' We shake hands. How a full wallet talks!

Foyer too grand a name: locks ripped from some post boxes, others rusted brown, two of four ceiling lights not working, damp on the wall, paint lifting, and a terrible musty smell. I peel off three hundreds and a fifty. They disappear into his hands like parking tickets into a pay machine.

'Cool, now just gotta check you.' He frisks me airport-style.
'Okay, we can go up. Sorry we have to walk, lift's bust, but good room and best girl!'

'Take it easy, man. I have to keep up my strength.' I grin.

Four floors, staircase full of graffiti and even mustier. Onochie panting after two floors, by the fourth he's grunting. Maybe he's new. He'll either become the fittest man in town or have a hearty. Bare corridor, rooms on either side, doors without numbers.

'Here we are.' He takes a key from his pocket and unlocks a door on the south side. God, do they lock them in?

We go inside. It's like walking into a Caravaggio painting: dark shadows, girl highlighted on a bed by a low-watt bulb, in knee-high boots and skin-tight red dress (the boots are scuffed); braided hairpiece, bright red lips, eyes as shadow-filled as the corners of the room. In the dark background a non-descript carpet that's seen better days, a cupboard leaning sideways, a bathroom, and double windows facing the back of the building. It could have been a suite once, it's so large.

'This is Lucy,' Onochie says, 'came in a few days ago, young and still a bit wild. The boss likes her kind, trains them to get top dollar – the word gets around you see. It's your lucky night, man, getting the first ride.'

Yeah, they've probably already taken their pleasure of her – pre-loved not second-hand, as they say about cars. She says nothing. I don't see anything in her eyes – is it shock or drugs?

'See you later, Onochie,' I wave him out to break the lecherousness of his leer.

I sit down on the bed. There's nowhere else. The room is for coupling, not erudite conversation, a fuck and forget place. I don't try to make eye contact, just as you wouldn't do with any wild creature. 'What's your real name?'

'It's Gugu, Gugu Mnyandu.'

'Where are you from, Gugu?'

'uMlazi.'

'Oh.' Grey and sprawling, with as many sections as letters in the alphabet – you don't want to go there. 'Your name in Zulu means precious. It's not how you're feeling I'm sure.'

She looks at me for the first time, dark eyes embers of anger. I expected fear. 'You come to sleep with me, why don't you?' She starts to undress, boots first (Zoe is the only woman I know who leaves her shoes until last, and sometimes she doesn't remove them at all, it drives me crazy).

'Sit down, I didn't come for that. Don't ask questions. I won't hurt you.' I turn my body so I'm facing the door. 'Where are your parents?'

'They die, first my father then my mother. The hospital says TB but maybe it is aids, I don't know ...' She shrugs, 'too many funerals.'

'Onochie says you're new. Where do you sleep, how are they treating you?'

'Like rubbish, we sleep in the basement some of us. We cannot leave, they stop us. Men like Onochie. We get thirty rand for food every day. They give us rock and pipes for free, but we have to pay one hundred for a room upstairs every time we go with a man.'

'You have to pay *them*?'

She nods fingering the sole of one boot that's coming loose from its upper. 'Some girls take men to the shelter not far away. They charge only twenty rand. The boss nearly kill one girl, he find out you see. No rock for a week and she go crazy.'

'How old are you, Gugu?' Her breasts are small.

'Fifteen.'

'If you stay you know what will happen, Gugu? One week a boyfriend will give you clothes and take you to restaurants, the next week he'll give you *whoonga*. Soon you'll look like an old woman. It contains heroin and rat poison, and antiretrovirals – the HIV-Aids medicine. And while your flesh and bones get eaten, they get rich.' It's been in the papers.

Her eyes are dark pools. 'That one, Onochie, I hate him. I hate them all.'

The door bursts open. A man glares at me. 'That's *my* woman! What the fuck you doing, man?' But he looks surprised. Probably that my trousers and my wallet are still on me and I'm not on her. Nasty little eyes, de rigueur jeans, sweat top, and sneakers. He shakes off his surprise and comes for me. The girl clutches her head and whimpers. I get up. 'Hey man, can't you see we're just talking? I paid for this, ask Onochie.'

'Do I look like Onochie? This is *my* girl.' He's determined to stick to his script.

'Hold it right there, I want to see Dragut.' It's my gambit. Everything depends on it: if he doesn't know Dragut I'm in trouble; if he does I stand a chance.

He stops, processing this turn of events, not a man who thinks on his feet. I press on: 'He'll sleep better if he hears what I have to say. I'd get him here if I were you.'

'Hah! What white man trickery is this? What information, man?'

'That maybe Tonderai Manyika is skimming him.'

It hits a spot. I hoping it'll kill his tiresome pretence. 'Why don't you phone him right now?'

Still he hesitates, full of suspicion. 'So what's your name?'

'James – Onochie knows.'

He calls. They speak, sounds like Ibo – rapid, urgent. I hope it's not about more than I asked for. How long does it take to say it in Ibo? My heart is at it again. I should be with Sister Amber having dinner and gazing into her eyes.

The girl on the bed could be sitting for a painter, she's so still.

We wait.

The door opens slowly, a head comes around. It's bald and bullet shaped.

*

We stare at each other. He's changed from earlier in the day: now in pin-striped shirt, leather jacket, dark trousers, and black shoes. He says nothing. I have to force myself not to look away or speak first. What if I call him Idi by mistake?

In a soft voice, not at all what I expected, he says, 'So you know Tonderai?'

'All I know is that he knows you and might be taking money that's not his.'

'What's in it for you telling me this? You don't know me. Is it a reward you want, sunshine?' His attempt at smiling falls flat like a bad joke.

'It's not money I want.'

The slender, long-fingered hand he runs over his pate is at odds with his bulk. 'So what is it about Tonderai?'

As he says Tonderai's name again I realise this man could be gay – nuances missed at first glance, binoculars not telling all. Dragut and Tonderai – the real reason Dunbar was killed? It comes as an epiphany. Tears bank up threatening to pull my poker face apart. Please let it not be that.

'Once he goes I will.' I point to the other man. 'I don't mind the girl.'

'I assume he's got no steel or lead on him?' Dragut asks the man.

'Onochie doesn't take chances, Boss. Or prisoners!' He gives me a parting shot, 'You remember that.'

Footsteps fading in the corridor, and Dragut says, 'Right, I'm listening.'

I don't want too much space between us for what I'm about to tell him. It could be my last words. I walk up to him slowly and unthreateningly, more in a confiding manner, as if I don't want the girl to hear. 'You see,' I say, my voice low, 'I don't care a damn if Tonderai is cheating on you, but I care a lot about friends of mine being killed.'

A slow dawning in Dragut's eyes as I carry on, 'You organised the hit on Chris Dunbar, didn't you, because Tonderai's nose was put out of joint? You had a man killed because of your bleating little spoilt brat.'

He is shaking now, his hand slides under his jacket. I snap a foot into his groin followed by a fist to his nose – things that would bring tears to any man. Not Dragut. As he clutches his balls he pulls out his gun, multitasking Caro would have approved of. 'You're dead meat, man,' he gasps. The girl shouts. Dragut pulls the trigger. I feel a jolt, no pain, just my hearing gone. It's me or him, call it primeval. I rush at him head first, arms around him and pushing with all my might. He loses balance but I don't let go. I want to run him into the wall, hard. Sweet momentum as in a rugby maul, but we crash into the window instead. I cannot stop. The pane and the frame shatter as Dragut goes through back first. Only then do I let go. I hear him scream all the way down into the dark space behind the building.

The girl is crying. 'For Christ's sake shut up!' I yell at her. 'If you stay here they'll hurt you. You must come with me. *Gugu, you understand!*' I look for the gun. It's gone, with Dragut.

She lets me lead her into the passage, shock rendering her as pliant and shaky as a reed. Warm blood runs down my left arm and side, a man's head pops from a door, 'What's up?

Thought I heard a gunshot, and screaming … hey, what happened to you?'

'There's a madman in the building with a gun.'

Another head peeps out from a room. 'No kidding man?'

'You think this is ketchup on me? Listen, if you wanna be a hero then bang on every door, warn everyone you see. Then run. I'll do the next floor, you the second, okay?'

Heads withdraw like cuckoos in a clock. I got to get us out, four floors to go, what if I black out? In the dim light I find the gash between my elbow and my shoulder, pumping blood. The girl stares at it. I remove my shirt, tear it with a strength I didn't know I had, and start tying a strip above the wound, close to my armpit. She takes over and finishes the job, her demeanour calmer.

I find her hand again. Don't stop, think on the run.

We reach the ground floor. 'Gugu, you wait here.' I point to a dark spot underneath the staircase. It's as though her helping me has steadied her.

Onochie is at the entrance.

I shout, 'Help me, Onochie! Please.'

He turns around and his eyes go wide. 'What's the trouble, man?'

I walk up to him swaying. 'Yeah, good room and best girl – ticks for both – but you said nothing about a man barging in saying it's *his* girl, shooting me, and taking my wallet. The old sting, eh, Onochie.'

'*Mba*, no, James, I'm shocked!' He reaches out to steady me.

'Well, he got hurt, I had to defend myself, you understand.'

His phone rings. As he puts it to his ear I give him an uppercut. His head jerks back and the phone flies. A second punch flattens his Adam's apple. He crashes down the steps onto the pavement. I sit on his chest, pressing the air from him. 'Your gun, Onochie, where's it?' He's wheezing too much to answer. I find it under his arm, shove the barrel into his mouth, and shout for Gugu.

I bend over, closer. 'Onochie, if I were you I'd let us go.' I don't wait for an answer and get up, holding the gun.

As we run up Rutherford I regret not parking down in Mahatma Ghandi.

The Esplanade, yacht masts on my left, Dick King on his horse[ii] riding south with me, shabby buildings, a few art deco gems, bloody traffic lights, gun on my lap, Gugu silent above the roar of the engine.

'Where you taking me?' she asks.

'To a better place, trust me.'

I take a left into Sydney – bad news for pedestrians at night but a one-way for cars with five lanes, straight and fast. Nausea pushes up inside me and I'm sweating. Open my window, don't black out, not here with blood all over, Gugu, and the gun. I take in gulps of industrial Congella air, and feel no fresh blood down my arm – should I be happy or worry?

Right into Rick Turner, up the hill, left again towards the college where Hugh and Marge, my adoptive parents, met and fell in love, past the school. I stop, rummage in the cubbyhole for paper and pen, and hurriedly write a note.

I pull up outside the red-bricked complex of three old houses. More trees than I remember after all these years. The jungle gym, swings, see-saw, and concrete tables and seats all still there, as are the outbuildings and washing lines behind the parking area. The only thing new is the steel palisade barrier around the complex with electric fencing on top.

I drive around the corner where the car is out of sight, and turn to Gugu. 'Gugu, listen carefully. I'm going to ring the bell and talk to them. Then I want you to go inside, without me. Don't be afraid, it's safe. Give them this piece of paper and this …' I pull out seven one hundred notes. 'They'll know what to do.'

Gugu fingers the notes like a distracted child, 'You are sure?'

'I wouldn't let you in there if I weren't.'

'But why you not come?' She clutches my arm.

I wince and pull away. 'You know why. Tell me, do you remember the name of the person the Boss and I talked about?'

She puckers her face. Her lipstick has smeared beyond her mouth, and she has some of my blood on her. 'No, I was too frightened. Why?'

'Good, I don't want you to remember it. Not even what kind of car this is.'

'Sure, but what must I say?' This girl forced into womanhood with indelicate haste. Underneath, the adventurous spirit of youth now blended with an understanding of danger.

'Well, you can tell them what happened, but why make unnecessary trouble for us? Onochie and his guys would be stupid to go to the police, they'd get bust. That place isn't only a brothel, Gugu, it uses people like slaves. And they're into drugs.'

She points at the cluster of houses. 'Those people, they will ask questions.'

I nod. 'Tell them you were held prisoner in the Point and escaped. You were trying to find work, right? You have no parents or home anymore. They beat you often. You were running and screaming in the road when I came along.'

Gugu's expression tells me I'm agonising too much. 'Most of it is true. It's not just a story. I will do it, no worries.' She touches my arm gently. 'You must go to hospital.'

A passing driver gives me a funny look. I'm not surprised – a shirtless, middle-aged white man with a black girl in a car at night, in this country. You don't know the half of it, my friend.

'Gugu, don't forget to say you don't want the police involved because you're afraid of Onochie and his men. What will the cops do anyway?' I laugh and she laughs too, for the first time. It has a nice sound. She should be laughing every day.

I ask for the matron on duty over the intercom. She holds her breath as I talk, the inevitable questions come, but I answer what I want to answer and tell her, 'Matron, the money is a donation to the home, indirectly for Gugu of course. Kindly leave an official receipt in an envelope at the spot requested in my note, in a plastic bag in case it rains. You'll hear from me again, soon. You're an angel to take her in.'

'You're very kind, but who do I make it out to?'

'Mm ... let's just say the Man from the Point.'

Gugu gives me an apprehensive little wave. I take another look at the board outside the buildings. *Durban South Childrens Home* it says. For the entire time I was there as a *homie* they never bothered with the apostrophe, one-thousand-and-fifty-three days to be exact, carved into my mind like Robinson Crusoe's notches on his wooden cross. Dizziness and nausea threaten to overcome me again.

CHAPTER TWENTY-SIX
Durban

ANC National chairwoman Baleka Mbete believes there is an internal plot to unseat President Jacob Zuma. Mbete said Zuma's detractors who had failed to oust him as party leader ... had now regrouped to plot his downfall.
— Editorial, *The Mercury*

When I reach St Augustine's Hospital ten minutes later and see the sign, '24 Hour Accident and Emergency', I can't drive in. I would have to answer too many questions, give all kinds of personal information before I'd get treatment.

I'm not sure I can make it to anywhere else, I feel so dreadful. It's raining now. Glistening tarmac and streaming yellow street lights. The car guard looks at me perplexed. Am I going to park or not? He doesn't know how confused I am. I've gone from corporate man to Harry Haller in one night, the man coming to Gugu's rescue, the wolf killing Dragut. I've been both parts my whole life without knowing it – a *Steppenwolf?*

Sudden clatter of a helicopter – sound of *Apocalypse Now* as it hovers over the hospital, spotlight sweeping the ground. There's no place to hide. I'm too weak to run.

Even when I realise it's the hospital emergency helicopter my heart doesn't calm down. If my situation weren't so precarious I'd think it funny. Is it a taste of what's to come – a life on the run? Maybe I'm just delirious.

*

Sister Amber opens the door. Her hand goes to her mouth. 'Oh my word, what happened, Mr Bland?'

As I lean against the frame I begin to slide. She catches me under the arms and pulls me inside. 'Here, let me help ... down the passage we go ... into this room ... there! Lie down.' All I can think of before I pass out is that's she's so strong because she does it all the time.

I come to, stabs of pain. Sister Amber washing the wound, I don't want to look. She's put a towel underneath my arm and has a bowl of water on her lap. 'Oh, you're with us again. I had to untie the tourniquet carefully – it could have started bleeding again. You'll be pleased to know the bone isn't damaged. You've lost some flesh, and of course blood. You'll need stitches though.' I could listen to Sister Amber's caring voice all day. 'Running water would be better, Mr Bland.'

She helps me to the bathroom and removes the shower spray from its hook. 'There must be a reason why you didn't go to hospital.'

I wince under the spray. 'It's the only way I could see you again.'

'Be serious. Aren't you going to tell? Where's your shirt?'

I can't tell her what happened. It would put her in the most difficult position. 'Lost my shirt, but I think I still won. It's a story involving crimes of passion, you see.'

Some of her hair has come loose. She gives me a look through her glasses. 'You and someone you mean? And crimes in the plural?'

I sense the woman in her talking, not the saint. It makes me feel better straightaway. 'Two gays, actually. I'm not fobbing you off. This is the stuff of novels, believe me.' Isn't it what Franny said?

Sister Amber looks puzzled. It strikes me suddenly she might think *I'm* coming out. I'm too weary to tell her I've never been inside.

She turns business-like. 'I'm off to the nursing home quickly. The wound needs antiseptic, antibiotic cream, and bandages. I'll be half-an-hour. Whatever you do don't let the bleeding start again.'

I'm lying on the bed. The gun in the car! I must hide it and clean the Astra. The events of the day feel as if they've played out over days not hours. Wonder how Gugu is – hopefully safe in her bed comforted by matron. A welcome sensation of being disconnected from the world comes over me like a warm blanket. I doze off.

*

'Mr Bland, this might sting a little, it contains benzalkonium chloride.'

She's back again, in her nice floral dress. What's with Lone Ranger females in their jeans and boots, off to shop in their four-by-fours with little Tontos in tow?

'Once it's dry I'll put on the antibiotic and the bandage. And then hopefully you'll stay in one piece.' She shakes her head. 'I have a feeling you're not going to get it stitched?'

I look away.

'It'll leave a bigger scar if you don't.'

I shrug. 'I've always wanted to look rugged.'

'You must stay here tonight. You shouldn't drive. Shower in the morning so I can re-apply the cream and put on a fresh bandage. Now, I'm going to make something to eat. You must be starved.'

'Before you go ...'

'Yes.'

'Are you ever going to call me Tom? Even Germans switch from *Sie* to *du* at some point, you know.'

She smiles at me. It's when I like her most, because to smile you have to come out of yourself a little.

In the spare room I think of her all warm in her bed just metres away. If I ever get married again I won't have any spare bedrooms in my house. I'll use the space for a library, a gym, maybe a billiard room-cum-pub.

*

I try to take it easy the next day but it's as though my mind is walking barefoot over scalding sand.

Off to the GM dealership near North Beach to buy two new mats for the Astra. It requires a full hour using one arm to remove the blood from the driver's seat with special stain remover. The gun I hide with Spirou's letter – two guns now. Soon my flat will be bulging with secrets.

I return the car to the rental company, and the woman asks if it performed satisfactorily. 'Like a bomb,' I say, 'excellent in sticky situations.' I'm shocked by my light-hearted, cavalier reply. Decades of corporate toeing-the-line, and suddenly a hyped-up senior – it's not what I expected. Neither could I foresee taking in my stride things others my age would find nerve-wracking. It's as if I've gone from accountant or actuary to adrenaline junkie in a matter of months.

I send an email to Tonderai to the effect that if he doesn't pay what he owes within a week, the syndicate would sue him, adding it would please his father no end. I inform him of the appointment of a managing agent who would be far less tolerant of arrears.

At the club everyone wants to know that happened to my arm. I say a little accident. Russ and Bones deserve better but I tell them all would be revealed in good time. They are suspicious and a little upset. They don't know the half of it (the phrase keeps cropping up these days).

It's as though I'm trying belatedly to take charge of my destiny – hubristic, I know, but I'm driven. Spirou had his appointment in the Namib Desert. Perhaps my own is waiting somewhere.

I go to the police station to see Harrisunker lest he becomes suspicious about why I'm not following up on Dunbar. For weeks it's been the same thing: I'd call or visit him enquiring if there's been a breakthrough, and he'd say 'we're working on it.' And I wonder how many other people across this land are doing the same at their police stations. Depressing to think the police are either overworked or undertrained or incompetent, or criminals themselves, and that when you look into their eyes you're not sure who is what.

'Warrant Officer, how are things?'

'Mr Bland, I wish I had good news for you.' The usual disarray around him, cup of tea with spill marks on the sill, sunken eyes with bags under them. But I for once, feeling in charge.

'So still nothing, eh?' I shake my head. 'Well, you know where to find me.'

I wonder if he's aware of Dragut's death (I'm assuming Dragut didn't survive). There's been nothing in the papers. Onochie and company probably disposed of the body quietly and quickly. I doubt any one of them is wearing black. Lucrative businesses have their own imperative. Maybe Harrisunker has been in the pockets of the gang all along.

Over dinner (at last a yes from her) Sister Amber comments that something about me has changed. 'You're not the same somehow … it's your look, the way you walk.' She laughs nervously. 'I've told you that before.'

'You said I reminded you of a prowler in a scary movie you'd seen.'

She lowers her eyes. 'I didn't say it was bad.'

'What then?'

'Okay, it was nice. There!'

'Is that all – just nice?'

'You're teasing me. Well, you know, it can be exciting.'

'Time for formalities to go, don't you think? The two of us could be in a Jane Austen story. No wonder they never made love until they were well and truly married – all that bowing and curtsying getting in the way.' With no tan Sister Amber's blush is obvious, and most agreeable as Ms Austen would say.

'Mister Bland, you're something else!'

The more I'm with Sister Amber the more I like her. Inside that starched casing of a uniform is a caterpillar waiting to become a butterfly.

*

I'm in the flat typing what is probably the most difficult letter of my life, using one-and-a-half arms. Blessed are computers, they'll inherit the earth. Without my tablet, scrunched-up and scrawled-on pieces of paper would be all over the floor. I think I have something at last.

Dear Caro,

Please don't read this letter as a plea from me to come back. I've accepted that we won't get together again, that it's over. Perhaps it's why I'm writing it, to tell you about things I should have told you long ago.

It's hard for me to tell you that my real name isn't Thomas Bland but Thomas Adendorff. And that my father was Maximillian Adendorff and my mother Rebecca. He worked the tugboats in Durban harbour, rising from ordinary seaman to bosun to mate but never to master because of what happened. I remember the name of his boat, the Coenie Aucamp. Tugboats tow and push vessels to safety, to keep them out of harm's way – God, the irony in that, as you'll see. My mother was bookkeeper for a small construction company. I was supposed to have a little sister but she was stillborn. You see, my parents became alcoholics, first my father then my mother, hers a case of 'if you can't beat them, join them'. Some alcoholics get silly, he became aggressive. That's how she lost the baby. I think he beat my mother into drinking. In those days the 'purge and puke' treatment was used for alcoholics (a mix of barbiturate and belladonna and toxic salts – a real shock to the system) but it didn't work. Then some rehab centres tried to dry them out but this also failed (they had to put my father in a straightjacket once, he got so violent). Soon they were more in than out of rehab. Of course both of them lost their jobs – tugboats require steady legs and hands, and bookkeeping a clear head.

I became a foster child at five. Trouble was my parents deluded themselves that they could beat the drink and look after me, so they refused consent for me to be adopted (I missed out twice in three years, although to be honest I wouldn't have adopted me either I was so difficult, a 'lost cause' a house mother said. Different foster parents meant changing schools often. I had to go where I was told. Not all of my foster parents were nice, but at least none were as bad as my own. In between foster parents I stayed at the Durban South Children's Home. I got to know Durban but made no real friends, and learnt to keep secrets figuring that the less people knew about me the less chance of bad things happening to me. By the time I met you it was second nature.

Your father never accepted me as Thomas Bland. Imagine his reaction if he'd known I was Thomas Adendorff, with parents like that! He would have ordered a hit on me rather than see you marry me. Yes, I should have told you, Caro, but I just couldn't. It was a combination of shame and fear of losing you. The double stigma of alcoholic parents (not recognised as a disease in those days) and foster child would have killed my chances with you. Forgive me for saying this but I doubt that you would have married the real Tom Adendorff – too much of a come down?

Funny how my father had a name fit for a Kaiser, and my adopted father, who was my rock, was lumbered with Bland. But to this day I thank the court that terminated my parents' biological right over me and allowed Hugh and Marge to adopt me.

I remember well arriving at the children's home the first time with wounds and scars. It made me some kind of hero with the other kids. Trouble was, although the flesh healed over time, the inside of me didn't. It's maybe why I didn't turn out to be a better man for you. But all that's in the past, and I can now only wish you everything of the best.
    Tom

CHAPTER TWENTY-SEVEN
Durban

The Statistician-General recently produced figures ... on unemployment among black youths that ought to give nightmares to those in government. The new democratic order has failed them. Frustration and anger will be simmering. What legitimate avenues remain for these young people? Their plight has potentially produced a ticking bomb.
— Editorial, *The Mercury*

I put the letter aside, aware that I'm not like Russ who has learnt to write about matters of the heart (it's probably why I could never talk about them either). At one point I nearly tear the letter up. I don't, but neither can I get myself to deliver it.

I drive around until I find a public phone that works, and punch in the number of the Children's Home. Matron comes on the line, courteous but business-like. I ask about Gugu. 'Ah, I'm glad you called,' she says brightly, 'Gugu is just fine. She's fitting in well.'

'I'm happy to hear it Matron, I was worried she might abscond for some reason. Please tell her I called.'

'You're not going to tell us who you are?'

'Not material, important is for Gugu to feel it's the best place for her, and for the home to help her with her schooling. I'd like to know the approximate cost of a child per month – food, clothes, school, everything. I realise you're an NGO working on donations and subsidies, so what I'll do is give donations equal to three months' costs at a time to cover her as an individual ...'

'It's extremely generous of you, bringing Gugu to us and now the donations. And don't worry, I'll keep tabs and leave receipts for you to collect – in our spot!'

'No, I must thank *you*. I'll be in touch. Give her my best.'

'She thinks the world of you, you know that?'

'Tell her it's mutual, for staying.'

At six the following morning I go to Caro's house, eye the mean mouth of the letterbox and push the letter inside. There, Sister Amber would say. A part of me feels unburdened, another apprehensive as I drive away. It could be the final straw with Caro, not that I've had many to clutch onto.

I spend the next two hours at New Pier catching crazy tubes and bombing out so often that Bones wants to know if I'm trying to write myself off. At least I can appreciate Bones's double entendre, unintended as it was.

*

We're on the deck, and I sense my friends aren't happy. 'Bru, you okay?' Bones asks. 'Yeah, what's up, man?' Russ says, 'it's like you're with us but also not, and taking those crazy waves with that arm.'

'Sorry, got a lot on my mind. It's Caro, and other stuff.' I sound cagey and this with my only friends (the temerity of Face Book yesterday informing me, 'you have more friends than you realise').

They stare at me as though I'm no longer the Tom they know. To me the deck isn't the same either. It feels smaller, precarious, no longer on foundations but adrift with only a table, umbrella, some chairs and me on it, and an empty horizon. I've probably caused confusion in Caro as well with my letter.

I change the subject. 'Look at this, have you seen it?' I point to the morning paper.

'Yeah, heard it on the radio,' Russ says, 'protests flaring up again, this time all over the place, police having to use live ammo in some cases – rubber and water not enough.'

'And the President ill again, stress they say. Anyone who doesn't know would think the country is exploding,' Bones says. 'I mean, we've had this stuff for years. Sounds like more of the same.'

'Maybe not,' Russ says. 'Until now they've been fragmented, no national leader, easily contained. What if it becomes a full-blown movement, like in other countries? They have little or nothing – young, jobless and landless, and until a few years ago, voiceless it seemed. And that in a democracy! No wonder the EFF has gained.'

'Yeah, if you have nothing, go with the party that promises everything,' Bones says.

'And those who do have jobs go on strike as if there's no tomorrow.' I feel weary. Maybe there's no tomorrow for me here either.

*

Harrisunker is on the line. 'Mr Bland, good day. I'm calling about Tonderai Manyika. I'm sorry to tell you he's late.'

'He always is, with his rent ...'

'I mean he's dead, Mr Bland, shot in a side-street off Mahatma Ghandi. When last did you see him?'

'What, I had contact with him just last week! I threatened to sue so he paid the outstanding rent. But this ...'

'You never liked him, did you?'

'He was difficult, always short of money, and made excuses. Would you be happy with a tenant like that? Any idea what the motive could be?'

'Well, his car keys were on him but not his wallet. We walked around the area pressing the remote until we located the car – a BMW. He was shot execution-style – someone settling a score maybe, but it could also have been a mugging.'

Yeah, whatever, but where to from here, Harrisunker? Nowhere, like with Dunbar? 'Here's a thought, Warrant Officer, maybe he took money that wasn't his to pay the rent, and he upset some people? Unsavoury types, you know, and they did a hit. Whatever, I represent a business syndicate and had no choice but to tell him we'd sue.'

'Been reading too many detective novels, Mr Bland?' Harrisunker gives a thin laugh. 'Yes, the area where he was found is bad, and he could have got mixed up with the wrong people. On the other hand, he might only have wanted sex. You'd be surprised who goes there – professional types, politicians, businessmen, all kinds. He wasn't on our radar for anything, and his father is well connected as you know. He probably was in the wrong place at the wrong time.'

'Yeah, like Chris Dunbar.'

Harrisunker ignores it. 'I'll have to go to the flat if you don't mind, have a look an' all. His father will have to ID the body and arrange for it to be taken back to Harare, also his possessions ... unless you want to assist with the ID?'

'On the first one, just say when and I'll let you in. On the ID I'll take a rain check, if you don't mind. Of course I'll advise our syndicate and the new managing agent.' I pause. 'So it's another murder case, and another docket. If you find out more please let me know.'

Hamlet comes into my head: *Let Hercules himself do what he may, the cat will mew and dog will have his day.* I imagine Harrisunker in his red-brick building that's like a slapdash Lego job. I have no further use for it. 'Goodbye, Warrant Officer.'

The next morning I'm in the flat long before the traffic to uMhlanga gets heavy, at Tonderai's desk and wearing a pair of yellow household gloves. The note is still there with Dunbar's details and Dragut's name. So much has happened since I saw it for the first time. I fold it carefully and slide it into my pocket, not touching anything else. I search the lounge: nothing in the couches, under the cushions, or behind the pictures. I check Tonderai's cupboards and drawers in the bedroom, putting everything back the way it was. Then I find it, among his colourful underwear: pebbles about three times the size of a matchstick head, wrapped in strips of black bag plastic, a rock pipe slightly longer than my thumb, and a cigarette lighter. No lowly *whoonga* for our designer dude – more like crack. Newspapers have been full of Durban's drug scourge. I leave Tonderai's paraphernalia for Harrisunker to find. I'm beyond caring whether he does or not. All that matters is for Dunbar and Spirou to rest in peace.

*

I often wonder what my true motivation was for starting this thing with Tonderai, watching him, following him to the Point then going back that night. To find out more, yes, allay or confirm my suspicions, and if it proved to be the latter, leaving it to others like Harrisuker to sort out? Would I have accepted that? I don't think so. And Dragut – would I have killed him anyway had he not crashed through the window? Did I not steer him to his death? I don't know the answers to any of this. It's too complicated.

*

Relief to be out on the promenade on rented bikes with Sister Amber, riding into a moderate onshore wind past the Casino's pastels towards Blue Lagoon, spring sun on our backs, and the whole nation seemingly on the move this Sunday: black, white and brown, all shapes and ages, on foot, bike, skateboard, and rickshaw. I'm in shorts and T-shirt, Sister Amber in jeans, sneakers and light jersey – as I recommended. It is probably Sister Amber's greatest adventure yet. I don't believe she's not ever made love, but maybe it was no great shakes, although you can never tell. Look at Zoe. She was a surprise a minute, on the upside.

Through wild strands of hair Sister Amber casts a look in my direction as if to say 'my goodness, here I'm riding a bike, all the way to the Umgeni and back!' Her face is flushed from pedalling, complexion of an English rose. I'm glad for her we'll have the wind behind us on the way back.

We have lunch overlooking Bay of Plenty, where the old Paterson groyne used to make for long, intoxicating rides to the right. Not to bore Sister Amber with.

'Your arm seems all right,' she says.

'Almost there, thanks to you.'

'But are *you* all right?'

'Well, funny you should ask about the part you can't see. As a matter of fact, I'm not.' It's scary territory. I feel like a WW1 soldier about to rush from my trench, towards an enemy I can't see. Scream as loud as you can to give yourself courage. I take a deep breath, and for the next ten minutes I tell her basically what I told Caro in my letter. She listens, no judgement in her eyes, no reprimand on her tongue. Oh, I think I could love this woman (I've become cautious about love, you see. I have to learn all over again, like a man with a prosthetic arm).

She puts her hand on my arm. 'It's become a big thing in your mind because you've held it inside for so long. Don't the same thoughts seem more troublesome in the night than during the day? It's a bit like that. I'm sure you feel better now having let it out.'

'Just don't call me Mr Adendorff, okay.' My smile feels plastered on.

'So you were hoping to get together again? What can I say? She also kept things from you, didn't she?' She starts picking at her food like an oldie at the nursing home.

'Yeah, and there I thought all she was hiding from me was her weight, meanwhile ... Have you ever missed someone, I mean really missed?'

She nods, 'For most of my adult life, yes ... my husband.'

I stop eating, 'Husband? You were married?'

'I married young, we had our honeymoon, and three weeks later he didn't come back one day. Just like that. In the morning he was there, in the evening he was gone. There was a terrible finality to it. It made the gap he left so much bigger. I mean, it wasn't as if he died slowly of some disease.'

'What happened?'

'Oh, car accident, he got a brief mention on page five of the newspaper – among the other accidents that day. Aren't you going to ask me his name?'

'I'm sorry, I never thought ...'

'I could be with a man?'

Sister Amber is a mind reader. 'Sorry again ... tell me his name.'

'It was Alastair.'

In the evening I take Sister Amber to a movie at the casino, and she lets me hold her hand. Here I am, at sixty feeling like sixteen, wondering what it's like to hold all of her. My mind goes a bit crazy at the thought, I must admit.

*

Writing and talking about my past after decades of silence have the effect of drawing up other memories like buckets from a well, and as clear as the water in it. How at age five I arrived at the home with scars, proceeding to add to them by doing dangerous things when told not to, like climbing trees and running along the top of the wall. I was told I was an unaffectionate, bad-tempered boy – I once hit the House Mother in the stomach and got four lashes for it. Other punishments included having my toys and dessert withheld for a week, putting the washing (enough for an army) through rubber rollers to squeeze the water out, turning the handle until my arms felt like coming off, being sent to bed early to read (I didn't mind this because it enabled me to escape). I got boils which had to be treated with Traxa, worms that needed Vermox, warts which had to be burnt off at Addington, German measles, colds and flu, jaundice, scabies – you name it. They even gave me Ritalin to curb my destructive, dangerous, and spiteful ways – their words (my habit of grinning while committing offences resulted in my being sent to Hunt Road for therapy – it emerged I was painfully shy of asking favours because I couldn't believe anyone cared about me, that I was like a prickly pear, hands off and all that stuff).

We were given jabs against a myriad of illnesses that stalked the home. How we did not die from these collective threats I'll never know. I was shunted from one foster parent to the next. In between, infrequently, my parents visited the home (once my father arrived drunk and had to be turned away). I lived for the ice cream cart that came by once a week. I could hear its bell a long way off, and I'd wait on the hot, shimmering tarmac clutching my coin. Oh, when that wafer magically appeared from the vapours of the freezer I could have danced.

*

Caro has instituted divorce proceedings. Letter from her lawyer giving as reasons the absence of communication, loss of love, and basic unhappiness (Rupert's firm is acting for Caro – surprise, surprise). There are unwelcome papers for me to sign.

I'm thinking of opposing it on the basis that she committed adultery and left the house to pursue it. Maybe I'll also claim damages from Cal for alienation of affection. But what's the point? Love isn't something to be forced. Was hiding my true identity all those years not a worse offence? And what about my Rabelaisian romps with Zoe and Lola, even if they were post-Caro?

The fact that she's using Cal's father's firm leaves a bitter taste in my mouth. Father and son one big glossy brochure, and to think Caro fell for it. I must have been a lousy husband.

In my flat I stack some magazines on top of the legal papers so I can't see them. Tomorrow is another day.

*

I wake up with new resolve. I phone Singapore Airlines to book a ticket and then spread the divorce documents out on the table to sign wherever there are crosses. The thought of breakfast is anathema, like the day in Zoe's flat when I heard the news about

Dunbar. I put the papers back into the envelope and drive to Caro's house to drop them off. That night I compose a long email to Franny telling her of my plans.

By the next day I have my e-ticket. At American Express I buy R75K's worth of US dollars in notes. Where I'm going it is green but primitive they say – only money changers, no banks. What better than greenbacks with their universal language? I try not to dwell on the fact that each dollar cost me a fortune in rand – *In God We Trust* it says.

The things in my flat that remind me of death – Hugh's ashes, Spirou's letter, my gun, *Steppenwolf* – I put into a shopping bag and hide in the gap between the top of the wardrobe and the ceiling. Onochie's gun I take out on my board underneath my rash vest, in a shoulder holster I bought for it, and drop it a good two hundred metres on the other side of the shark nets.

CHAPTER TWENTY-EIGHT
Durban, Amber

A visibly stressed President Zuma ... delivered a State of the Nation address in which he trotted out the old mantras. (It) cannot alter the realities of a declining economy, massive unemployment, lamentable labour relations, appalling non-achievement in government at all levels, downgraded international credit ratings, and a seething discontent throughout society.
—Editorial, *The Mercury*

At North Beach I rent a bike similar to the one Tom chose for me weeks ago. I give the man my driver's licence to keep for the hour.

'But what's your name,' he asks.

'Oh, it's Amber.'

Enjoy the ride, Amber.' He's over-friendly. Immediately I feel vulnerable. I peddle away hastily, aware that my front wheel doesn't quite look in control.

I decide to ride south, to uShaka, a shorter stretch than the one to Blue Lagoon, and not as isolated. A sparkling sea, expanses of beach, the wind light in my face, piers, lifeguard towers, a few walkers, joggers, and cyclists. Did I come here to feel Tom's presence, the place in Durban I associate with him most? I feel instead his absence, the strange sensation of a gap next to me as I ride, and me filling it with images of him. I want to warn him about the three approaching cyclists riding side by side, the female jogger, but depress the urge feeling foolish. Just after South Beach I draw up at the railing and stare at the sea. It is now afternoon where Tom is, six hours on. Is he surfing right now? How often does he think of me? The ocean between us is vast.

I do not see the man coming up behind me, and hear only the voice: 'I gotta gun in my pocket. Don't scream, don't run, just gimme the bike.'

I'm so shocked I can't move. Rough hands remove mine from the handle bars. To make sure I understand, he adds, 'If you shout I kill you.' His tone is flat, lifeless. It's more a statement than a threat, of what will happen should I disobey. It implies choice when actually I have none. Still I don't move or try to catch anyone's eye. There seems to be a lull in pedestrian traffic.

'Take it and go,' I try to keep my voice calm. For a bizarre moment I want to tell him it's a woman's bike and he'll look ridiculous on it.

The sound of breaking waves; over it I hear the soft swoosh of tyres on the promenade and my heart thudding as he rides away, the saddle far too short for him.

*

At the police station all they want to know is if I'm okay. If there's no injury, why bother with a charge sheet, they ask? To summon a car and cruise the Point area searching for the man seems too much trouble (they tell me a car isn't available anyway). The bike rental company needs only a case number for insurance purposes. I feel immeasurably frustrated in this no-can-do place – a microcosm of what's happening all over the country, a chipping away at the whole idea of justice, replaced by the notion that crime pays.

Much later in my flat, still shaking, I think of Tom, and how it would not have happened had he been with me. It makes me miss him even more. How I wish he had put his arms around me when he said goodbye. I could see in his eyes he wanted to. I was too shy to make the first move, regretting it later with all my heart. What if he likes his island so much he decides to stay, or stays so long he loses whatever feelings he had for me? There is so little to keep him in Durban anyway, apart from his few friends.

In the middle of the night I wonder what Tom would say about today. That it is simply one of life's curveballs, as he calls them? He seems to attract them. He's like a planet without a moon to mitigate the number of meteors crashing into it. Is it why I find it so exciting to be around him? He's like Harrison

Ford in a movie: the decent, ordinary guy that somehow gets in the path of danger, and then comes up trumps. The difference is the movie I can switch off, or view in instalments if it gets too scary. If today is what real-life hazard is about I don't want any part of it. Alistair being taken away from me three weeks after our marriage was enough. I've stayed out of harm's way for decades since then, accepting the limits of my existence, working and living behind walls and electric fences, venturing out on the roads only when necessary.

Everything in me says I should use this opportunity to get used to being without Tom. That I should be thankful he left me without words of endearment or commitment, words that might have created expectations, stretched thinly and hopefully across this great sea.

CHAPTER TWENTY-NINE
Grupuk, South Lombok, Indonesia

L ocals and visiting surfers know it as Grupuk. Its official name, Gerupuk, is reserved for maps and the crude sign nailed to a tree at the entrance to the village. I guess it's a vowel less to twist your mouth around.

First-time visitors can be forgiven for feeling intimidated when they arrive, mostly on mopeds: young Sasak dudes giving them the once-over and demanding 'toll' money – five thousand Rupiah, which sounds a lot but isn't once you do the conversion (why Indonesia persists with all the zeroes I don't know – a Rupiah millionaire here means nothing). The village is easy to control. It has one main street – if you can call the pitted, dirt-baked thoroughfare a street – running parallel to the sea for less than a kilometre before being stopped by a hill. Its buildings – generally decrepit except for the mosque and a few homestays and eateries – form a single line on the sea side, extending inland for about fifty metres before petering out. Udin reckons no more than twelve hundred people live here – it's more like surviving from what I can see.

Today is my seventh day and the men wave me through knowing I'm with Udin. Kojak, Udin's guard, greets me: military-style blue trousers tucked into boots, security badge on his cap and white shirt, knife in a sheath hanging from his belt. *'Berembe kabar?'* he asks me, standing ramrod straight and saluting me. I'm undecided whether he likes me or not. When he showed me his knife on the second day there seemed to be no difference between the glint of the blade and the look in his eyes.

'Solah, tampi asih, I'm fine thanks,' I answer, parking my moped exactly where he shows me. Udin emerges from his board rental shop to shake my hand. We go through the same greetings.

'Mister Tom, you better now?' Udin asks. Fortyish, with a body that once must have been well defined, spiky black hair, tan skin, colourful sarong, T-shirt and sandals – standard island attire.

'Fine thanks, but no salads from now on or brushing my teeth with tap water.' I pull a face – two days of stomach hell and plenty of rehydration powders, bananas and steamed rice. To say nothing about my sore ribs from all the paddling – a nice kind of pain because it means long rides: just twelve at a hundred-and-seventy metres each equate to two kilometres of paddling, and that in a single surfing session.

Badri approaches with a stack of T-shirts. 'New stock, very nice,' he holds one up, 'blue like water you can see right down, like your eyes, Mister.' His weathered face cracks into a smile – a fisherman before tourists started coming to Lombok, now a salesman and making a better living, the story of so many of the villagers and I'm happy to be a part of it.

'I'll have a look when I get back, Badri.' I've already bought two.

Udin shouts in the direction of his house. 'I'm calling Doni, no school today. You go with him, okay Mister Tom?'

'No worries.' I like his kid.

'Same board, see here, I keep it for you.' He points to a nine-foot-something longboard scarred like an elephant that's seen many fights. It rides a lot better than it looks.

Doni bounces towards us, past the old woman sitting on an upturned bucket chewing betel, her mouth red. He hits a puddle (they say the season turns in October), spraying the air brown and causing her to shriek and gesticulate. Doni is like a puppy that runs, eats and sleeps with little in between. He beams, 'Hello, we go now?' He looks like his father but has the sturdy, muscular build of most Sasak boys in their teens. Today he's wearing a blue cap with orange brim, sun glasses with yellow frames, a flowery sarong, and a red and black Quicksilver shirt. Somehow he pulls it all together, making him look cool. Ah, the forgiveness of youth.

'Check Don-Don first, if no good go to Inside,' Udin says as I walk towards the stone-wall and the steps leading to the beach. 'Overhead today I hear, maybe double by Monday. Learners will be at Kiddies' Corner, make you happy.'

Dugouts at anchor in this quiet corner of the bay, dogs curled up in the sand's warm hollows, children hopping and jumping on finger-drawn squares on the sand. At the water's edge countless sardine heads, the bodies drying on plastic sheets in the sun near Udin's house.

Doni has put my board crossways on the dugout which he calls a *perahu*: narrow, with two benches, two small masts (to erect canvas for shade), bucket for emergencies, rusted anchor in a prow surprisingly proud for such a rudimentary craft – a touch of artistry carved from the hard wood. He starts the Yamaha. I clamber over the bamboo outrigger and hop on, waterproof bag over my shoulder with sunscreen, towel, wax, and bottled water. I feel my heart beating as we put-put past lobster farming platforms, Don-Don which looks tame today, into clearer water and the rising sun, to Grupuk Inside.

'Where's school, Doni?'

'Praya, I stay with uncle, no senior school in village.' Doni squints, his glasses more show than substance.

'You play football?' Who doesn't in these parts of the world?

'Nah, I am *pepadu*.' He brings an arm up and strikes down on some imaginary target.

'What's that, Doni?'

'Stick fighter, I want to be famous stick fighter.' His dark brown eyes shine. 'Every day I train.'

He tries to explain in his broken English, getting up and steering the boat with one foot while demonstrating strikes with the *penjalin*, or rattan stick, and defensive moves with the *ende*, or cowhide shield. The dugout rolls with his efforts. I put a hand on my board to keep it steady. I've seen pictures of stick fighting in travel magazines. Even in this narrow space, with one foot steering, Doni's movements are graceful and his balance amazing. Do I detect a touch of bravado, of showmanship trumping substance? It doesn't matter. His youthful exuberance is what I like. Nostalgia sweeps over me as I watch him.

'You show me one day, Doni, where you have contests. You take me?' I'm relieved his attention is once again on where he's going.

He nods vigorously. 'Yes, yes, to Seger.'

'You must be good at surfing. You surf together, you and Udin?'

'Nah, Papa never has time, always fixing things – engines, boats, the house, the shop, the moped.' He shrugs.

Udin can surf most days if he really wants to but he doesn't, caught up in pressures I thought were only city afflictions. I must claim back some of my dreams, before it's too late, make a start on this island. Far out, massive headlands rise like sentinels on either side of the bay's entrance. Blue water, green hills, the sky – unstained as yet by man, the village an incongruous, flimsy footprint in the corner and, gazing down on it all, Mount Rinjani, patient as all volcanoes are, signalling bottled-up anger once in a while but keeping the moment of eruption entirely to itself. I feel small here but, strangely, not threatened, grateful to be alive in the presence of awesome nature. And full of hope.

*

Bru and Bru

Russ please print a copy for Bones. Kuta in south Lombok where I'm staying is seriously chilled. What a favour Dunbar did me when he told me about it. It's nothing like Kuta Bali. Why they also called it Kuta here I don't know, maybe they thought the Bali link was cool (it isn't in my opinion). You have to stay in town in a homestay (their name for b&bs) to appreciate it.

It's not everyone's cup of tea (i doubt Caro would have liked it) – a ragtag bunch of people outside the airport building gawping at tourists, litter along the roads, chickens on suicide missions (guaranteed free range on menus, ha, ha), ramshackle buildings, and the town which, in Russ's absence, i'll try to describe: with no visible street names, no stop signs or traffic lights, no pavements, no road markings, potholes like you can't believe, a million mopeds, stray dogs (i haven't seen one being walked by its owner, called by its name, or stroked), skittish cats that for some strange reason have only half a tail, water buffalo and bleating goats, restaurants and homestays, clothing and surf shops, and dusty second-hand books in deep corners of shops where mosquitoes hide. Buildings are low-slung and people laid-back (about ten thousand, called Sasak, basically Muslim with elements of Buddhism, Hinduism and traditional practices thrown in). Now here's the thing: after some days, including riding the 8km gauntlet every day to Grupuk to surf (potholes even worse) Kuta's appeal starts to come through. It's as though suddenly you don't see that a person is unattractive anymore and you're aware only of something nice inside, maybe because it isn't phoney or plastic or ritzy. It seems unaware of itself, doesn't look into the mirror asking if it's beautiful, or dynamic, or good at this and that, so that after a few days it changes in front of your eyes from scruffy to quaint (charming would be taking it too far). The only things here that make your heart rate go up are big waves, not the Sasak who are gentle and helpful, and won't kill you for your cell phone or tablet, or rape you because you happen to be a woman. Yet there's poverty, you see it all around, but not a single beggar. You explain that. Maybe because people here look after their own so that no one is left down and out. A different culture I guess: no alcohol, praying every day, at peace with the unbeliever (they seem too unvarnished and unworldly to pretend at this).

I'm telling you all this so you can understand how different it is. And that includes the surfing: one prevailing wind, not two like back home (so you can surf every day), rock and coral bottoms not sandbanks (got to watch it though!), water so clear you can see all the way down, and the best longboard break I've experienced (8 out of 10 surfers ride short boards so guess who gets the waves). My only complaint is too many people out sometimes but hey, i'll take it, and anyway on big days the learners vamoose. Got much more to tell but bushed right now. Hope you guys are keeping well. Haven't picked up any bad news on SA but then i'm totally in another world and happy to stay in it for as long as I can

Cheers, Tom

I'm tempted to ask Russ to drop a copy off at Sister Amber's as she also doesn't have email, but decide it's a bad idea. I also don't phone. What would I say anyway? That I think of her often, and miss her? It wouldn't be conducive to clearing my mind of the many bothersome things, or making good decisions.

*

I spend my days unconnected to the world. No disturbing newspaper headlines (even if there were, I wouldn't understand the Bahasa Indonesian and Sasak languages), bamboo and coconut-skin beads on my wrist instead of my watch, and my tablet locked away while I surf the real thing not the net. I rise at dawn with the first call to prayer, sleep through the midday heat, have my last meal when light fades, check emails once a week, never switch on the TV. Sometimes I surf in the afternoon until the hills on my right turn dark and the western sky an exuberant red-pink, like bubble gum or candy floss, and I'm aware of nothing but being there on that balmy sea with all its beauty. Then a last wave and a slow paddle back to Udin's *perahu* anchored safely away from the white water.

The season is changing, the wind becoming more offshore. It rains more frequently, straight down as if buckets are being poured onto the earth. Holes in the road become small brown dams, and mopeds – with driver, wife, and sometimes children – splash passers-by. Cats and dogs seek cover, water-buffalo stand meekly in the wet, and leaves bend into tiny waterfalls. Soon the sun breaks through and the world is bright once more. I'm at one with this new rhythm to my life that's more primeval than anything I've known, even eating closer to nature than before: deep-coral papaya, bananas twinned like Siamese, pineapple, avocado, eggs, green tea with lime and honey, barracuda, tuna, mahi-mahi, crab, chicken, water spinach, boiled potato, steamed rice; no red meat, bread, cake or dairy. With wonderment I realise that the only processed thing I'm putting down my throat is Bintang – my beer at the end of the day – and the creeping stiffness in my finger joints is no more.

*

This morning as I'm waxing my board Badri goes and stands in the middle of Udin's parking lot facing Kojak who is in his cubicle. Badri smartly brings his feet together soldier-like, leans forward, and performs a slow, exaggerated salute with his *left* arm, fingers quivering at the temple. He makes sure he gets Kojak's full attention before allowing his weathered face to wrinkle up in mirth. We all crack up with him, Kojak the only one not amused. I'm surprised Badri has survived what appears to be a regular performance.

'Mrs. Tom is in Kuta?' Udin asks as he pulls the starter cord of the outboard motor.

'There's no Mrs Tom, Udin.' I slide my surf cap on and smear my face and the top of my hands with sunscreen.

'She is dead?'

'No, no, just gone, left me a while ago.'

'It is not good, not good.' Udin looks pained as if the thought of his wife ever leaving has occurred to him only now.

'And your wife's name?'

'She is Nining, she everything to me, Mister Tom.'

Swells twice my height today, I see them from far away lifting majestically and in eerie silence as they approach the land for a final assault, utterly disdainful of the humans in their path on such flimsy craft. Many don't reach us, venting their anger much earlier against the yellow-brown headlands, throwing massive white plumes into the air. At our take-off point two hundred-and-fifty metres from shore we wait for the ones that come through, mindful of the coral and the rocks, and the hill on our right sticking out like a carbuncle. The sound of many tongues floats across the water: an unlikely coalition of German, French, Commonwealth English, Japanese, Sasak, pale Poles and Russians; bursts of paddling, surfers sweeping across walls of water, defiant cries as fins knife the waves until the blue, severed by the wake, turns tumbling white.

*

If during the day I am able to dispel thoughts of Caro and Cal, Tonderai, Dragut and Harrisunker, I can't stop the dreams. As unnerving as my real experiences have been, my dreams are making things worse, maliciously distorting reality to the point of farce, except I can't judge them as such while I'm dreaming, only when I wake up, making me welcome the early call of the muezzin. As if to compensate I also dream of Amber – that she uttered my name for the first time when I said goodbye. 'Take care, Tom,' she said, her green eyes a mix of worry and sadness. Waking up then is sweet because that's what really happened. My name never sounded so good, as when she said it.

CHAPTER THIRTY
Kuta, South Lombok

It is a sad commentary on our state of affairs when the South African Policing Union has to call for increased training in public order policing – in other words riot control – because of an anticipated increase in service-delivery protests. SAPU says it needs 10 000 officers ... It has 4 000. Ironically, this potentially dangerous shortfall is the outcome of an incompetent administration.
— Editorial, *The Star*

The missed call on my phone one morning startles me. I check the number. It's as if Caro has walked into my room. She leaves no message. I test myself, saying aloud, 'I am not dreaming!' I try to surf it away but feel so disorientated I fall off and ride out the white water lying down on my board. Nathan, a fellow longboarder, wants to know if I'm all right. I eat only half my banana pancake, and ask for another green tea with lime and honey so that I can feel its warmth.

I tell myself it's an intrusion, and unwelcome in the extreme. I get another missed call from the same number the next morning. Is she terminally ill, has someone died, does she want money after all (she stated she wanted only her freedom, that the house was hers anyway, and Franny no longer our responsibility). Still I resist the urge to contact her – I've given her what she wanted, and I must now stay out of her life, rebuild mine.

The resentment I feel gives me strength. But her calls, like corrosive sea air, are tarnishing my idyllic existence.

*

Dear Tom,

i was so hoping to talk to u but your phone seems off all the time, so i'm trying email. Russ wasn't very helpful when i asked if u were okay – he said yes, very, and fourteen hours away by plane (still the smart Alec of old i see). Bones didn't say anything
     anyway, i prefer not to use email for what i want to say, it's too important. where are u and when are u coming back (they didn't know or wouldn't tell).
     Caro

*

Caro,
can't imagine what it is u want to tell me if it's not about illness, death or divorce. therefore if it's not about any of these would u mind letting me get on with my life. correction, i also don't want to hear about the last one
     let's keep the thing clean, no hard feelings, but no contact please. i've signed everything i was asked to sign. sorry caro, u can't upset my life again
     Tom

*

I now leave my phone switched off all the time, in case Caro susses out my location and the six hour time difference. I'm drinking more than a beer a day, large Bintangs to boot. It's easy with someone like Nathan who thinks nothing of downing four or five biggies in an evening, making my two or three seem restrained. Having other surfers in the bar doesn't help. Take the other night: Nathan and I watching rugby league on TV, three other Aussies next to us, topless and with tattoos on their backs, one tattoo, FREEDOM, stretching from one well-developed lateral muscle to the other. And Nathan – paunch developing below his hard chest – telling us about Bondi's rail of knowledge, where surfers gather and what they say is retained by the rail, a kind of storage point for their collective wisdom you can tap into even if you're the only one there (he forgets I've heard the story a couple of times and that surfers are prone to bullshitting). But Nathan is a good sort — a cut above the 'blow-ins', as he calls backpackers – works like a dog driving heavy vehicles in Western Australia's dusty mine belt, making enough money to buy a place on the east coast and surf Indo twice a year. And me, after a fourth beer without food in my stomach, declaring a propos nothing that 'karma can be a bitch, you don't always get out what you put in.' It elicits puzzled looks but everyone is happy to drink to it anyway.

A day later, after a surfing session and a late breakfast of double scrambled eggs, toast, and green tea, I see Russ's email: 'Bru, check the news if you haven't already.' I go on the internet: South Africa's President stepping down due to ill health, his Deputy about to be sworn in, people taking to the streets, peacefully at the moment, as a warning to the government to deliver on its promises, police outnumbered, uneasy standoff, no comment from the ruling party. Are they confused, complacent, or worried? The country and the markets are holding their breath. Is there a connection between this and Caro calling me?

Balmy day, twittering birds, cocks crowing, mopeds and people about, Fiji fan trees, coconut palms, yucas, pink and red frangipanis, and small, gentle Julie asking, 'More tea, Mister Tom?' I'm nettled by the news.

Festive sounds in the street, I get up and walk outside. Wedding procession, bride in front, groom trailing, both dressed in gold from their pointy shoes to their ornate umbrellas, sedate, impassive faces heavily made-up, while the line moves rhythmically to music from two big speakers on a cart being pushed and pulled at the same time. Four marching drummers add to the din, enchanted westerners snap digitally from the side. Happy days! I think of Russ and Bones, and Sister Amber, and wish they could be here, and Dunbar and Spirou from the dead.

Little Sophie and her friends are selling beads. I see her often – waif-like, pretty, and sharp. 'You want some more, Mister?' She's already had to fix one because of my clumsy pulling of the strings. 'What you got, Sophie?' She holds them up, neatly arranged on a display board. Her friends chime in, 'See my beads, Mister! You buy from me today!' I buy two from them and another one from Sophie. She's my favourite.

In the following days, in the midst of my tranquil world, terrible images unfold on the small screen of my tablet: stones thrown at cars, tyres and debris set alight blocking roads, billowing toxic smoke, police firing water cannon and tear gas, then live bullets, bodies joining the rubbish in the streets, trouble spreading like pox across the land: Kennedy Road, Harrismith, Khutsong, Gugulethu, Zakheleni, Oliphantshoek, Bekkersdal, Roodepoort, Soweto, Langa, Macassar, Ermelo, Grahamstown, Khayelitsha, Balfour, Marrianridge, Bronkhorstspruit, Klipspruit, Shaka's Kraal, Noordgesig, Ficksburg, many highways – no one can predict where next. In cities and towns people remain indoors hoping the uprising is quelled, no matter the cost or the consequences. The police try to respond with restraint. In many cases it's not possible, resulting in more deaths. Airports, harbours, and freeways are secured. Violence stutters to an exhausted, inconclusive halt. No one is convinced that it's permanent.

I call Silk Air in Mataram and book the next flight back to Durban via Singapore. In my room I check my finances – enough for another three weeks, but in what frame of mind? I email Franny, certain that she'll demur at my decision, and pack away my sarongs and surfing gear, what's left of my smoky, limp rupiah notes, and rands with Mandela's inspiring face and the big five, feeling the call of Africa but with sadness and trepidation.

At the airport I check the news. A state of emergency has been declared in South Africa. The last time it happened was in the mid-eighties, when P.W. Botha wagged a defiant finger at the world. The irony of another emergency a quarter century after the end of apartheid – this time about the pocket not the ballot – weighs on me like a ton of white water.

Flight attendants prepare for take-off making everyone feel it's just fine to fly in the stratosphere in a thin steel tube. And I reflect on John Donne saying no man is an island entire of itself, and Axel Heyst, who had to confront this reality on his island, not far from here come to think of it – same archipelago, lush bamboo, teak, mahogany, and palm, same trade winds and beautiful seas.

CHAPTER THIRTY-ONE
Durban

He was murdered because he was a decent, upstanding comrade, widely believed to be trying to expose corruption. He had to go.
— Mary de Haas, at the time ANC Regional Secretary, Sbu Sibiya, was assassinated outside his Durban home.

I'm supposed to be coming home to summer but I land in a winter of disquiet, life seemingly carrying on as if nothing has happened except everyone knowing it has. High-off-the-ground, alien-looking craft visible on the roads as we near the city: Buffel and Nyala personnel carriers and Ratel fighting vehicles, conspicuous in this urban environment despite their camouflage. My taxi driver is reluctant to overtake them or engage with me. It's a homecoming both strange and unsettling.

The flat is musty, surfaces are dusty, my view of the sea is blocked from the residue on windows, and I'm uncertain about my reasons for coming back – Sister Amber, my friends, Caro, my father's ashes, feelings for my tormented country? I shake off the gloom, open the windows wide and take a shower, the water from the geyser still cold, bracing and tingling on my skin. Then I check the Jeep in the basement and reconnect the battery.

*

She stands in the door in the evening light, eyes and lips open in surprise and I, uncertain what to do, pulling her towards me and covering her mouth with mine.

'Oh, it's you, Mister Bland ... Tom!' It comes out muffled, the rest of her not pulling away from me.

'I had to come back. I was worried. What a thing, my God.'

'I missed you. Here, let me look at you ... oh my, you're so brown, and lean! Not eating enough I suppose.'

I remove her glasses and put them on the entrance table and kiss her again. Her arms go around my neck and we just stand there, the uncertainties during the flight – the prospect of awkward hellos, and slipping into the old confines of our relationship – all evaporating. I would prefer never to see her in uniform again. And the bun, when she's not working, must definitely come down.

She pulls away. 'I'm dying to hear about your trip. Feel like taking me out for a bite?'

She's holding my hand as if to make sure I don't disappear again too soon.

*

Amber is as worried as I expected her to be. 'Heaven know what's going to happen. Some people are shutting themselves off, a kind of mental laager I suppose. I'm not like that.'

'Makes one feel vulnerable, I know.'

'I would have understood it had you decided not to come back. I mean, everything you've been through, and now this. But I knew I'd see you again.'

I'm looking at a woman who seems to have made up her mind that I'm to be trusted. It's been a long time coming, her letting me into her world. It's me who's finding it difficult to open up. The many days of few words on the island: in my room, in restaurants, even with Udin and his friends, and at the backline with other surfers. I'm not complaining. The absence of TV, of social media, not texting, not checking emails compulsively – it was manna for the soul, the kind of freedom the modern world seldom allows. But it isn't helping my frame of mind now. Add to this Caro's attempts at making contact.

I pour the wine. 'I'm hoping the new man will make a difference. He knows what he must do to get things right.' I shrug. 'Whether he has the will and the support is something else. The status quo has become too lucrative for too many people.'

'Will you go back? Your island sounds wonderful.' She lowers her eyes but not before I see the sombreness.

'I'm not sure, Amber. It's too big a question right now.' I put my arm next to hers. 'Wow! Look at that. You really must let me take you into the sun and the sea.'

Her eyes look bruised. How can I tell her I must know what Caro has on her mind, that I regret not heeding Caro's pleas to leave the country long ago? Cal would never have got a look in and we'd still be together. But it's like saying what if *he* had saved Caro from the sea instead of me? What-ifs can be toxic once they get hold of you.

*

At the North Beach backline with Russ and Bones waiting for the next set, like old times except it isn't – too much has changed, in my life and in my country, love and loyalty betrayed, death visiting me all too frequently, my dreams damaged. The fact that the city's skyline is still the same after forty years, except for the Point and the Moses Mabhida stadium, shows a lack of confidence, explaining why people have been moving north. Even this sea – saviour and inspiration to me in my youth – isn't the same: waves don't run like they used to, and the once golden sands have become grubby. I keep it to myself, it's too raw, my feeling of irrelevance too strong, as though I'm a stranger to it all.

Then Russ asks, 'So when are you going back to paradise, bru?'

It's what Amber wanted to know. *'Fragen Sie den Papegai,'* I say lightly. 'Ask the parrot!'

'Trying to be funny?' Bones says.

'No, it's a Richard Stark book I picked up in Kuta … you know, new languages exercise the brain.'

'Explain it to me before the next wave,' Russ says, 'I haven't got all day.'

'Ask the parrot. Think Numo. He wouldn't have had the foggiest with that question either.'

'You're full of shit, bru,' Bones says, 'and leave my parrot out of it.'

'Too much time on your own, methinks,' Russ says, 'forgetting about your friends, eh.'

Their hackles are up, but on the deck others are hanging on my every word. Russ and Bones calm down. 'What about johnnies there?' someone wants to know, 'and box jellyfish, some the size of a thumbnail but poison worse than a mamba's?' Another says, 'And fucking volcanoes going off, jeez.'

I laugh. 'Hold it guys, I can add venomous sea snakes, stonefish, blue-ringed octopi and earthquakes, but you know what? When you're sitting out there, the water glassy so you can see the coral down below, and sometimes a parrot fish or a turtle, and the sets pop up as if ordered and there's no aggro about whose wave it is, you just don't think about those things. Sure, sometimes at night they cross your mind but the days are just too good. I mean, where can you surf *every* day for weeks on end?'

'Yeah, it's like having crayfish all the time,' Bones says.

Russ corrects me, 'Actually, the word is octopuses, not octopi.'

*

Blow me down if Amber doesn't ask the same thing over dinner, 'Aren't there dangerous things in those waters, Tom? I thought about you, getting hurt with no one to help. No decent hospitals or doctors I would imagine.'

The wine has given her cheeks colour (she never uses rouge, just a little lipstick), pink blouse, black jeans, in the candlelight her eyes intense green.

'Maybe my karma has got better,' I say, 'a change in my fortunes, who knows.'

Her laugh is a happy sound, mood-soothing yet quickening my heartbeat. I feel slightly heady. Amber has become less Sister Teresa and more Jennifer Lawrence (an older, even fuller version I should add). We've kissed a few more times since my homecoming, but she always steers things back to my trip or the state of the country. Talk now is that the President is stepping down from being the active head of state but staying on as a figurehead, making the new president more of a prime minister. – This is because he's done only two-thirds of his term. (Or is it because so many people in public life depend on his patronage?) Why can't Big Men of Africa walk away from their positions, the way retired people do in companies? Why are there not more Mandelas on this massive continent? I sense no clean, new beginning here, only a rehash of things unsatisfactory. I sip more wine.

Thirty minutes later Amber and I are making love, just like that, my last apprehension put to bed as it were. A little awkwardness on her part initially, and an unnerving quietness, but soon her breathing and sighing telling me how much she wants me. And I so awestruck by this circumspect woman giving herself to me that I treat her with a mindfulness I never knew I had. She's extraordinarily smooth and white except for her glowing cheeks and green eyes, no perfume on her, only the smell of nature. Most amazing is that she doesn't mind the bedside lights on. It's all too much.

*

No festive air with the holiday season and the warm weather upon us. Travel plans are cancelled, people not wanting to be on the roads or in the open. The state of emergency, allowed under the constitution for twenty-one days to begin with, is extended by the National Assembly for three months to ensure restoration of peace and order – in the interests of the country, they say. The army continues to exercise its powers, banning marches and large gatherings, imposing curfews, detaining some protest leaders, with lawyers demanding they be treated in accordance with the provisions of the constitution. Although the government does not attempt to muzzle the media or target individual journalists as happened in the nineteen eighties, it rails against what it calls irresponsible, unpatriotic reporting. Finally it declares its intention to introduce restrictive laws. The rand drops against the dollar, and the JSE slides further. Exchange controls are tightened reducing the amount citizens can take out – measures used by the apartheid government to shore up things, now adopted by the ruling party. It makes me feel less guilty that I opened a Singapore bank account on the way back with the balance of my travel money.

As cracks in the country's unity appear about how to address the underlying causes, Amber and I draw closer – out of defence as much as deep desire (that she knew about Socrates should have been a sign months ago that we'd get together). To her compassion for all living things, including monkeys, earthworms, cockroaches and mosquitoes (our only disagreement so far) she's added something else: passion (again, looking back, it was probably always there, just suppressed). It has come slowly, not like a flame reacting to fuel, more like growing love having to find expression. It's an experience new to me, being with someone whose feelings are awakening without haste, and it leaves me with a sweet mix of certainty and anticipation.

Were it not for Amber I'd be at sea more than ever, wrenched loose to drift from the moment I saw Caro and Cal embracing through my binoculars. I surrender to Amber's seemingly endless capacity for understanding, and tell her how I got shot and Gugu ended up at the children's home. I hold nothing back about Tonderai, Dragut and Dunbar, and Spirou's suicide, unwilling to let our relationship go another day with secrets between us.

Only one more thing I must tell her: where I stand with Caro. I'm wrestling with it, uncertain what it would do to her. I consider leaving it for another day, maybe forever, out of fear of wounding her very soul when my feelings for Caro will, in all probability, die a slow, deserved death.

CHAPTER THIRTY-TWO
Durban

Two years? That's it? I'm guessing. Everything takes a bit longer than you think ... It's possible that the ANC can just miss the fate that I've said they were heading for, but I doubt it. Equally, I don't think it's the very worst by a long way. I think if they were to refuse that deal then, sure, you would see chaos.
— R.W. Johnson, in an interview at the time his book, *How Long Will South Africa Survive, the Looming Crisis* was launched.

The new president, Paul Avhadali Ramasodi, waits until the New Year to assert himself, promising the poor they'll inherit the earth, and the corrupt that hell, fire and brimstone await them. Russ reckons that's really smart because it's the time of year when people want hope and new beginnings (especially after a miserable Christmas). Bones just wants to be in the water, away from it all.

On the deck everyone is a political buff, the articulate getting by without shouting or gesticulating, those short on vocabulary having to use expletives and sheer decibels. Consensus is that the new man will need all the help he can get. Russ points out he'll get it from the private sector, opposition parties, trade unions, the churches, media, and the minister of finance, the public protector, and the reserve bank governor. Against Ramasodi, although they won't say or show it, will be the black moneyed elite, and the top echelons in national, provincial and municipal government – collectively the beneficiaries of black economic empowerment and the tender system.

People leave the deck either more muddled or more enlightened. What Russ says blows over the heads of many in the breeze, with others listening attentively. Russ thinks about things. Maybe he should establish a rail of knowledge at the club, to rival Bondi's; give the Aussies a run for their money. Most worrying is his observation that South Africa reached a tipping point a few years back, and that a new president won't be able to change things.

I check on Gugu. She comes out to my car parked around the corner, and hugs me. 'You've been away, but funny, I didn't worry.'

Two women now who've said they knew I would be back. Does Caro think it too? Gugu is looking healthy and happy. She tells me she likes school. It's what I want to hear. It will be her salvation. I tell her not to waste energy thinking about the country as she can't do anything anyway. 'Get your matric, Gugu, and get a good one so you can go to university. Think of yourself as special, because you are.'

Amber springs another surprise. When I remark that she must surely believe in God because she does so much good, she says: 'You don't need God to tell you what's right and wrong, you just *know*.'

'But do you believe there's a God anyway? You know, for other things?'

'I wish I could say yes. He knows I tried, heaven knows I did. But in all these years he never sent me a sign of any kind. And I wonder about all the bad in the world, and where he is, if he's there at all. You know Tom, sometimes I think we made him – for our own selfish reasons – not him us.'

'Amber, that's quite a thing to say!'

'It gets worse. If what I'm thinking has any truth, it means the existence of God is dependent on us, not the other way around.'

I've always stayed on the side-lines with religion and politics – I can't handle overzealousness and over-promising. It's what I have a brain for – to think for myself – and right now it's overheating. 'Well, if I take what you say to its logical conclusion, it means if man is wiped out in a nuclear war or natural catastrophe, God dies too?'

'I suppose so, in the meantime there's you and there's me,' she says, smiling.

I want to say it's the only thing that keeps Steppenwolf at bay, but don't. My admiration for Amber knows no bounds. It's remarkable that she's able to carry on in spite of feeling ignored by God, motivated only by her own sense of what is right and wrong.

*

I don't have to wait long to find out if Caro knows I'm back. We're on the deck as usual after a good surfing session feeling relaxed, the state of emergency something we no longer think or talk about every day, perhaps because our lives are so confined anyway. I'm facing the sea, and Bones and Russ the door leading onto the deck. And Russ kicks me under the table, on my shin, hard enough for me to know something's up. He gazes at the door. I turn around. It's Caro. None of us move. Is she brave – the deck a kind of lion's den for women like her – angry, or desperate? I try to gauge the meaning of her look but am not nearly calm enough. All I see is that she's wearing a pink dress and nice shoes, not track pants and Reeboks, and her bob is freshly done, like she wants to look good. And she does, better than I can remember her (I kept no photos of her or the house). I wait.

'Tom, can we talk somewhere, please?'

'Sure, let's go for a walk. Sorry, guys.'

They're hostile towards her out of concern for me. Outside we walk without talking in the direction of New Pier so that any curious eyes from the deck will quickly lose us. I'm aware only of her and still manage to be out of step, my strides longer than hers. It was never a problem in the days when we were in love and held hands. I shorten my step; got to synchronise and get the discussion off to a good start.

'How did you know I was back, Caro?'

'Saw you in your car, I know the car.'

'Oh.' I want to add 'so?'

'Yes, you were with someone.'

This time I say it. 'So? You were also in a car with Cal.'

She ignores the barb. 'Well, very strange – you and a young black girl in a side street. It's not the fact that's she's black, you understand.'

'Is that what you came to see me about, Caro?' We're not off to the good start I wanted.

We step onto New Pier – creator of waves, protector of surfers together with the shark nets. My world Caro boldly has stepped into. Just to tell me I was with Gugu? Spring high tide and the waves are smashing against the end of the pier, soaking the wooden rails. In monstrous conditions I like to go as far as I can to the end of the pier, feel the might of the sea close up, the shuddering of the structure below my feet.

'No, I wanted to tell you that Cal and I are no longer together.'

I take a deep breath. 'Why tell me Caro, I mean, what does it matter now?'

She's holding the railing, knuckles prominent, the wind blowing her bob apart. She hates it, I know.

'I wanted to say I made a mistake. Cal isn't for me, never was.'

She's looking far out, to the ships at anchor waiting to enter the harbour. I take her by the shoulders to face me. 'Why, why are you telling me this? I'm just coming right!'

'I want you back, Tom.' Tears are streaking down her face now like rain on a pane in the wind.

*

I let the weeks drift by in a kind of mental fog, suspended between Caro and Amber, studiously avoiding hasty decisions I might regret later. I say nothing to Amber about Caro and nothing to Caro about Amber even though I know it's prolonging the agony. My favourite demon – guilt – is playing havoc with my sleep. I have another conversation with Caro, on the pier which she appears to accept as neutral space, like the UN in New York. She repeats she wants me back, and when I ask, 'both Tom Bland and Tom Adendorff?' she bursts into tears saying my letter initially made her feel betrayed, let-down, angry, and only later, after our divorce, started to haunt her, to the extent that Cal asked if there was someone else (hearing this gives me enormous emotional satisfaction). She says Cal proved to be different from the man she remembered, that he had become an emotional cripple (by this time I'm completing sentences for her). I nearly ask if she kept him for so long because he was so good in bed. It reminds me of the time she said good lovemaking is like good food: respect the ingredients, spend time prepping, plate up with panache, and then tuck in. That Caro dumped Cal makes me hopeful he was a dunce at these things, but how much better was I, if at all? Doubt has a habit of finding its way into my head with Caro.

I ask her to give me time to think, for her to understand I've been living with the pieces of our relationship. How do you restore to its original state a beautiful vase that's been dropped from a dizzy height? Beautiful to me, perhaps to her something from the flea market – it's the whole point, isn't it?

Alone in my flat I'm more confused than ever. When I'm with Amber she sometimes gives me her considered look, but thankfully stays clear of asking if anything is wrong.

*

The new President seems determined to walk the talk, putting together measures to combat corruption in national, provincial and municipal government, labelling nepotism, cronyism, cadre deployment, and *tenderpreneurialism* – the practice of awarding state tenders based on personal connections and corrupt relationships – as the greatest risks to the country's young democracy. He threatens to name and shame offenders, vowing to stop the practice of transferring and sometimes promoting transgressors to other departments (a central database would see to that). The best person for the job would become the only selection criterion, regardless of race, gender or religious persuasion, effectively saying goodbye to affirmative action after a quarter of a century. He talks of a pact between government, labour and business, modelled on best practice in countries like Germany and Ireland – to facilitate investment from abroad, improve service delivery to the poor, create jobs, and provide proper education and training for our youth. He promises to end the state of emergency in the coming months provided there's no more violence. Do justice to what Madiba gave us at great sacrifice, he intones. Locally and overseas Ramasodi is lauded. The rand swings up sharply against major currencies. And I feeling distinctly uncomfortable because it's going too well – if there are dissenters they're too quiet. I say nothing for fear of being called a spoiler.

*

Another meeting with Caro, this time at my request, New Pier again, the air still and heavy when we set out from the North

Beach parking lot, now the wind pushing from the south-west – a buster in the making, unsettling and exciting all at once.

We stand on the pier with our backs to the wind. 'I said I need time, Caro,' I tell her, 'but not in Durban where I can't think straight anymore. I have to go away.'

She turns towards me, mouth trembling. 'We can work through it here, together, can't we?'

'I don't think so. For the sake of both of us I don't want to make the wrong decision.'

Across the sea, horses galloping in the direction of uMhlanga, chests heaving and pumping, white manes flying. She says something, but it gets lost in the wind. 'What?' I shout. Her answer is to move closer, close enough for me to feel her. Our eyes meet, flashes from long ago – a treacherous sea, she holding onto me, something connecting us against the elements. She's forgotten what she said, or doesn't care. I want to take her in my arms, break this impasse, but all I say is, 'Let me do this on my own. We'll talk again soon.'

'Where are you going? Is there someone else?'

I answer both questions as matter-of-factly as I can especially regarding Amber, hoping it would soften what I'm saying. I want to apologise but don't. I must tell things as they are, and no more secrets. She's silent, taking it all in.

'Is it over between us then, Tom?'

'I wouldn't have asked to see you if it were. I'm just confused. Look, nothing's far away. You'll hear from me, I promise.'

We walk back. She takes my hand, either frightened the wind will blow her away, or wanting me to remember her special touch. Thirty-six years of living with her and I can't tell which it is.

*

Over dinner, indigestion burning a hole in my stomach, I say to Amber, 'We need to talk. I have something to tell you.'

'I've been waiting for it, Tom. Is it what I think it is?' She's composed except for her eyes – that bruised green again, like grass crushed by a boot. Am I such a heel?

'I didn't look for it. It's the last thing I expected. It came as a shock.'

'You mean Caro? Yes, I sensed something. The fact that all this time you never mentioned her meant it wasn't over. Not like when people openly talk about their exes.'

I tell her what happened. I don't say I probably would have contacted Caro had she not sought me out at the club.

'Do you still love her?'

It's the question I've been afraid of, whether from Amber or myself. 'I honestly don't know.'

'That's what you want to find out?'

I nod. 'I need to clear my head once and for all.'

'And me?'

'I've loved you for much longer than you realise. The fact that Caro has re-appeared doesn't make me un-love you, or make me love you less. I don't go hot and cold like a geyser.'

'So you could end up loving two people – equally, or in different proportions?'

'Jeez, Amber, you're worse than Socrates!'

'I like to get an idea of where I stand in the scheme of love.'

'You don't seem very upset?'

'Who says I'm not?' She puts her knife and fork down, suddenly looking washed out, vulnerable, like she does when death visits the nursing home and chalks up another victory.

I lean across the small table and take her face in my hands. 'I want to kiss you.'

'No, let's just be friends until this thing goes one way or the other. How do you think I feel?'

'A platonic relationship? Impossible!'

'Yes Tom, *spiritual*. Try it for a change. It came to me at the home, years ago, when I needed it most, and thank God I still have it.'

Once again I'm relegated to sleeping in a spare room, through my own doing I have to admit. Making my bed in my flat and lying in it is the prospect I face until I leave for Lombok.

CHAPTER THIRTY-THREE
Durban, Caro

'Caro, you know your own mind, and we respect that, but your mother and I want to know if you'd reconsider your decision.'

Daddy looking strangely uncomfortable in his own study – on the edge of his chair, his elbows on the desk – exacerbated by the fact that he transplanted the formality of his old Berea home to this townhouse: book shelves that need a ladder to reach the top row (and he's eighty, for God's sake!), heavy curtains on the bay windows, dark Persian carpets, brooding landscapes and portraits, a separate round table with four fat-legged chairs covered in dated brocade, for meetings with his financial advisors, he says. Set me up years ago with my own interior decorating shop yet ignoring my advice – that's Daddy.

'You mean wanting Tom back?'

His eyes go dull olive when he's upset – the same dead hue as the protruding veins on his hands and temples. He's never been a shorts and T-shirt man (another thing he dislikes about Tom), and as for sandals, he'd rather get corns and callouses than wear them.

'Yes, now that you've left him. Surely it tells you something, Caro – doesn't it confirm what I said long ago when you married him?'

'You said we didn't go together and that I could still call it off. It stressed us all out.' I smile at him. It's in the past. It upset him that I went ahead. Now he sees another opportunity. 'Have you thought, Daddy, that wanting him back tells *me* something?'

He gets up and runs a nostalgic hand along the row of dentistry books, pausing and patting them as one would do with faithful dogs. 'Does he know all this yet?'

'Yes, I told him the other day, face to face. It's done, I'm afraid.' He's checking how far this thing has gone, and whether it's salvageable.

'What did he say?'

'He wants to think about it. You must understand, Daddy, how it must have hurt him. What Cal and I did was unforgivable – some friend, some wife.'

My pride won't allow me to confess to Daddy that Tom, to my surprise, didn't jump at the opportunity. It perplexed me. I thought it might be because of this other woman, but there was something more: a touch of his old resoluteness?

'Quite a flip-flop, Caro, if you don't mind my saying so: swept up by Cal one minute, deeply regretting it the next, accompanied by much anguish I should add. I know you've explained it to Mummy and me, but I don't understand it. Am I missing something?'

Decaying body but still the sharp mind, from the beginning his own man, first as *the* dentist on the Berea, then early retirement to play the stock and property markets, amassing a tidy fortune in the process, scathing of those who depended on others for their salary and prospects.

'Please sit down, Daddy, and I'll tell you. It's a long story.'

Wearily he sinks into his chair, leans back, and waits. I go and sit on the corner of the wide mahogany desk so that it isn't between us, and tell him that the man I married is actually Thomas Adendorff.

*

He closes his eyes, lowers his head, as if what he's hearing is a weight too much to bear. Alcoholism, child abuse, a children's home, foster parenting, adoption – all of it confirmation to my patrician father of the abject moral failing of the plebeian class, and of the unsuitability of Tom for his only daughter.

'I've not told you this, Caro, but Cal came to see me. He had a one-way ticket to London in his hand, and said he'd tear it up if you'd have him back. He'd relinquish his work, and devote his life to you. I must say, he sounded passionate. You know I've always liked him. He's *our* kind, Caro.'

'Oh, Daddy, don't do this, please. Is this why you asked me to come over?'

He nods. 'You have the house, the car, and money to live. I'll give you more, to buy things, go on boat cruises. You wouldn't want for anything, and you wouldn't have to ask Tom for a thing, or rely on Cal financially. I don't think you realise just how well off you'll be when I go. So just give Cal a chance, on your terms of course. What have you to lose?'

I cannot stop the tears, or face my father any longer. I leave him sitting in his leather chair that has become too big for his diminishing frame.

*

Back at my Berea home I pour myself a whisky, go to the balcony and stand at the railing watching evening descend, waiting for the moment when the lights go on – to let us see where we are going, and to comfort us in the night. God, how I need it tonight – the terrible conversation with Daddy, and the knowledge that both Cal and Tom will fly away soon, Cal if I don't take him back, Tom to decide if he wants me back. I feel a kind of panic rising, and pour another whisky to try and still it. Hanging over everything is a country on the edge. What have I done? No one to talk to, a father who's floating above it all in his usual proud way, a house so empty it's as though my thoughts are echoing. Should I not also leave? The thought of going into the world on my own is frightening and depressing. Maybe I'll go with Cal, to London, and never come back.

I can't sleep. More drink won't do it for me. I won't let it. On the balcony again, staring across the undulating carpet of suburban light to where it comes to an abrupt halt at the ocean's edge, some four kilometres away. Cal and Tom right there within walking distance of each other, one in a flat the other in a serviced suite, with me making up the old triangle.

*

I must've slept because at three I'm awake again, wondering what Tom's woman is like. Amber, he said. A photo won't tell me what she's really like. I'd have to be with her, *feel* her presence, not to make friends but to know what I'm up against, and get a sense if she has what it takes to keep Tom. She cannot possibly understand him the way I do. I think he still loves me, and it gives me hope.

I lie there thinking of them making love. Have I not created a second triangle, this time with another woman? What a fool I've been. My pillow is going wet with tears.

*

In the morning I know what I have to do. I phone Daddy and tell him to tell Cal to keep his ticket, and go back to London. I give Daddy a chance to say his say while I'm holding the phone away from my ear, until it's my turn to talk again: 'Daddy, listen, I made Tom feel worthless when actually he was worthy of so much, and Cal wasn't, and I'm going to make up for it, oh, yes I am! Cal is all veneer – his looks, his clothes, his language, that earring, how he smiles. I was seduced by it, by a man who spends too much time in front of the mirror and too little on people, when all along I had someone like Tom. I know Tom has issues, but at least I understand them better now…'

'My girl, don't you think you ought to take stock …'

'No, no, enough time has been wasted! I'm going to send him an email saying all of this, for him to think about while he's on that island. I'll give him all the space he needs, because I don't want to lose him again. And Daddy, I love you, whatever's been said and whichever way this thing goes. Oh, I feel so relieved!'

Some things in the past are best not to dwell on because they are uncomfortable truths. For instance the way Cal cowered after Tom shot him with the water pistol. It makes me wonder if Cal would have brought me back safely from that raging sea the way Tom did? Would he have overcome the terrible childhood Tom had? I've never thought of it until now. Come to think of it, I wonder if Cal has it in him to come up trumps on anything if he were really put to the test.

CHAPTER THIRTY-FOUR
Durban

There's no reason now to delay my return to Lombok. I first sell the share portfolio I built up over the years with my work bonuses, then the remainder of my share options, asking for the proceeds to be credited to my money market account. The profit from the sale of the uMhlanga flat I leave in my savings account. My provident fund I also don't touch. One step at a time, I can take out more at a later stage. I can't help wondering if it will be like keeping valuables in a safe on the Titanic.

When all the money is in, I instruct the bank to transfer to my Singapore account an amount that would enable me to live on Lombok for a considerable period. I buy an air ticket to Lombok and then order a hundred thousand Rand's worth of US dollars from American Express.

Russ and Bones aren't surprised I'm going back to Lombok. They're envious. 'Jeez, imagine surfing every day!' Bones says, 'no easterly to mess things up.' 'Yeah,' Russ says, 'politicians and the easterly – boy, do they fuck things up. You won't have any of it there.'

'Any time you feel like visiting, let me know,' I say.

Bones has a heavy, down look. I know what he's thinking. He can't stop his thoughts from showing – a kind of mental incontinence, I guess. 'I'll have to paddle over,' he says, shrugging. 'Bru, I'm just glad you can go. You've had a hard time, and what's happening here you need like a hole in the head.'

I take out an envelope. 'Keep this safe, Bones. When you're ready, get Russ to help and then let me know.'

Bones opens it, stares at the pages, not comprehending what he's reading. He hands it to Russ. 'Tell me, is this right what I'm seeing?'

I give him the answer, 'Yes, it's an open ticket to Lombok. Any time you want to activate it I'll do it for you.'

They say cowboys and surfers don't cry...

*

I phone about a 'for sale' ad I saw at the club. I listen. It's what I'm looking for.

A day later I'm trying out the surfboard: 9 feet 6 inches long, just over 23 inches wide, 3 inches thick, concave underneath in front, reinforced rails, centre fin bigger than normal – a classic nose rider, with the famous spider logo on the front. I have it packed to export specifications by Safari, without fins and leash which I'll put in my luggage.

A day before my departure I take the board to King Shaka Airport and hand it in at South African Airways Cargo who mark it for Johannesburg. At the flat I pack my things, this time including Hugh's ashes.

In Johannesburg I collect the board and check it in as luggage at the Singapore Airlines counter. As I sink into my airplane seat at last, flight attendants brushing past me with exotic looks and accents, and passengers fussing in their seats with pillows, blankets, and earphones, a feeling of not having had enough oxygen for weeks comes over me. It's as though I'm breathing properly only now, and I imagine myself already out in that blue bay, embraced by green hills, ochre headlands, and a majestic sky with divine colours splashed over it. Just for me.

CHAPTER THIRTY-FIVE
Kuta, South Lombok

In Lombok I slip into my old routine, and even avoid getting Bali belly. I got handshakes from the male staff at the homestay, and women smiled their welcomes. Udin hugged me, 'Mister Tom! *Antih lemak yak tulak malik!*' If Udin was pleased to have me back, Doni would have knocked things over had he been a dog. Badri put his shirts aside to greet me. Kojak shook my hand without hardness in his eyes. To each one of them I said, '*Tampi asih, berembe kabar.*' I was home.

It wasn't like that at Praya airport. Customs officials must've decided I was an ageing drug mule, and with grim thoroughness searched first my luggage then my board bag, using rough fingers and hand-held machines, all the while chatting in Sasak which caused sweat to break out over me. I felt guilty even though I knew perfectly well I was innocent. It didn't look like it though. One of them found the hessian urn with Hugh's ashes, prodded and sniffed it, giving me a triumphant, tight little smile. His colleague wet a finger and tasted the ash. 'No, no! It's my father!' I shouted. I was about to add, 'fucking cannibals', the f fluttering on my lips before I flicked it away. I was lucky: a fellow passenger who spoke Sasak and English saw my distress and explained the ash was my father's. Were it not for him I probably would have had to produce the death certificate, get an import licence (for a deceased person with zero import value, who won't apply for asylum or an extended visa, or take anyone's job – the mind boggles). What helped, the Englishman told me afterwards with typical humour, was that cremation is a Muslim custom, and I didn't arrive with the actual body. A couple of days later I took Hugh's ashes in a bag to Grupuk Inside, paddled to a quiet spot east of where the *perahus* lay, and gently scattered them while saying a few words. I could not have found a more serene place on earth, and it felt good setting him free into what I can only call the vast, mysterious oneness of things.

*

When I'm not surfing, and especially at night, I think of Amber and Caro, and try to give them equal time so as to remain objective. I'm alone with no one to talk to; on the plus side, no one can influence me. Then I get an email from Caro that tilts the balance – imploring, loving, and almost heart-breaking in its directness and honesty. If I'd been at home I might have been tempted to talk things over, and then what? Make up, make love, and move into the house once more? I'm paralysed by this whirl of thoughts. All I can manage is to say thank you, Caro, for your nice email, I'll call soon.

At the end of ten days I conclude neither of them would like Lombok – Caro too fussy, and upscale, Amber too unused to the great outdoors, and frightened of the unknown. It's a pathetic result considering the time I spent on it. I remind myself it isn't about Lombok, but which one I cannot live without, *wherever* it may be. I'm vacillating, delaying the decision, any peace of mind gained from closing the final loop on Hugh reduced to nil by the whole exercise.

Since my last visit the summer rain has turned the island extra green. Now once again it's changing: drier skies, more of the surfers' wind, the sun a powerful Van Gogh-yellow. I have no sense of spiteful or bad karma, of untowardness darkening the heavens. My new board is a dream at Grupuk – taking me on long rights with one foot on the nose. I sleep with the *Indo Surf and Lingo* tide table next to my bed, in tune with everything around me.

Doni asks me to come to a stick-fighting tournament at Seger in which he is competing. I can hardly find a parking spot for my moped. People stand four-deep around the arena. The grassy slope that overlooks it is also packed. Yamaha bunting flutters in the breeze, drum beats dominate the music, and the referee does a graceful solo dance in the centre, creating anticipation. At last it is Doni's turn. He and his opponent prance around dressed only in sarong and head cloth, wriggling their shoulders and hips, grinning at the crowd. The referee brings them together, reiterates the rules, and blows his whistle. Doni's adversary doesn't know the word retreat. Doni delivers some good blows but his taller opponent goes at him with rapid overhead strikes, forcing Doni to hold his shield high while he retreats. He steps outside the boundaries and the referee brings them back for a restart. The same thing happens in the next two rounds. Doni throws ghastly grins at the crowd meant as smiles of confidence. He bounces back in the third, landing some telling blows and doesn't retreat. But in the final two rounds he is outgunned again. It seems de rigueur to still swagger and smile, but his attempts are taking strain. Afterwards he doesn't seek me out, walks quietly to his moped and drives off to Grupuk, shoulders slumped over the handlebars.

The next time I see him, I shake his hand and tell him what matters is that he saw the contest through to the end, that he is still young, and tomorrow is another day.

*

It happens on the other side of the Indian Ocean, on a day so lovely on my island I want to give thanks with poetry and quiet tears of joy. Late afternoon, the sun already behind the hills of Kuta, dogs resting in the streets, birds into their evening song, mopeds on last errands, and the faithful gathered in mosques or on mats in quiet rooms. And like an angry leopard the line leaps out at me, 'South Africa's President Assassinated.'

My hands shake, I have to put my tablet down before I can read more. President Paul Avhadali Ramasodi and a number of his entourage, bodyguards, and police died this morning in a hail of automatic and mortar fire in Groutville, Kwadukuza (formerly Stanger) on KZN's north coast. Ramasodi was on his way to open a new hospital and pay his respects at the grave of ANC icon Albert Luthuli. A terse government statement has labelled it a heinous crime against the people of South Africa and their hard-fought democracy, and that it would not rest until the perpetrators have been brought to justice. The assault occurred on a three kilometre stretch of road linking the N2 to the R102. Witnesses say the presidential convoy passed some houses and the Groutville High School, crossed a railway bridge, and was approaching a T-junction that would have taken it onto the R102 when it was fired upon from a line of pine trees barely twenty metres away. It is speculated that the convoy had been forced to slow down as a result of a series of pronounced road humps leading up to the T-junction, and that the dense bush around the pine trees gave the necessary cover to the attackers. Chief Luthuli, revered Zulu teacher, preacher, and politician, winner of the Nobel Peace Prize in 1961 for his non-violent resistance against apartheid, and president-general of the ANC for 15 years, ironically also died violently when he was allegedly run over by a train in 1967 not far from today's attack on the President.

A political analyst pointed out that of the ANC party's twelve leaders, five were Xhosa, four Zulu, and three Twana-Sotho, and that President Ramasodi did not belong to any of these groupings (opposition parties liked to say he was of Ngona stock, historically spurned as sorcerers; Ramasodi always avoided the subject in interviews). It is speculated the real reason for his visit to Kwazulu-Natal was to increase his popularity among Zulus in that province. Ramasodi was not fully trusted there, and people feared he might re-open corruption investigations against his predecessor and others in government.

Messages of condolence are pouring into the Union Buildings from all over the world. The nation is stunned, the hopes of millions dashed on a quiet country road in a matter of minutes. People are massing on the streets in greater numbers than ever – a spontaneous combustion needing no clarion call or exhortation – defying emergency regulations. Rioting has broken out again, more bodies on the streets, tanks stationed at vital installations, buildings and freeways. The rand has plummeted like a bird shot in mid-flight.

I call Amber. 'Tell me you're okay! Are you at the home?'

'Yes, yes, I'm so glad to hear your voice. It's dreadful, Tom, isn't it?'

'Please get yourself here, I'll organise a ticket. *Please.*'

'I'm not sure. Aren't you coming back?'

'Been there and done it, Amber. It doesn't mean you can't fly to *me.*'

'Oh dear, and leave these poor people in the home?'

'The poor here would thank you more, Amber, believe me. Women die in childbirth, and babies don't make it past their first year. Medical staff is thin on the ground, health education is badly needed. You'd be like an angel to them, they'd love you. *Please, Amber!*'

'Is it because you want me over Caro, or because you're worried about me? Like you were for Gugu?'

'Normally I'd revel in a woman's jealousy but now's not the time, Amber. Isn't it enough that I love you and worry about you? Look, I'm going to arrange a ticket regardless and email it to you at the home.'

'But they'll see it on their computer!'

'Well, warn them before the day is out that you're leaving. Pay your rent for at least three months, from your savings. Tell me you *do* have a passport. Yes?'

'I have one but I must check the validity, used it years ago to go to Mozambique with friends.'

'Your Indonesian visa you can get on arrival. Does it mean you're coming then?'

'I'll have to think about it, Tom. It's such a big step, please understand … dropping my life's work, and all these old people, just because I'm worried about myself.'

*

I wish she'd put herself first for once. More rioting and looting, this time local mobs targeting foreign-owned businesses in Soweto, started after a Somali trader shot a looter breaking into his shop. The fact that the owner didn't have a licence for the gun incensed the crowd even more. Snake Park, Naledi, Zola, Emndeni, White City, Meadowlands, and Dobsonville are overrun by the young and unemployed, the army and police reluctant to confront the large, violent groups, and opting for containment by encircling the worst-hit areas. Could they be siding with the locals? Immigrants have long been seen as muscling in on jobs. In Durban, attacks escalate against Congolese shop owners and car guards, and in Cape Town structures suspected of housing foreigners are razed. More unlicensed guns come out, leading to more deaths and fury. Thousands of Somalis, Malawians, Zimbabweans, Congolese and Mozambicans flee to churches, mosques, temples, and refugee camps set up for them.

The police present as an achievement the fact that they have not shot anyone to death this time around, adding that the rioters' actions speak of criminality not xenophobia, and the might of the law would be brought to bear on them. The government also denies it is xenophobia. It's as though any acknowledgment would stain the country's vaunted democracy and bill of rights.

Their anger ignored and unquenched, locals turn their attention to the emotionally-charged issue of land, grabbing vacant stretches along roads and freeways outside cities. Rickety structures are erected overnight in a frenzy of building with no water and electricity supply. The police and army can't stop it, unable to be in so many places at once. Motorists are forced to slow down or stop as a result of stones, bricks, and burning tyres on the roads, only to be attacked by the mobs. Trucks are waylaid, requiring armed escort. The price of food shoots up.

All I can think of is, what if enough of the country's three hundred and eighty-seven townships – those apartheid wounds and scars still so visible – collectively rise up? They may be out on a limb thanks to the old government's policies, but today are part of the heartbeat of the new South Africa. Destroy or cut them off and the body will die.

I call Russ. He says he's okay and no, he's not flying anywhere, maybe Bones but not him. He'll take his chances. I tell him about Amber, and ask, 'Will you take her to the airport for me, please? That's if she decides to come.'

'No problem. Let me know. Awesome how one can communicate nowadays in a revolution! The French and the Russians must've run around like headless chickens without cell phones, Face Book, and YouTube – not that this isn't an omnishambles.'

'Oh, for the Hong Kongers who protest but clean up after themselves, and don't loot and destroy. Bru, take care, you know where I am if you want to come over. Give my best to Bones.'

I send Caro an email saying I hope she's all right and that she still has my promise to give our relationship the consideration it deserves (am I too frightened to shut the door because I'm dreading the thought of never seeing her again? I saved her life, and she gave me a life – does it mean these things bind us until death do us part? Like Hugh and me?)

*

I'm battling to crack open a crab's claw for its sweet meat which, I suppose, is small beer in the big scheme of things. I'm in Santana's restaurant: open sides, palm-trunk pillars, bamboo roof struts covered with ylang-ylang; on the pillars some weird masks, and a painting with three eyes, and on my plate chilli crab with salsa sauce. Not to forget Rif the cat, stub-tailed and grey-brown like dirty dishwater, who is waiting patiently for throw-downs.

No crustacean implements or extra-large serviettes, just a bowl of lemon water. I place the flat end of a spoon on the claw and press with all my might. It cracks all right but flies onto the table next to mine, bouncing onto the floor near Rif who can't believe his luck.

Giggles from the table, and a woman says, 'That was brill, I was hoping I'd get it.' Fortyish, face a little coarse but enough laugh lines to redeem it, broad Aussie accent. Her friend is a redhead with sun spots and a curvaceous mouth, dressed in shorts and a flowery vest.

'Sorry ladies.'

'No worries,' says the redhead. 'Is it good?' She says it as if we're in bed.

'Awesome, east coast crab, ask for the biggies, lots of flesh.'

'I'm Ruby,' she says, 'and this is Charlotte. You're South African I think? I hear the accent often in Perth.'

'I'm Tom. Yeah, you might hear a lot more of it soon.' They giggle again. 'Anything the matter,' I ask testily, now that my country has come into the conversation.

'There's salsa all over you.'

I look down. It's as if I've crawled from a crashed car.

'Mandela was my idol,' Ruby says, 'I wonder what he'd think now.'

'He was mine too, and I think he'd be very sad,' I say.

Ruby gives me high fives, and Charlotte asks, 'How do you feel about it, Tom?'

It's a toss-up whether I make light of it or tell it as it is.

'It's a dream shattered, for all of us. The country held such promise. I suppose the signs were there all along, people just didn't want to see them.' I stay away from my own broken dream. That dreams are not to be trusted isn't something you share with just anybody.

We order more frosty Bintangs, and they also have chilli crab. Both are from Perth, Charlotte a nurse, and Ruby a chef on the mines. Ruby makes us laugh about how she has to feed hungry miners who, with bellies full, invariably want to get lucky with her. I tell her she must write a book about it, citing Russ. When Charlotte talks about her job I think of Amber, wondering when I'll hear from her, if at all.

A large man at another table holds a wriggling crab next to his face and asks his wife to take a picture, probably for his friends back home. Like some fucking trophy hunter. He's no quiet American.

I need to get out, be under the stars, and go with what they tell me. I say my goodbyes to a disappointing look from Ruby and walk the kilometre to my homestay. The night is my friend here, not my enemy. On the other side of the ocean it's still afternoon, and I wonder if my country has had another bloody day.

In the morning well before the crowing cocks and the calls to prayer, with thousands of sandals still lying outside doors, Amber's SMS finds me.

CHAPTER THIRTY-SIX
South Lombok

Amber emerges from the airport with her trolley to curious eyes from the motley crowd, disconcerting to visitors until they realise it presents no threat. She looks overly warm in her blue jersey and jeans, bun wound up tightly. Her tentative expression dissolves when she sees me, her smile reaching out then her arms. In that moment I don't care how many people are watching, or that we might upset Muslims mores.

'It doesn't feel quite real, having you on my island.'

'Couldn't sleep on the plane, thought of you all the time. Oh, to think I did it!'

'You also didn't think you'd ride a bike to Blue Lagoon and back.'

I take her trolley. We stay close. She whispers shyly, 'You look so good.' People move out of the way; hungry, longing stares, as if we've stepped from a movie screen. Hardly Clooney and Alamuddin, to be sure, but then everything is relative.

'The place feels so different. You think I'll be okay?'

'I know you'll be. One can live gently here. It's needy, yes, but not overbearingly so. They try to sell you things but there are no beggars. You feel you *want* to help.'

I stop and take her in my arms again. 'We'll have to buy you some island clothes, you know, shorts, vests and sandals, some beautiful sarongs.'

'I'm way too white!'

'We'll change that, Amber, you'll see. There are beaches here to die for.'

*

We're riding to Selong Belanak, Amber clinging to me as if we're on a rollercoaster. She's in a sarong and T-shirt, and smeared with sunscreen and mosquito lotion, hair loose in the wind (I persuaded her that buns are too uptight for island life; actually, she never put it back up again after the first night). Amber has taken to living here better than I expected, treating it as one big adventure, admitting she's always been too cautious – with an undefined angst to boot – and that she would never have come here on her own. Then she'd hug me and thank me. She never mentions Caro, maybe feeling that possession is nine-tenths of the law. And, as I expected, the Sasak people love her, sensing her compassion and genuine interest. She remembers their names, asks about their families, schools, and general conditions on the island. She helps out at the clinic for a few days a week, amazing everyone with her sure and kind touch, and not wanting a cent for her work. To some she's an angel descended from heaven, in her lovemaking increasingly far from it, to the point where she wakes up some mornings all shy and demure, and fearful as though expecting to be struck by lightning. One morning Doni took us on the *perahu* to Grupuk Inside, where she watched me surf. Udin had erected canvas shade for her and hung a ladder down the side so she could swim and climb back on, but Doni still fussed over her.

Only when Amber stopped talking about the nursing home did I realise she had cut that umbilical cord. With our country it hasn't been that easy. We check the news while we try to get on with our lives. An uneasy calm has descended over South Africa, the state of emergency keeping a lid on things with the help of the army until a new leader is appointed. All the recently announced clampdown on the media is doing is to support the illusion of calm – citizens have no idea what's going on (I expect controls on the Internet to follow, in the name of security, of course). The clampdown came after a frenzy of speculation on the identity of the President's assassins: a ruling party faction, opposition party rebels (following poor showings in local elections), a right-wing cell trained in the use of such stratagems and weapons, militant trade unionists, the black elite, organised crime, and the chilling thought that some of these elements might have worked together. It went on and on until the government stepped in. If there's a future for my country I cannot see it.

The hills are more forested now, the valleys more fertile with corn, rice, tobacco, and vegetables everywhere. The road is so windy only a few sections have dotted lines in the centre. In villages, rice has been put out to dry on huge mats protruding into the road. Unlabelled bottles of fuel are for sale on open racks, small shops are crammed with drinks, cigarettes and sweets. Running roosters play chicken with cars and mopeds, while people move unhurriedly in the heat. Possessions are pitifully few, yet I have no worries whatsoever about being mugged in the event of a breakdown. How can cultures with poverty be so different?

At Selong Belanak beach Amber slips off the moped and runs down the white-powder sand into the turquoise shallows, yelling at me, 'Need water wings? Don't worry, I'll look after you!' From disliking sand, sea and wind, she's become a tyke, aiming straight for the water whenever she sees it, and then not wanting to come out. She's no longer pale. Her cheeks are permanently rouged from the sun, her hair more curly and lustrous. In the sea we embrace, break away and cavort, lie on our backs and drift, take in the grand sweep of the beach, the verdant flat land beyond the high-water mark, the Jabon hills in the distance. A line of water buffalo passes us on the beach, taupe hides aglow in the sun, unfazed by a long-necked horse and its bareback rider galloping past them in a spray of silver.

I take her to Kuta's Sunday morning market, a throbbing, chaotic place. We see not more than three other westerners. Families and produce are piled onto mopeds, horse-drawn carriages, and vans. Along narrow pathways and under low roofs, stalls display the island's bounties in sacks, buckets, and baskets, and on mats, wooden blocks, and banana leaves: pungent-smelling dried fish, fresh-eyed tuna and barracuda, octopuses like slimy mops, fruits, spices, and vegetables – some very strange – tobacco, Gudang Garan cigarettes, and corn on the cob. Limp rupiah notes change hands with breath-taking rapidity. Through this bedlam Amber walks with child-like wonder, not letting go of my hand. I buy some *serabi* – Indonesia's version of a samosa, filled with rice and meat – which beg to be eaten on the spot. Then *lunis* for dessert – flour, rice, and coconut milk pancakes served with coconut sugar syrup – and we lick our fingers.

We spend our days as though we're in paradise, as though they'll never end.

*

Another day about to break, familiar sounds finding their way into my half-awake state: the call of the muezzin, mournful so early in the morning, the crowing of roosters, high-pitched twitter of birds, deep barking of dogs. I must get up. A languorous stretch, a savouring hand on Amber's hip, then sliding out of bed. Swig from the water bottle, brush my teeth, grab my gear, and depart like a ninja – master of quiet exits practised over many years. Follow the pocked road to Grupuk. A few other mopeds with boards clamped to the side, girls at the back. Closed-up shops, curled-up canines, water buffalo turning shining eyes my way like torches, the ocean thundering on the reefs to my right, ahead of me the first brushstrokes of orange and yellow in the sky.

At the village Udin is getting ready for the daily influx of surfers. 'Doni will take you today, Mister Tom. Drop you at Inside and come back for you, okay?'

'Sure. Where's he going?'

Doni puts his head down, hiding his eyes beneath his frayed blue and orange cap. Udin's voice is stern: 'He lost my anchor in the bay, very expensive. He must find it, dive down.'

'It's a big bay, Udin.'

'He put a buoy to mark spot. Maybe two hours, Mister Tom, okay?' He turns to Doni. 'You got the goggles, boy?'

Doni holds them up, and a rusty spade.

On the *perahu* I say to Doni, 'Old caps are like good friends, aren't they, go everywhere you go.'

He laughs as he avoids catching an anchor line with his left outrigger. Dugouts dot this still corner like a marine parking lot, its people hunters and farmers of the ocean for centuries and today also ferrymen to surfers. Without the sea they'd shrivel up like seaweed in the sun.

I imagine Amber curled up, still asleep. Or is she already up and about, ready to go to the clinic? I must find a place to rent that's more economical than the homestay's daily rate. Other living costs, including food and moped hire, are more than affordable. As regards clothes, I'm in a place where I'm not judged by what I wear, and dressing like a local is cool. And I

Curveball   229

think of Caro, and my promise to her weighing on me now in my Garden of Eden – a dilemma entirely of my own making.

My spirits are lifted by the glassy sea at Grupuk Inside, the small cluster of anchored *perahus*, and no more than a dozen surfers at the backline.

Doni cuts the engine about a hundred metres away, balancing astern on sturdy legs like a young Ahab. 'I come back for you later, Mister Tom.'

'Where is it you're going, Doni?'

He waves in the direction of the left headland towering jaggedly. 'I find the buoy. It is orange, like this.' He holds up his cap then makes his way nimbly to my board, toes clutching the thin rail like claws.

'Take your time, Doni. Just get the anchor.'

He lowers my board into the water. I jump in, secure the leash to my ankle and paddle towards the line-up. The backs of the waves are high enough to block the shoreline entirely from my view, triggering that old, delicious rush.

PART THREE

GRUPUK BAY, SOUTH LOMBOK

CHAPTER THIRTY-SEVEN

The tsunami swells come, not more than two metres high but kilometres wide, unlike anything I've ever seen, four of them at intervals of between five and ten minutes. As we go up and over them, it's as though their energy radiates all the way from the seabed, not like the surface waves I know, giving the feeling of a thick wall of water passing through. My heart is thumping. I realise that being this far out has saved us, but when the waves approach land they will look and behave differently.

A deceptive peace now lies over the sea making me want to paddle back and find Amber, but it isn't safe, not for a long while yet. And I have Doni to think about.

On the danger scale sharks are like tadpoles against a tsunami. Uppermost in our minds is what destruction has been wrought along the shore. Doni and I discuss it in hushed tones, as though reluctant to further tempt the force that picked our island from among thousands for such violence. Tears come to Doni when he talks about his family and his friends. And I tell him about Amber, and Russ and Bones, and how I lost Dunbar and Spirou. I even talk about Caro, and Doni asks awkwardly, 'Will you go back if ...' He means if Amber is dead. Were it not for her clinic day she could still be on the third floor of our homestay, safer, and also much closer to Ashtari's hill than to the sea. Anguish and uncertainty gnaw at me.

After an hour I cannot wait any longer, exacerbated by a concern that currents could develop and take us even further away from land. We start the long paddle back. I glance over my shoulder frequently, wishing for eyes in the back of my head to keep a closer watch on this capricious ocean.

*

We pass Grupuk Outside on our left. I can't make out whether the ochre cliffs have been affected or not, they're already so scarred. I scan the corner of the bay but the village is still too far away. Our paddling becomes more urgent, our breathing more laboured. Closer in, to our left, buildings are still intact on the hill, giving me hope. Until I see the village: bare walls, remnants of roofs sticking out at crazy angles, *perahus* and lobster platforms piled up, incongruous like fish on dry land. 'Ah, look, the mosque!' Doni exclaims – enough of its arches gone for the dome to have collapsed, and his world with it, his eyes turned old in a single day, stopping his young tears from flooding out and bringing relief. Udin's surf shop, his brightly painted little house one street back, the surfing school further down, the homestays and restaurants that overlooked the water – all gone. It's as though a giant claw curled itself around the village and crushed it, with no intention other than to destroy it in the shortest time possible. I can't see where the road used to be, just stripped trees and debris now all the way to the foot of the hills. Higher up people are moving about, their cries rising and falling in the breeze.

At the wall we climb off the board into chest-high water, and feel our way up the stone steps to what was Udin's parking area, treading carefully through the sludge and the wreckage, personal belongings, remains of furniture, mopeds, surfboards, and bodies of villagers and their animals. I cannot imagine life here again, the destruction is so complete. I see the old woman with her red betel mouth, still staring at nothing. And Kojak, his big knife still on him, lying in the muck – no tsunami could bend his resolve to remain at his post, it could only take away his cap. I never knew he had so little hair.

Doni heads for where his home once was, like a pigeon programmed. 'Doni, wait, there's nothing! Go to the hills, you might find them there. I'm going to Kuta, but I'll be back.' I put my board down and hold him to me. Will he ever cry again? I stroke his tousled hair. 'You're a man now, Doni. I'm proud of you. You have a friend, understand, whatever happens.' He clings to me then shakes his head as if he knows he has to face reality.

I watch as he makes his way to the base of the hill. He stops and bends over. In the sultry air his shout sends shivers through me: 'It's Separ! He's dead, Mr Tom!'

*

I'm walking through a wasteland stretching as much as two hundred metres inland, baggies and rash vest clinging to me, board underarm, and my moped somewhere under the muck. Above me the sun still a way to go before the sky turns red, pink, and mauve, and I have eight kilometres to Kuta, probably more because the Mandalika road will be impassable, necessitating a detour. I contemplate dumping my board but its sturdy, familiar feel comforts me. Did it not bring me and Doni through the valley of death? Did Paul Revere[iii] and Dick King not feel the same about their horses after their epic rides? I make the decision right there that one day it will hang on a wall in my home in memory of this day.

At Tanjung Aan I remove my rash vest, now wet with sweat, and tie it around my waist. In the brown watery landscape, dwellings lie smashed like birds' nests after a gale, the bodies of buffalo, dogs and humans semi-afloat, soon to bloat in the sun. The road is submerged, forcing me to veer inland through bush. There I take a break, my throat parched and my heart heavy. The sun, undisturbed above all the destruction, begins its trajectory down.

*

I'm walking in the dark now, thickets no more than blobs in the moonless night. I hit one and recoil with pain. Rock and stone cut through my soles. There is no light or sound, not even the rustle of wind. It's as if the night itself has been overcome by the ocean. I stop again and lie down this time, my head on my board looking up at the dense black sky. How different from a few hours ago when I gazed at its blue infinity with wonderment. I want to sleep and not wake up, so I won't have to face this smashed world.

I get up. Nothing now to tell me where I am, if I go too far I'll miss Kuta. Will I find her? Did Separ use precious time calling the clinic when he could have been saving villagers? Is that why the water got him? I would forgive him even if Amber hasn't made it.

My feet hit tarmac. No potholes – it has to be the airport road, the Awang stretch. Somewhere I know there's a link to Kuta.

*

I see it, cordoned off, lined with mopeds and people, faces registering shock and relief, clutching their children, each other, staring dully at the flashing red lights of ambulances and police vehicles. Others sit or lie in silent exhaustion, eyes closed. Belongings are scattered everywhere. I get strange looks – one tourist shakes his head and whispers to his girlfriend. I don't know where to begin, afraid of what I might hear. I ask a Sasak woman the time. It's eight, she tells me. Where the lights of Kuta once were is only darkness, as though it was never there and existed only on the pages of a novel.

'How much of the town is left?' I ask a westerner, a burly man with a beard, in sleeping shorts and vest.

'Dunno mate, but I don't think much. Didn't stand a bloody chance, too flat and close to the water, know what I mean?'

'You know where the clinic used to be?' Visitors with Bali belly often went there. My use of the past tense disturbs me.

'Yeah, but I can't tell you anything, sorry mate. Looking for someone?'

I nod. 'How did you get out?'

'I know about tsunamis. When the birds stayed in the air in tight circles and the water buffalo started making strange sounds I got worried. Grabbed our passports and money and my missus and got on the moped. Many weren't so lucky. Can you fucking believe it there's no early warning system!'

'How much time did you have before the first wave came?'

'It seemed like no time, but actually it could have been forty minutes. You see that police vehicle? You can report missing people there. They're making a list.'

It would have taken Separ fifteen minutes to reach the village. Again I wonder if he made the call, or got through. Even if he had, the clinic was some way from the Ashtari hill. Amber would have had to run well over a kilometre. But like Kojak, Amber wasn't the kind to abandon her post. The knowledge weighs on me. I have the terrible choice: look for her in town – what's left of it – or go straight to Ashtari.

*

I continue on the airport road, more of the same: people everywhere with nowhere to go, staring at any flashing light with weary hope. When I ask for water I get only a shake of the head. I'm at the big roundabout now: airport right, Kuta left. To reach Ashtari I'd have to go through Kuta, but the road here is also cordoned off, uniformed men eyeing me suspiciously. I have flashes of my ordeal at the airport but am having none of it. Forget Kuta. I plunge into the bush, the board's nose first. The men don't stop me. I must look crazed.

Halfway up the hill the thick undergrowth suddenly opens up onto the Ashtari road. It's as if my entire body is on fire. I hide my board marking the spot with a little pyramid of stones, and think of Namibia – how far away my old life! As exhausted as I am I start running, the image of Amber pushing me towards the dimly lit building on the hill. With rasping breath I take the staircase two steps at a time, into the space I know so well: fans on the ceiling, floor mats and cushions in the centre, tables along the side, and walls of glass – bohemian feel, tranquillity borne of quiet minds, but tonight filled with distress. Only a few candles in this large room, flickering shadows play across my vision. No Amber. I imagine going down the hill to retrieve my board but not ever my life. There's only you and me she once said.

I look again, checking heads one at a time. Still I can't see her. I close my smarting eyes. Was my decision right to come here? Did I choose Ashtari because I couldn't bear seeing her among Kuta's dead? If she is not here, all I would have done is to delay the inevitable.

I climb up on a banquette against the wall, onto the cushions with my bloodied feet, and shout, 'Amber, Amber, here, it's me!' Heads turn my way, eyes dead as if made of glass, only a few registering pity for this half-naked man with torn skin towering above them.

She rises up from among the crowd, peers in my direction, glasses gone, white coat streaked with dirt. 'Amber!' I shout again. Has she been there all along, sitting down? Everything is swaying now, my sight is blurred. I'm struggling, and can no longer tell what is real and what isn't. Am I awake or dreaming? Is what I am seeing my imagination, by morning no more than a callous chimera?

I see a sea of people parting, my hand going out to her and leading her to the deck outside, to lie together on a beanbag in the corner and look up at the night sky. And I hear words that have been a long time coming: 'When the sea shook, Amber, I thought it was the end. It was as though my entire life had been building up to it, to punish me, test me, give me a chance at redemption – I don't know. And then the calm, like the eye of a cyclone, and the realisation that I no longer cared about anything except you, and I was done even with Caro.'

She says nothing, lies with her head nestled in my neck. I don't stop: 'I thought, Amber, what if you lived and I died without the chance of telling you this, or you died and I lived knowing I never told you? I couldn't imagine dying more tormented … what a fool I've been.'

The night is dense with no beginning or end to it that I can see, so close and so far at the same time, embracing me yet not sharing anything, and I say, 'The ghosts will go, Amber, just stay with me. Will you?'

I feel her fingers interlocking with mine. If this is a dream after all, I won't let it fade with time. When I wake up I'll write it all down.

PART FOUR

JABON HILLS, SOUTH LOMBOK
SIX MONTHS LATER

CHAPTER THIRTY-EIGHT

I think the reason why Robinson Crusoe kept meticulous track of the days was because he was lonely. I mean, that's how Friday got his name.

On my island I'm not lonely, so the days of the week and the months don't really matter. I live by the seasons, the winds and the tides, and by a voice inside me the sound of which I've come to like. And the voices of others, like little Sophie's today, because no man should be an island.

Munching the chocolate I gave her, she thanks me, '*Tampi asih*, Mister Tom.' Now eight, eyes and skin the colour of deep-roasted cashew, favourite cap with 'monster' on it, T-shirt too big, neat sarong, sandals showing pink toenails.

'Well, you're special, Sophie.'

'Is that homework?' She looks at the tablet and papers on the table.

'I suppose you can call it that. I'll put it all away in a minute.'

'But you don't go to school!'

I shake my head. 'No, it's for my friend Russ, he's coming next week. He writes books you see, stories, and these notes are for him. They're about my life. It's for his second book.'

'Is it about fairies?'

'You're smart. It is, sort of, because the things that happened to me are difficult to believe, even for me.'

'Why? ... Oh, sorry, you want some?' She holds out the chocolate, making sure not too much is protruding from the silver paper.

I snap off a piece. 'Well, considering I'm just an ordinary man ... I mean, I was expecting my life to be so different. I'm not explaining it well, Sophie, sorry.' No epic sweep to my life, to be sure, like in *Gone with the Wind* or *Dr Zhivago*, yet Russ quite inspired even though I'm decidedly ambivalent. For one thing, do I reveal all about Dragut and Gugu? Detective Warrant Officer Harrisunker could be on my case again. Then there's Spirou's letter, and my time with Zoe. Caro and Cal's betrayal, on the other hand, should be told, if for no other reason than to exorcise it once and for all.

Thinking about the book, I might have to omit parts, or have it published upon my death (nothing like Mark Twain's request for his autobiography to be published a *hundred years* after his death – I must remind Russ).

'Will you fix these beads please, Sophie, my wrist is not happy without them.'

'Ah, that's why I got my kit. Strings must be same length when you pull. See here, this one too short, that one too long.' She takes from her bag a pair of scissors, string, and some loose beads. I never tire of watching her tiny white teeth and fingers and big toe work together to string the bamboo and coconut-skin beads of the island. Saturdays are her days with me, ever since her parents died. Doni also visits often, as do Udin and Nining. Doni is now a favourite *pepadu,* or stick-fighter, among the locals. At the February tournament, preceding the Festival of the Sea Worm, he beat his opponents in a manner that was awesome, telling me quietly afterwards, 'For saving me, Mister Tom, on that day. I not scared since then, never! *Terima kasih!*' We hardly ever talk about that day. It's just there, with us, always.

I take in the grand curve of the bay below me, deep blue far out, turquoise inshore, powder-fine white sand. 'Let's go for a swim.'

We pack our things, and I take her hand. We pass the longboard mounted on the wall and Sophie noisily sucks in air, feigning fright at the spider on the nose (as much as it fascinates her she's shown little interest in the inscription below the board). I have other boards I don't mind risking on the reefs.

In the mirror I glimpse the stranger who's been me all my life: the lean face with a few extra lines now, blue eyes set deeper than I recall, the jawline easier – a presence less disquieting than before. I could get to like this man; we might even ponder the past without old heartaches getting in the way, drink to each other. I squeeze Sophie's hand, and smile down at her.

As we get to the door Numo shouts, 'She's home, she's home!' Smitten by the thought, it swings its head from side to side, eyes rolling.

Sophie looks at me. 'Please can she come with us, *please*, Mister Tom?'

I know Sophie isn't talking about the parrot. I nod and lift her up high. Their excitement became mine the moment we heard the moped outside.

GLOSSARY

ANC. African National Congress: founded in 1912 to fight for the rights of black South Africans by peaceful means. Following the Sharpeville massacre in 1960 the organisation turned militant, pressuring the Nationalist government to cede power in 1994 which allowed Nelson Mandela to become the country's first black president.

Antih lemak yak tulak malik. Sasak for 'glad to have you back again'.

Berembe kabar. Sasak for 'how are you?'

Bier vom Fass. German for 'draught beer'.

Bigaz. Shona slang for 'big'.

Biltong. Dried strips of beef, the South African equivalent of American jerky and Swiss Bündnerfleisch.

Bosbefok. 'Bush-crazy' in Afrikaans – a type of psychosis that some South African soldiers developed after long periods in the bush on the country's borders 1960 – 1990.

Braai. Afrikaans for 'barbeque'; from 'braaivleis': literally 'barbequed meat'.

Chidhina. Shona slang for an old-style cell phone; literal meaning 'brick'.

Chimbeva. Shona slang for a smaller, modern, expensive cell phone.

Dokkies. Durban Teachers' Training College in Umbilo.

Ende. The cowhide shield used in stick-fighting contests in Lombok.

Foamie. Surfer slang for a white water wave, i.e. a wave that has broken.

Fragen Sie den Papegai. German for 'ask the parrot'.

Hamba kahle. 'Goodbye, go well' in Zulu.

Hearty. Durban beach slang for a 'heart attack'.

Homestay. Term for a B&B in Kuta, Lombok.

Homie. A boy or girl from a children's home in South Africa.

Inkosi ikubusise. 'God bless you' in Zulu.

Johnny. Surfer slang for a shark.

Katidza. Shona slang for 'tea'.

Kiff. South African slang for 'nice', 'cool'.

Kugula ukugula. 'To be sick', in the Ndebele language.

Larney. English South African slang for 'smart', 'fancy'.

Lunis. Indonesian pancake made from rice, flour, and coconut milk, eaten with coconut sugar syrup.

Madziro. Shona slang for 'ATM'; literal meaning 'wall'.

Mafella. Shona slang for 'fellow'.

Malini? Zulu for 'how much?' (the cost of something)

Mamparra. Afrikaans for a 'stupid person', 'idiot'.

Miff (adj.). Surfer slang for 'unpleasant', 'bad'.

Mbongo. Shona slang for 'money'.

Mlungu. 'White person' in Zulu.

Moer die ou ballie. Afrikaans for 'hit the old guy'.

Vhuzhi. Shona slang for 'car' (from the sound produced by a car).

Oke. Afrikaans slang for 'fellow', 'chap'.

Penjalin. The rattan stick used in stick-fighting contests in Lombok.

Pepadu. Sasak for 'stick fighter'.

Protea. South Africa's national flower.

Raven ou. Durban Indian slang for a 'black man'.

Rock. A form of cocaine that can be smoked.

Roggenbrot. German for 'rye bread'.

Sadza and matemba. Cattle hooves and yam (for human consumption).

Sasak. The people and language of Lombok, an Indonesian island.

Sawubona, unjani? Zulu for 'good day, how are you?'

Serabi. Indonesian version of a samosa: triangular pastry filled with rice and meat.

Simple and klaar/finish and klaar. Afrikaans for 'end of story/discussion'.

Smuggies. Smuggler's Inn, a pub in the old Point Rd., Durban, notorious in the 1960s and 70s.

Solah, tampi asih. Sasak for 'I'm very well, thank you.'

Steenbras, kabeljou (kob), blacktail, galjoen. Fish prized for their flavourful meat, found off Namibia's west coast.

Sugars. Heroin mixed with cocaine and used with other drugs like marijuana, sometimes bulked up with rat poison; inhaled.

Tenderpreneurialism. The practice in South Africa of state tenders being awarded based on personal connections and corrupt relationships.

Terima kasih. Bahasa Indonesian for 'thank you'.

To be late. Durban Indian slang for 'deceased'.

Tonaz. Shona slang for 'town'.

Tonfa. Okinawan martial arts weapon: a stick 38 – 50cm long, with a perpendicular handle a third of the way down.

Ubuntu. African word meaning 'humanity to others', 'unselfishness'.

Vasbyt. Literally 'bite hard' in Afrikaans: to show fortitude, perseverance.

Vis-en-kuier. Afrikaans for 'fishing and socialising'.

Weissbrot. German for 'white bread'.

Welwitschia. Hardy, weird-looking plant endemic to Namibia's arid west coast.

Whoonga. South African drug consisting of rat poison, soap powder, and antiretroviral medicine (used to prolong the life of HIV sufferers); a highly dangerous concoction.

Wuss. South African slang: someone who lacks backbone, a weakling.

Zanu-PF. The ruling party of Robert Mugabe in Zimbabwe.

SOURCES OF MEDIA QUOTATIONS

Page 2: *The New Yorker,* 21 April 1962, page 32. Geoffrey T. Hellman's article, 'Bond's Creator', on his interview with Ian Fleming.

Chapter 2: *Time Magazine.* Author/correspondent Alex Perry's article, 'The New Struggle for the ANC', 24 Dec 2012.

Chapter 3: *South African Civil Society Information Service (SACSIS).* Professor Jane Duncan, 'A Culture of Political Assassination,' article published on SACSIS website, 2 Nov 2010.

Chapter 4: *The Mercury.* Editorial, 9 Dec 2013, three days after the death of Nelson Mandela.

Chapter 5: *Statistics South Africa. General Household Survey,* 19 June 2014, on the quantum leap in the number of people receiving grants from the state.

Chapter 6: *Independent Online News (IOL),* 22 Feb 2015, concerning the excessive use of consultants by the first two tiers of government in a single financial year (2012/13). If monies spent on consultants by the third tier, municipalities, are added the amount would be much higher.

Chapter 8: *Time Magazine.* Author/correspondent Alex Perry's article, 'Africa Rising', 3 Dec 2012.

Chapter 10: Clem Sunter's and Chantell Ilbury's website, 'Mind of a Fox',10 Oct 2012. Article by Clem Sunter, pre-eminent South African scenario planner and strategist, 'Looking over the edge of a cliff'.

Chapter 12: *The Mercury,* 14 Oct 2013, on the occasion of Julius Malema launching his Economic Freedom Fighters Party (EFF) at Marikana, site of the 2012 mine massacre by police.

Chapter 13: *The Mercury,* 14 Oct 2014. Max du Preez in an article on increasing social unrest in South Africa's disaffected areas.

Chapter 16: *The Mercury,* 24 Jan 2014, quoting Durban psychologist Shaquir Salduker on the increasing incidence of mental health illness in SA.

Chapter 17: *Business Report.* Ellis Mnyandu, Editor, on government's need to address the growing discontent in the country, 17 Sept 2012.

Chapter 18: *The Mercury,* 5 Aug 2014. Max du Preez on the danger posed by extra-parliamentary politics in South Africa.

Chapter 19: *Crime Stats South Africa.* Average number of carjackings per month in the year 2014/15, an increase of 14.8% over 2013/14, extracted from the South African Police Service Crime Statistics report, 29 Sept 2015.

Chapter 20: *Institute for Security Studies (ISS).* Article by Lizette Lancaster, 26 Oct 2012, quoting research by the South African Law Commission on low conviction rates for violent crime.

Chapter 24: *Business Day.* Moeletsi Mbeki, South African author and political economist, warning of South Africa's impending 'Tunisia Day,' article published 10 Feb 2011.

Chapter 25: *SWEAT website.* The Sex Workers' Education and Advocacy Taskforce is an NGO to improve living and working conditions of sex workers in South Africa, a country where sex work is still regarded as a crime.

Chapter 26: *The Mercury,* 14 April 2015, on an alleged plot to unseat President Zuma.

Chapter 27: *The Mercury.* Editorial, 29 Sept 2014, on South Africa's new democracy having failed the country's unemployed black youth.

Chapter 28: *The Mercury.* Editorial, 19 June 2014, on President Zuma's State of the Nation address.

Chapter 30: *The Star.* Editorial, 4 Sept 2014, on the unpreparedness of South Africa's police to control the anticipated increase in service-delivery protests.

Chapter 31: *Time Magazine.* Alex Perry, quoting political-violence specialist Mary de Haas in his 24 Dec 2012 article, 'The New Struggle for the ANC', on why Sbu Sibiya, ANC Regional Secretary, was assassinated.

Chapter 32: *BizNews.com.* R.W. Johnson interviewed by Andrew Donaldson on his book, 'How Long Will South Africa Survive? The Looming Crisis' (Jonathan Ball, J/ohannesburg, 2015), posted on 1 June 2015.

NOTES

[i] Tom – humorously or not – temporarily casts himself as Harry Haller, the protagonist of Hermann Hesse's *Steppenwolf* (orig. German *Der Steppenwolf*), named after the lonesome wolf of the steppes. *Steppenwolf* portrays the protagonist's split between his humanity and his wolf-like aggression and homelessness. (Wikipedia)

[ii] Richard Philip "Dick" King (1813–1871) was an English trader and colonist at Port Natal, a British trading station in the region now known as KwaZulu-Natal. He is best known for a historic horseback ride in 1842, where he completed a journey of 960 kilometres (600 mi) in 10 days, to request help for the besieged British garrison at Port Natal (now the Old Fort, Durban). (Wikipedia)

[iii] Paul Revere (December 21, 1734 O.S. – May 10, 1818) was an American silversmith, engraver, early industrialist, and a patriot in the American Revolution. He is best known for alerting the Colonial militia to the approach of British forces before the battles of Lexington and Concord, as dramatized in Henry Wadsworth Longfellow's poem, 'Paul Revere's Ride'. (Wikipedia)

THE PUBLISHERS

Proverse Hong Kong (PVHK), founded by Gillian and Verner Bickley, is based in Hong Kong with long-term and developing regional and international connections.

Proverse has published novels, novellas, non-fiction (including autobiography and biography, history, memoirs, sport, travel narratives), single-author poetry collections, children's, young teens and academic books. Other interests include diaries, and academic works in the humanities, social sciences, cultural studies, linguistics and education. Some Proverse books have accompanying audio texts. Some are translated into Chinese.

We welcome authors who have a story to tell, wisdom, perceptions or information to convey, a person they want to memorialize, a neglect they want to remedy, a record they want to correct, a strong interest that they want to share, skills they want to teach, and who consciously seek to make a contribution to society in an informative, interesting and well-written way. Proverse works with texts by non-native-speaker writers of English as well as by native English-speaking writers.

The name, "Proverse", combines the words "prose" and "verse" and is pronounced accordingly.

THE INTERNATIONAL PROVERSE PRIZE FOR UNPUBLISHED BOOK-LENGTH FICTION, NON-FICTION OR POETRY

The Proverse Prize, an annual international competition for an unpublished single-author book-length work of fiction, non-fiction, or poetry, the original work of the entrant, submitted in English (unpublished translations welcomed) was established in January 2008. It is open to all who are at least eighteen on the date they sign the entry form and without restriction of nationality, residence or citizenship.

Founded by Gillian and Verner Bickley, the objectives of the prize are: to encourage excellence and / or excellence and usefulness in publishable written work in the English Language, which can, in varying degrees, "delight and instruct". Entries are invited from anywhere in the world.

The Prize
1) Publication by Proverse Hong Kong, with
2) Cash prize of HKD10,000 (HKD7.80 = approx. USD1.00)

Extent of the Manuscript: within the range of what is usual for the genre of the work submitted. However, it is advisable that novellas be in the range, 30,000 to 45,000 words; other fiction (e.g. novels, short-story collections) and non-fiction (e.g. autobiographies, biographies, diaries, letters, memoirs, essay collections, etc.) should be in the range, 75,000 to 100,000 words. Poetry collections should be in the range, 5,000 to 25,000 words. Other word-counts and mixed-genre submissions are not ruled out.

International Proverse Prize Annual Entry Deadlines (subject to confirmation and/or change)

Receipt of Entry Fees / Entry Forms begins	[Variable, no later than] 14 April
Deadline for receipt of Entry Fees / Entry Forms	31 May
Receipt of entered manuscripts begins	1 May
Deadline for receipt of entered manuscripts	30 June

**The above information is for guidance only.
More information, updated from time to time, is available on the Proverse website: proversepublishing.com**

**WINNERS OF THE PROVERSE PRIZE 2015
Gustav Preller and Lawrence Gray**

**PREVIOUS WINNERS OF THE PROVERSE PRIZE
WHOSE ENTERED WORK HAS ALREADY BEEN
PUBLISHED BY PROVERSE HONG KONG**

**Rebecca Tomasis
Laura Solomon
Gillian Jones
David Diskin
Peter Gregoire
Sophronia Liu
Birgit Linder
James Mccarthy
Philip Chatting
Celia Claase**

THE INTERNATIONAL PROVERSE POETRY PRIZE
(SINGLE POEMS)

An annual international Proverse Poetry Prize (for single poems) was established in 2016. The international Proverse Poetry Prize is open to all who are at least eighteen years old whatever their residence, nationality or citizenship.

Single poems, submitted in English, are invited on (a) <u>any subject or theme, chosen by the writer</u> OR (b) <u>on a subject or theme selected by the organizers</u>.

Poems may be in any form, style or genre. Each poem should be no more than 30 lines.

Entries should previously be unpublished in any way (except in the case of unpublished translations into English of the entrant's own work already published in another language, providing the entrant holds the copyright).

In 2016
cash prizes were offered as follows:
1st prize; USD100.00; 2nd prize: USD45.00;
3rd prizes (up to four winners): USD20.00.

If there are enough good entries in any year, an anthology of prize-winners and selected other entries will be published.

In 2016, judging took place at the same time as the judging for the Proverse Prize for unpublished book-length fiction, non-fiction or poetry.

Judges: anonymous (as for the Proverse Prize for an unpublished book-length work).

Max number of entries per person: No maximum.

No poet may win more than one prize.

The above information is for guidance only.
More information, updated from time to time, is available on the Proverse website: proversepublishing.com

FICTION PUBLISHED BY PROVERSE

Those who enjoy **Curveball** may also enjoy the following novels, novellas and short story collections (listed separately).

A Misted Mirror, by Gillian Jones. 2011.

A Painted Moment, by Jennifer Ching. 2010.

Adam's Franchise, by Lawrence Gray. Scheduled November 2016.

An Imitation of Life. 2nd ed, by Laura Solomon. 2013.

Article 109, by Peter Gregoire. 2012.

Bao Bao's odyssey: from Mao's Shanghai to capitalist Hong Kong, by Paul Ting. 2012.

Black Tortoise Winter, by Jan Pearson. 2016.

Bright Lights and White Nights, by Andrew Carter. 2015.

cemetery – miss you, by Jason S Polley. 2011.

Cop Show Heaven, by Lawrence Gray. 2015.

Death Has a Thousand Doors, by Patricia W. Grey. 2011.

Hilary and David, by Laura Solomon. 2011.

Hong Kong Hollow, by Dragoş Ilca. Scheduled, 2017.

Instant messages, by Laura Solomon. 2010.

Man's Last Song, by James Tam. 2013,

Mila the Magician, by Zhang Jian (Catherine Chin). 2014. (English/Chinese bilingual edition).

Mishpacha – family, by Rebecca Tomasis. 2010.

Paranoia (the walk and talk with Angela),
      by Caleb Kavon. 2012.

Red Bird Summer, by Jan Pearson. 2014.

Revenge From Beyond, by Dennis Wong. 2011.

The Day They Came, by Gérard Louis Breissan. 2012.

The Devil You Know, by Peter Gregoire. 2014.

The Perilous Passage of Princess Petunia Peasant,
      by Victor E. Apps. 2014. (Young adult fiction.)

The Village in the Mountains, by David Diskin. 2012.

**The Monkey in Me: Confusion, Love and Hope
      Under a Chinese Sky**, by Caleb Kavon. 2009.

The Reluctant Terrorist: in Search of the Jizo,
      by Caleb Kavon. 2011.

Tiger Autumn, by Jan Pearson. 2015.

Tightrope! A Bohemian tale, by Olga Walló.
      Translated from Czech by Johanna Pokorny, Veronika
Revická & others.
      Poetry translated by Justin Quinn, Veronika Revická.
      Edited by Gillian Bickley & Olga Walló,
      with Verner Bickley. 2010.

University Days, by Laura Solomon. 2014.

Vera Magpie, by Laura Solomon. 2013.

SHORT STORY COLLECTIONS

Beyond Brightness, by Sanja Särman.
Scheduled November 2016.

Odds and Sods, by Lawrence Gray. 2013.

The Snow Bridge and other Stories, by Philip Chatting. 2015.

The Shingle Bar Sea Monster and other stories,
by Laura Solomon. 2012.

FICTION – CHINESE LANGUAGE

The Monkey in Me, by Caleb Kavon.
Translated by Chapman Chen. 2010.

Tightrope! A Bohemian Tale, by Olga Walló.
Translated by Chapman Chen. 2011.
Chinese translation supported by the Ministry of Culture
of the Czech Republic.

~~~

FIND OUT MORE ABOUT OUR AUTHORS BOOKS AND EVENTS

Visit our website:
http://www.proversepublishing.com

Visit our distributor's website: <www.chineseupress.com>

Follow us on Twitter
Follow news and conversation: <twitter.com/Proversebooks>
OR
Copy and paste the following to your browser window and follow the instructions:
https://twitter.com/#!/ProverseBooks
"Like" us on www.facebook.com/ProversePress

Request our free E-Newsletter
Send your request to info@proversepublishing.com.

Availability
Most books are available in Hong Kong and world-wide from our Hong Kong based Distributor,
The Chinese University Press of Hong Kong,
The Chinese University of Hong Kong, Shatin, NT,
Hong Kong SAR, China.
Email: cup-bus@cuhk.edu.hk
Website: <www.chineseupress.com>.
All titles are available from Proverse Hong Kong
http://www.proversepublishing.com
and the Proverse Hong Kong UK-based Distributor.

We have **stock-holding retailers** in Hong Kong,
Singapore (Select Books),
Canada (Elizabeth Campbell Books),
Andorra (Llibreria La Puça, La Llibreria).
Orders can be made from bookshops in the UK and elsewhere.

Ebooks
Most of our titles are available also as Ebooks.